Picture Perfect

Books by Janice Thompson

Weddings by Bella

Fools Rush In
Swinging on a Star
It Had to Be You

Backstage Pass

Stars Collide
Hello, Hollywood!
The Director's Cut

Weddings by Design

Picture Perfect

Picture Perfect

A NOVEL

JANICE THOMPSON

Revell

a division of Baker Publishing Group
Grand Rapids, Michigan

© 2013 by Janice Thompson

Published by Revell
a division of Baker Publishing Group
P.O. Box 6287, Grand Rapids, MI 49516-6287
www.revellbooks.com

Printed in the United States of America

Library of Congress Cataloging-in-Publication Data
Thompson, Janice A.
    Picture perfect : a novel / Janice Thompson.
        p.   cm. — (Weddings by design ; #1)
    ISBN 978-0-8007-2152-7 (pbk.)
    1. Wedding photography—Fiction. 2. Weddings—Fiction. 3. Christian fiction. 4. Love stories. I. Title.
    PS3620.H6824P53 2013
    813'.6—dc23   2012034581

The author is represented by MacGregor Literary Agency.

13   14   15   16   17   18   19   7   6   5   4   3   2   1

To the faithful prayer warriors on my dream team. You helped me breathe Bella back to life. What fun to see her through Hannah McDermott's eyes! Thank you for your prayers, your encouragement, and your ideas. This book is as much yours as it is mine.

In memory of the great Bing Crosby, whose movies and melodies filled my heart as a child. I couldn't pen a story about Irish Americans without including some of his best-loved songs as chapter titles.

So the last will be first, and the first will be last.
Matthew 20:16

Prologue

Going My Way

May your troubles be as few and as far apart as my grandmother's teeth.

Irish proverb

My life has been a series of *almosts*.

Take, for instance, the time I *almost* made the cheerleading squad in high school but lost out to my archnemesis, Jacquie Practically-Perfect-in-Every-Way Goldfarb. Then there was the time Matt Hudson, the hunkiest football player at my high school, *almost* asked me to the prom but ended up going with Jacquie instead. Oh, and we can't forget the time I *almost* got a photographer's dream job, shooting superstar Brock Benson's wedding. Yep. Another *almost*. That time, the opportunity of a lifetime slipped through my fingers and into the open palms of my chief competitor, Drew Kincaid of Kincaid Photography.

Some people are haunted by memories of things they've done. Me? I'm haunted by all of the things I nearly accomplished but missed by a quarter of an inch. That's why, when faced with yet another unbelievable opportunity—a profile piece in *Texas Bride* magazine to promote my new Galveston-based photography business—I couldn't blow it. No more *almosts* for me. This time I would hit the finish line a winner. My meeting with the *Texas Bride* reporter would transform my career and propel me into the limelight, winning me the favor of the island's top wedding planner, Bella Neeley. If I could just keep from messing it up.

Oh, but this time I wouldn't! In fact, I could almost hear my grandpa Aengus cheering me on from the great beyond: "Hannah Grace, if you're lucky enough to be Irish, then you're lucky enough."

I didn't happen to believe in luck, but if being Irish meant I stood a better chance at succeeding in business, I would embrace my heritage as never before. I would bathe with Irish Spring soap, dress in the vibrant colors of the family crest, skip through fields of shamrocks, and listen to my father's nightly tales of Clan McDermott's glory days. And I would do it all with a smile on my face and confidence in my stride.

From his mansion up in heaven, Grandpa Aengus smiled down on me, his gold-capped front tooth gleaming like the precious stones in the pearly gate. I could sense his pleasure as I made up my mind to do the McDermotts proud. Like my warring ancestors of yesteryear, I would fight to the finish, wielding my bloody sword—er, my two-thousand-dollar digital camera with stellar resolution and optical zoom—until I took the prize. I would come out a victor in the end, or make a fool of myself trying.

Either way, I wouldn't go down without a fight. A true McDermott never did.

1

Too-Ra-Loo-Ra-Loo-Ral

May you have no frost on your spuds,
No worms on your cabbage.
May your goat give plenty of milk.
If you inherit a donkey, may she be in foal.

Irish saying

There's no denying the fact that my grandpa Aengus shaped the way I look at life. The man had a saying for everything. If I fell and scraped my knee, he mended it with an Irish proverb: "For every storm, a rainbow, for every tear, a smile." If I woke up with a head cold, he had an Irish remedy: "A good laugh and a long sleep are the two best cures." If I got into an argument with my BFF, he offered sage Irish wisdom: "Don't give cherries to pigs or advice to fools."

The man firmly believed that anything good that came to him in this life was in some way tied to his great fortune at being born Irish. No one ever debated him on that point. No one in the family, anyway. Since his passing three years ago, those quirky proverbs and blessings have brought those of us who loved him an ongoing sense of comfort and peace.

My father, God bless him, has done his best to keep Grandpa's sayings alive, but he usually ends up botching the proverbs. Still, a botched proverb is a proverb, so, on the third Saturday in September, as I buzzed down the road, I decided to give my dad a call. Surely he could come up with words of wisdom. I desperately needed them before meeting with the reporter from *Texas Bride* magazine.

My father answered with a jovial, "Hannah Grace! How's my girl?"

The moment I heard his voice come over the car's Bluetooth speaker, I wilted like a flower in an underfertilized garden. Something about my dad's happy-go-lucky tone always made me feel young again. Vulnerable. Once a daddy's little girl, always a daddy's little girl, right?

I turned my focus to the road, paying particular attention to a group of tourists on the edge of the seawall snapping photos of the murky gulf waters as they rolled in and out in predictable fashion. Funny how people liked to capture every little moment on film—the good, the bad, and the ugly. Even the mundane.

My hesitation must've prompted some worry on my father's end.

"You okay, Shutter Speed?"

I laughed at his funny nickname. "Yeah. Mostly." A lingering sigh followed. "Just needed some sage advice."

"So you called me?" His chuckle lifted my spirits. "You

must be desperate. Or forgetful. I've never been very good at advice, remember? I'm pretty sure I'm the one who told my friends to buy stock in Enron years ago, wasn't I? And I'm the one who convinced your mother to buy that over-the-top Christmas sweater you girls all make fun of. Oh, and remember that whole Y2K thing? Got people worked up for nothing and felt like a fool in the end."

A girlish giggle escaped on my end. "Yeah, but you've been forgiven for all of that. And I do need some words of wisdom, Dad. I'm just about to head into an interview with an important reporter and need to know how to change the subject if she brings up Sierra Caswell's wedding. I don't want to blow this. Bella Neeley from Club Wed will read this article, and I need to impress her."

"Wait . . . Bella Neeley, that's a name I know. But who's Sierra Caswell?"

"The bride I told you about a couple of weeks ago. The one with all the attitude."

"Ah. The country-western singer?"

"Yes."

"Why are you so worried about the reporter's questions?"

"Because I need to do my best to protect Sierra's privacy, and I'm afraid I'll blow it. You know? Sometimes we get to talking and things just slip out. I've got to be careful not to let that happen. You know me, Dad."

"Gotcha. You're a chip off the old block."

"Yep. But Sierra's a high-profile case, and she hasn't been easy, so I'm afraid I might accidentally spout off if the reporter gets too nosy." I turned onto Broadway. "You're not going to believe it, but Sierra's publicist sent me a note saying that I have to Photoshop out any wrinkles around her eyes." I thought about the email I'd read on my phone just this morning. The whole thing seemed ludicrous, even now. "Seriously? Who has wrinkles at twenty-six?"

Oh, wait, I did. And they deepened every time I thought about Sierra's wedding. Instead of seeing the event as a blessing to my career, I felt a strange and ominous sense of foreboding every time I imagined the big day. But I tried to push those feelings aside. They were just feelings, after all. And as a woman of faith, I knew better than to put much stock in feelings.

"Grandpa Aengus never had a wrinkle till he turned seventy-five."

My father's voice brought me back to reality.

"Then again, his hair turned gray at twenty-two," my father continued, "so he always looked older than his age, even without the wrinkles. From what I hear, it never really bothered him, though."

"Still, some people worry about such things, especially people in the public eye. Sierra's famous, you know. She had a top ten song on Billboard last month, and she just recorded the new theme song for *Stars Collide*."

"*Stars Collide*?"

"My favorite sitcom. The one about the talent scouts. You know?"

"Oh, right, right."

I had a feeling he didn't have a clue, but I kept going anyway. "My point is, she's famous. So landing this gig is critical to my career. It will put me in good standing with Bella Neeley, and if I can stay in her good graces, my studio will become famous."

"And this Sierra person holds the key to all of this? She's really that important?"

"Definitely. You can't pick up a magazine without seeing

her name in it. And she was on *Entertainment Tonight* just last week. But she's a pain in the backside to work with, like I said. Talk about a diva. I was really excited to get this gig, but it's been nothing but trouble so far. Even Bella has struggled with her, and she's handled every bridezilla known to mankind. If she's having trouble, can you even imagine *me* trying to manage it?"

"From what I've heard, Bella's one tough cookie."

"Oh, she is. But she's as sweet as sugar too. And right now she adores me. I'd like to keep it that way."

Up ahead the light turned red and I waited, though waiting didn't come naturally to me.

"How could she help but love you? You're a McDermott." He took a swan dive into one of his usual Irish tales about the joys of belonging to the clan.

As always, when he got to talking about our heritage, his brogue thickened. The *g*'s disappeared from the end of his words. The *r*'s were pushed. The *h*'s disappeared altogether. Words like *thirty* became *tirty*. The letter *i* became *oi*. In other words, we were no longer Irish. We were, without apology, Oirish. And very happy about it, from the lilt in Dad's voice. He continued to share his heart about how easy it would be for Bella to love me and my work.

"Hey, Oi read the *Daily*, kiddo. Oi know tat Bella named you one of te top five photographers in South Texas. Tat's got to be great for business, right?"

He had no idea. Picture This, the Galveston studio I'd opened just a year and a half ago, stood a chance at blossoming into something of great beauty now that the coordinator at Galveston's premiere wedding facility had taken notice of me. How many months had I prayed for such a miracle? Seemed like forever. And with one word from Bella, the Red

Sea had parted at last. I would forever be grateful. But I had to be proactive. Nothing—I repeat, nothing—could mess this up. Not now, after I'd worked so hard.

A little sigh escaped as I thought it through. "I just have this horrible feeling that the situation with Sierra Caswell could undo all of my hard work. She's a royal pain. I've never met anyone so self-focused."

The light turned green and I put my foot on the accelerator, ready to move forward—both physically and emotionally.

"Ah." My father paused. "And you need to make sure you don't give any of this information away to the reporter, should she ask."

"Right." I eased the steering wheel to the left, careful to avoid several parked cars on the side of the street. The closer I got to the Strand, the worse the traffic.

"Well, you know what your grandfather would've said on a mornin' such as this, don't you, darlin'?"

The lilt in my father's voice made me smile, and a sense of calm settled over me as I anticipated his next words. "Nope, that's why I called you."

My dad chuckled. "Your grandpa would've said, 'Put silk on a goat and it's still a goat.'"

I eased down on the brakes as I approached the Starbucks parking lot. "You're calling Sierra Caswell a goat?"

"Well, if the silk fits . . ."

Okay, that got a chuckle out of me. I turned my car into the lot, then slipped it into park and leaned back against the seat. "Don't know how you've done it, Dad, but you have. You made me laugh. And feel much better about the situation." Nothing new there. This daddy's girl always felt better after a heart-to-heart, even a quirky one involving goats.

"I didn't give you a lick of advice, but I've managed to

distract you, and that's exactly what you need to do with that reporter. Pull a Grandpa Aengus on her. Respond with an Oirish proverb. She'll think you're brilliant."

"I'm not so sure about that."

"Well, you are brilliant, Shutter Speed. You're from good Irish stock, after all. Now get in there and knock 'em dead." He cleared his throat. "Well, um, not really. But you know what I mean. Let your confidence ring out loud and clear. Just give the reporter enough information to let your competitors know who's who and what's what. The rest will take care of itself."

As he said the word *competitors*, my thoughts shifted at once to Drew Kincaid. Would I ever get past the nerves when his name was mentioned? Okay, so my father hadn't actually mentioned my hunky competitor by name, but he might as well have. Why did Drew unnerve me so?

"You still there, kiddo?"

My father's voice roused me from my ponderings and forced my attention to the matter at hand. "Yeah. Just thinking about what you said. Wondering how I should go about putting Drew Kincaid in his place so that I come out looking like a pro and not some sort of bitter competitor with a chip on my shoulder." *Which I probably am, but I'm working on it.*

"Kincaid?" A string of words in lyrical Gaelic flowed on my father's end, followed by, "That's the competition? A Kincaid?"

"Yeah." I sighed. "Kincaid Photography."

"Well, why dinna ye say so?" Brogue now thicker than before, my father took off on a passionate rant. I couldn't make out much until I heard the words "fight till the death." Only *death* sounded more like *det.*

"Wait, what are you saying, Dad? We have some connection to the Kincaids?"

His tirade drew to an immediate halt. "You mean you really don't know? You haven't heard the story?"

"No."

"It's quite a tale, the story of the clash between Clan Kincaid and Clan McDermott. Are ye sure yer up for it?"

Have I ever been up for any of your Clan McDermott stories?

A quick glance at my watch told me I'd arrived twenty minutes early for my appointment. Probably just enough time for one of Dad's tales. "Sure. Fill me in."

His brogue deepened even more as the story began to unfold. Before long I felt he'd transported me all the way across the Atlantic to the green hills of Ireland, the lilt in his voice dancing across the phone line. "We're talkin' generations of fightin' that took several lives. Almost wiped out both clans. Worse than the Hatfields and McCoys."

I gasped at this news. "Over what?"

"Land, a' course. What else?"

"There were no cameras involved? No photography businesses?"

Dad grunted. "A' course not. We're talkin' hundreds a' years ago. No such thing as cameras back then."

"What happened?"

"The Kincaids lost their land in a bloody battle between the clans and vowed to fight till the death to get it back. So far they haven't been successful. In fact, tempers still flare in the old country whenever a McDermott and a Kincaid cross paths." He slipped into Gaelic, words laced with passion.

"No way." My heart quickened at that news. "Are you sure about this?"

"Check it out in the history books. You'll see it's quite a story. So don't fret over this Kincaid fellow. He comes from a long line of losers."

"Wow."

"You're a McDermott, darlin'," my father said. "We McDermotts always come out on top if we don't give up. So don't go down without a fight. Remember that and you'll go a long way in this life. Remember what your grandfather always said too: 'Enthusiasm is like a fire that needs an occasional poke with a stick.'"

He laughed and I joined in. In fact, I could almost envision my grandfather's face.

"Just stir the embers," my dad said. "Keep the flame lit, Shutter Speed."

"Gotcha." I released a slow breath. "Thanks again, Dad. Give Mama a kiss from me."

"Always happy to kiss your mother." He half mumbled something in Gaelic, then the call ended. I could almost picture him doing a little jig across the house to sweep Mama into his arms.

Ah, romance! When would it knock me off my feet like that?

Never, if I spent eighty hours a week focused on my business. Still, what else could I do? We McDermotts didn't go down without a fight, as Dad said. Not that I needed to fret over the whole Drew Kincaid thing, apparently. Like my clan members, I would win the battle. I would claim the land, conquer my foes, and take some impressive wrinkle-free photos of the biggest diva in country music history.

And somehow manage to impress Galveston Island's top wedding planner along the way.

2

The Little Things in Life

May those who love us, love us.
And for those who don't love us,
May God turn their hearts.
And if he cannot turn their hearts,
May he turn their ankles,
So we may know them by their limping.

Irish saying

After touching up my lipstick, I headed into Starbucks dressed in my most professional attire and carrying a portfolio that would've made a novice photographer shamrock-green with envy. Why, then, did I have to blow it the moment the reporter walked in the door by rambling as if I'd consumed nothing but caffeine all day? Oh, right. Because I hadn't.

The cup of cinnamon dolce latte that I purchased trembled in my hand as I took the seat across from the frazzled blonde reporter who introduced herself as Dani. She gave me a pensive look as she pulled an iPad out of her purse and turned it on. "Start over, Hannah," she said, her thinly plucked brows elevating as she tried to keep up with me. "But slow down this time. I don't want to miss a thing."

After clearing my throat, I began my speech again, this time pacing my words. "I was just saying that wedding pictures don't tell the whole story. Not even close." Taking a sip of my latte, I tried to look poised and professional. Unfortunately, my acting skills had never been very good.

"Meaning?" She typed a few words into her touch-sensitive keyboard, using the two-finger method.

I released a slow breath and delivered my carefully rehearsed speech. "Photographers work hard to capture the glorious moments. The radiant smile on the bride's face as she takes her first step down the aisle. The look of wonder coming from the groom as he catches a glimpse of his bride for the first time. The backdrop of a gorgeous wedding facility—especially if it happens to be Club Wed, the prettiest place to get married on Galveston Island."

Dani looked up from her iPad and sighed. "Don't you just love Club Wed? My sister Sharlene got married there a few years ago. Her ceremony made the papers because it was their first official themed wedding."

"The boot-scootin' country-western one?" I could hardly believe it. That wedding was infamous.

"That's the one." She grinned. "Now you see why I'm so interested in the place. I'd like to get married there myself someday."

"Who wouldn't? But you'd better go ahead and book it

now if you're serious. I hear they've got a waiting list a mile long."

Dani released a little sigh. "Well, I'm not exactly engaged yet. Just wishful thinking on my part. Every girl wants the perfect wedding."

"Of course. Club Wed is definitely the best venue on the island and the perfect place to capture those rare, once-in-a-lifetime photos."

"Like?"

"Like . . ." I paused to think it through, my eyes fluttering closed as the images presented themselves in my mind's eye. "Like the close-up of a lone tear as it slips down the cheek of the mother of the bride. And that made-for-the-camera moment when the bridesmaids and groomsmen take their places alongside the bride and groom, forming a perfect V-shape with the minister at the very center." At this point, I added all the dramatic flair I could muster as I punctuated each word. "*These* are the things we attempt to catch through the eye of the camera."

"And you do a lovely job." Dani continued to type in her notes, then glanced my way. "I looked through the photos you sent. I've never seen such beautiful wedding portraits, and I'm not just saying that. They're exquisite."

"Aw, thank you." Her words boosted my confidence and almost made me feel worthy of this interview. Almost.

With a bit of maneuvering on her screen, she pulled up the photos I'd emailed, and we both leaned in to have a closer look. I couldn't help but smile as a picture of my most recent bride filled the screen. Dani gave me a little wink as she enlarged it with a swipe of her fingers.

"I've already talked to my editor. *Texas Bride* is going to feature some of your photographs along with this interview.

Quite an honor." She reached into her bag and came out with some legal-looking papers. "Of course, you'll have to sign these copyright release forms and mail them to me. You okay with that?"

"Sure." I was completely overwhelmed by this amazing opportunity.

I turned as the barista called out someone's order—a caramel mocha macchiato. My stomach rumbled, another reminder that I needed real food, not more coffee.

Focus, Hannah. You may never get another chance like this.

I released a slow breath and faced the reporter once again. "As I was saying, there are some not-to-be-missed photo ops at a wedding, but I think it's only fair to add that there are a few things we photographers deliberately leave out, things the average wedding guest never sees. This is what makes or breaks a photographer, in my opinion. And I would like to think that's what sets me apart from the competition." My eyes fluttered closed again, and an image of Drew Kincaid flitted across my mind. Remembering my father's story about the Kincaids and McDermotts, I trembled. Better stay focused on the interview, not my competition.

"Things you leave out?" Dani's brow wrinkled. "Like what?"

I opened my eyes and offered a confident smile. "Oh, say, the bride screaming at the bridesmaids just minutes before she walks down the aisle, or the flower girl throwing a fit in her beautiful dress. The caterer realizing she forgot to bring the duck a l'Orange, or the florist scrambling to make an extra bridesmaid bouquet with only seconds to spare. I've seen all of that and much more."

Should I tell her about the drunk-as-a-skunk father of the bride who'd shown up fifteen minutes before his daughter's scheduled ceremony? I'd poured three cups of hot coffee down that man's throat to prep him for his walk down the aisle. Nah. Better not share that story just yet.

"Ooh, your life sounds so glamorous." Dani entered more notes, then looked up, her eyes narrowing. "What else have you got?"

I thought for a moment. "Well, I worked one wedding where the four-tiered cake toppled just before the reception. Thank goodness I got a couple of pictures before it hit the floor. See what I mean? It's all about knowing what to shoot and when. I always get a few shots of the cake before anyone arrives, just in case."

"Wow." Dani gave me an admiring look. "You've got this down to a science."

"Yep." I chuckled. "I've learned a lot from Bella Neeley, the coordinator at Club Wed. She's the best in the business." *Please make sure you print that.* I flashed Dani a smile, but her gaze had shifted back to the iPad. "We've done a couple of weddings together, and I'm so grateful for the things she's taught me. She's such a wedding pro, loaded with great information about the biz."

"Speaking of the wedding business, one of Bella's brothers is a photographer too, isn't he?"

"Yes, Joey. I've never met him, actually. He and his wife just moved to Italy to help with the family's wedding facility in Naples."

"Sounds like a dream job." Dani sighed.

"No kidding." I smiled, in part because losing Joey to Italy meant Bella would be calling on me more to take photographs at Club Wed. I hoped so, anyway. It probably wouldn't hurt to mention her name a couple more times in this interview, just to be safe.

Dani shifted in her seat as the already crowded coffee shop took in extra patrons. As the table next to us filled with teenagers, the noise level rose, and so did the pitch of Dani's voice. "So, you were telling me about things *not* to capture on film at a wedding."

"Right. Well, I shot this one wedding where the mother of the groom refused to be escorted down the aisle because she hated her future daughter-in-law."

"What did you do?"

"Bella gave me the idea, actually." *Score! Another shameless plug for the woman who holds my career in her hands!* "We spent a couple of minutes before the wedding showing the mother photographs I'd just taken of her son in his tuxedo, looking content and happy. That won her over."

"Perfect. You're a master."

"Aw, thanks. I try." Another story came to mind. "This is the worst one of all. I worked an over-the-top wedding for a well-to-do Houston family where the best man and matron of honor were having a romantic tryst." I took a sip of my coffee to wash away the bitter taste that filled my mouth at the memory of the event.

"They met at the wedding and fell in love?" Dani giggled. "How sweet."

"Actually . . ." I leaned in to whisper the details so that the family at the next table wouldn't overhear. "They were married to other people. I happened in on them in the chapel after everyone else had gone to the reception hall."

"Oh, ouch."

"Right. I'd gone back in there to snag a few photos of the unity candle and candelabras. Found something else entirely."

A shiver ran down my spine as I relived that horrible moment. "I'm just saying some things are best not committed to film." I picked up my coffee and took a sip, now deep in thought. Placing the cup back on the table, I continued. "After years in the business, I've become skilled at knowing which shots to catch and which ones to avoid."

"It's truly an art form, then."

"I'd like to think so."

The deep bellow of a ship's horn sounded, and I glanced out the window of the Starbucks. Across the street, well within eyesight, a massive Carnival cruise ship pulled out of port. Twisted memories snaked through my mind as I watched the cruisers wave their goodbyes from the top deck. How many times had I stood in that spot, camera in hand? Another blast of the ship's horn startled me back to attention. I rubbed my eyes, feeling a headache coming on.

"Hannah?" Dani gave me a curious look.

"Yes?" I turned to her with what I hoped would look like a confident nod. "Sorry. Just thinking about those cruisers."

"Oh, that's right." She gave me a pensive look. "I think I read somewhere that you once worked on a cruise ship, taking photos of the passengers. Is that right?"

"Yes." Not that I wanted to talk about it. I wouldn't garner much respect from Bella or from future clients if *Texas Bride* printed the details of my very messy breakup with the cruise director of the *Clarity*. I cringed just thinking about it.

"Now tell me about . . ." Dani glanced at her notepad, then back up again. "Drew Kincaid."

"Drew Kincaid?" I tried to maintain a calm expression, all the while sword fighting the demons of envy that danced in front of my eyes. "What about him?"

Dani referred to her notes. "Well, I see that the two of you have quite a competitive thing going on. Kincaid Photography took the number-one spot on Bella's list, after all. You took the number two. Want to tell our readers about that?"

I'd rather not, thanks.

Who cared if my blue-eyed distraction made it to the top of Bella's list? He wasn't the one shooting Sierra Caswell's wedding, now was he?

Swallowing hard, I chose my next words carefully. "I've known Drew about a year and a half. He's very good at what he does."

"Better than you?" she teased.

"Hardly." I bit back the rest of the words that threatened to escape. "I mean, I'd like to think I've got a few tricks up my sleeve."

"Like the one where you make the competition disappear?" She gave me a wink.

"That's the idea."

"Well then, why don't you tell our readers about some of those tricks you've been hiding. Let's start with the wedding you're photographing the first weekend in December. Everyone in town is talking about it. Must be quite an honor, working with Sierra Caswell." Dani's eyes sparkled. "I mean, a mega country singer like Sierra's been photographed by hundreds of photographers all over the world. How are you going to capture her on the big day?"

With a net and a rope?

How could I explain the situation and still come out smelling like a rose? Frankly, I couldn't wait for this wedding to be behind me so I could move forward with a saner, happier bride-to-be, someone who treated me with respect and kindness.

Divert her, Hannah. Come up with one of Grandpa Aengus's proverbs. Something witty.

"Every dog is bold on its own doorstep," I managed. Where the words came from, I couldn't say.

Really, Hannah? That's the best you've got—that stupid "dog on the doorstep" proverb?

"W-what?" She looked my way, the lines of concentration deepening along her brows and under her eyes.

I swallowed hard, feeling like an idiot. "Oh, I'm just saying that, um, the boldness I feel—or, rather, the sense of confidence I have in photographing Sierra Caswell—is much the same as a dog on his doorstep." I gave a weak smile, though I felt like a blithering idiot.

"Are . . . are you calling yourself a dog?" Dani looked more confused than ever.

"Oh. Well, no. Not really. Just saying that I am confident I'll do a good job of capturing photos of Sierra on her big day."

"Ah. Well, why didn't you just say so?"

Because I was trying to distract you. And apparently it worked.

I somehow diverted Dani's attention once again by talking about the most recent wedding I'd photographed, an Irish shindig featuring my younger sister Deidre as the bride. That seemed to put the reporter at ease. For a while. She finally came back around to her questions about Sierra Caswell, and with a smile plastered on my face, I answered to the best of my ability.

At three o'clock, just as several patrons headed out of the coffee shop, Dani glanced at her watch and gasped. "Oh, I can't believe we've been here this long. Do you mind? I really need to . . ." Her words drifted off as she glanced at the door.

"You have another appointment?"

"Yes, actually, I—"

"No biggie." I rose and reached for my purse and portfolio. "I've got to get back to work. Can't wait to see the article in print. And I'll be sure to fill out the copyright permission forms so you can use those photos. I'll sign them and fax them back to you this evening."

"Great. I appreciate it." Her gaze shifted to the door of the coffee shop as it swung open.

My breath caught in my throat as the ever-gorgeous Drew Kincaid stepped inside. Ribbons of sunlight reflected off his stunning blond hair. He flashed that cool smile of his, and those blue eyes shimmered with mischief as he walked toward us.

"Well now." He stopped at our table and focused on me. "Never expected to see you here, Hannah." He turned to Dani, still offering that boyish grin, his firm mouth curved as if on the edge of laughter. "And you must be Dani. From *Texas Bride*?"

He extended his hand, but my focus was on the broad shoulders and muscular arms. Why did the competition have to be so . . . hot? He looked devilishly handsome and forced my attention away from the conversation at hand. I did my best to shift my gaze, but how could I, with that deep blue shirt matching his eyes so perfectly? And why did his face have to be bronzed by the wind and sun? Who had skin like that in late September?

"I—I'm Dani." The reporter took his hand, almost knocking over my coffee in the process. "Nice to meet you."

His smile widened, his teeth strikingly white against his tanned face. "Well, I hope I haven't missed all the fun." Drew pulled up a chair between us and took a seat, then plunked his portfolio on the table.

"Oh, Hannah is full of stories. But I guess it's time to shift gears." Dani flashed a nervous smile and fussed with her hair in a flirtatious fashion. "I hope you don't mind, Hannah. I just figured, well, both of you made the list . . ."

Yes, both of us had made the list, all right. Despite my best attempts to nudge out the competition, Drew had somehow won the top spot. Seemed like he always managed to steal my thunder. But not for long. No, if I played my cards right with Sierra Caswell, I would eventually knock him off his perch. If I kept my cool and handled things like a pro.

Deep breath, Hannah. Think about the McDermotts of old. Didn't they end up with the land? Of course they did! This is going to end well, as long as you don't crater.

I fidgeted with my necklace, a lovely silver cross Grandpa Aengus had given me for my thirteenth birthday. I happened to glance down and did a double take as my eyes landed on my feet. On my left foot—a comfy black flat. On my right—a luscious brown strappy sandal.

What in the world?

I looked again, just to be sure. Yep. Two mismatched shoes stared back at me. So much for looking and acting like a pro.

Stay calm, Hannah. Stay. Calm.

I shifted my gaze back up to Dani and Drew, but they were both staring down at my feet, cockeyed grins on their faces. Now what?

"I, um . . . it's Wear Your Mismatched Shoes to Work Day. I'm surprised you two didn't get the memo." I reached down to grab my now-lukewarm coffee and offered Dani what I hoped would look like a confident smile. "Well, thanks for your time. Have a good day."

"Happy to meet you."

Judging from the fact that she never even looked up from my feet, I rather doubted it.

I gave her a curt nod, then pivoted on the heel of my black flat, caught the toe of my brown sandal on the leg of Drew's chair . . . and promptly dropped my cup of coffee into his lap.

3

I'm a Dreamer, Aren't We All

There was a young lady named Rose
Who had a large wart on her nose.
When she had it removed
Her appearance improved,
But her glasses slipped down to her toes.

Irish limerick

There are those moments in every young Irish woman's life when she wishes that whole leprechaun legend was true. I found myself wishing that very thing after dropping a cup of coffee in Drew Kincaid's lap. Oh, if only I could turn into a leprechaun! Then I could disappear at will. That's exactly what I wanted to do after making a fool of myself in such a public way—and in front of a reporter, no less!

But dropping a cup of lukewarm coffee in Drew's lap hadn't

been bad enough. Oh no. I'd followed that act with the grand finale—trying to clean up my mess with several napkins.

Note to self: never attempt to clean another human being's pants, especially in a public forum.

Oh, how I cringed thinking about it. I wanted to curl up in a ball and admit defeat. Instead, I squared my shoulders, pretended the whole thing never happened, and got right back to work. In fact, I pretty much saturated myself with work so that I could forget about the whole thing. Many times I prayed, *Dear God, please don't let that reporter include my dog proverb in her article*, followed by, *And if you could somehow coax her into leaving out the mismatched shoe issue, that would be great too.* These urgent pleas were capped off with, *Oh, and the coffee incident. Yes, Lord, the coffee. Please, please make sure that whole fiasco doesn't appear in print.*

Other than those few things, I felt the meeting with the reporter went great.

Two days later, I pulled my car into the driveway at Club Wed. My three o'clock appointment with Bella would prove to be a challenge, no doubt, since we planned to meet with Sierra Caswell via Skype.

I did my best to remain calm but found it difficult. Meeting with Sierra online felt safer, at least. Connecting with her in person put the fear of God in me and made me question my decision to photograph this wedding in the first place.

Pulling the key out of the ignition, I drew in a deep breath. My gaze shifted to the pristine wedding facility where so many glorious ceremonies had taken place. The butterfly farm in my stomach took to flight as I saw Bella Neeley walking across the lawn, headed right for my car. The gorgeous brunette's long, dark curls reminded me of a character from a painting. She wore the prettiest blouse—sort of a teal blue—along with a fashionable pair of skinny jeans. And her trademark cowboy boots, of course. I couldn't help but notice them because the inlaid stones caught the sun and made them glisten.

Bella carried her infant daughter in her arms. And her toddler—what was his name again?—had somehow wrapped himself around her right leg. He jostled up and down as she made her way toward my car, his unruly brown hair standing atop his head—half trendy, half mop top.

I opened the door and stepped out, all smiles, then offered a little wave to win over the rambunctious youngster. The boy released his hold on Bella's leg, then hid behind her, obviously terrified by my presence. Not quite the reaction I'd hoped for. I reached down to fuss with his hair, messing it up even more, and offered a cheerful, "Hey, you!"

He spouted something in Italian, and Bella's eyes widened as she turned to admonish him. "Tres Neeley! I've told you a thousand times not to say that!"

Tres. That's it.

The youngster's lip curled down in a pout, and his gaze shifted to the ground. "But Uncle Laz says it." The child's words had a bit of a Texas twang to them, which I found endearing. A little odd after the outburst in Italian, but endearing.

Bella groaned and looked at the baby girl, who stirred awake. "Do you mind?" She placed the little doll in my arms, and I shifted my attention to her captivating brown eyes and lush eyelashes.

Wow. This one's a beauty. A little on the chunky side, but a beauty.

Bella knelt down and scolded Tres, who offered up a quiet apology in Tex-Italian.

"There, now. That's better." Bella rose and sighed as she looked my way. "Just about the time you think you've got a handle on life, you throw kids into the mix. I hope you'll forgive the fact that I've got them with me today. D.J. will be here soon to pick up Tres. They've got father-son plans tonight."

"Sounds like fun."

"Yeah. Tres always loves spending alone time with his daddy—who wouldn't in a family this big, you know?"

"Oh, well, I . . ." How could I explain that I got alone time with my dad most every day?

"Anyway, Tres has been looking forward to this all day, so I hope D.J. gets here soon. He's got a construction job on the west end of the island, but he knows we've got this meeting about Sierra's wedding, so he should be here any minute, I promise."

"Oh, no problem."

"Speaking of Sierra, I got a call from her publicist today." Bella headed toward the wedding facility, tossing her hair over her shoulder as she glanced back at me. "You won't believe how picky they're being about her photographs. Only certain angles, certain areas of her body. It's crazy. Her publicist said something about some legal forms he's planning to send your way. Hope you're okay with that."

"I'm sure they're just the usual privacy forms. No big deal." *And by the way, did you realize I'm still holding your baby?* My purse slid off my shoulder and into the crook of my arm, but I kept walking.

"Ah. Wonder why he called me, then?" Bella paused at the veranda and shrugged. "Oh well."

I did my best not to groan aloud. Frankly, I wasn't sure which bothered me more—the fact that Sierra's publicist had the nerve to be so picky, or the fact that he'd called Bella, not me. Who was shooting this wedding, anyway?

Deep breath, Hannah. Don't read too much into this.

"We can talk about all of this when we meet with Sierra online." She glanced at her watch. "We can hash it all out then." Bella swung wide the front door to Club Wed and ushered me inside.

I held fast to the baby girl, who now gazed up at me with such longing that I actually heard my biological clock ticking.

Tick-tock, tick-tock. Give the baby back to her mother.

I pressed the little darling into Bella's arms. "It stinks that Sierra's going to be in Nashville until two days before her wedding."

"True, but what can we do? She's in the middle of a recording session right now. Thank God for video chats, right?"

"Right."

I took in my surroundings. As always, the beautiful old Victorian home captivated me with its charm and intricate details. The gingerbread trim. The carved wooden door. The peekaboo stained glass window above the front door. The divine chandelier in the lobby. Original wood floors, polished until they gleamed. A girl could get used to a place like this.

I heard the strangest sound off in the distance. I listened more intently. A voice singing. What was that—"Amazing Grace"? Yes, "Amazing Grace." Sort of. Certainly not like any version I'd ever heard.

Bella must've sensed my confusion. She laughed and pointed at a large cage in the adjoining room. Inside it, a colorful parrot trilled with delight, then hollered out, "Go to the mattresses!"

"Sorry about Guido." Bella chuckled. "He shifts back and forth between choirboy and mobster."

"Ah." I took a couple of steps toward the parrot, hoping to get a closer look, but he let out an ear-piercing *rat-a-tat-tat* sound that reminded me of a machine gun going off, and my heart sailed to my throat. The baby began to cry at once, and Tres put his hands over his ears and winced.

So much for befriending the family's bird. I'd have to win Bella's approval some other way.

She released an exaggerated groan. "I'm so sorry, Hannah. It's my day to watch Guido, but he doesn't make it easy on me. Ever since Uncle Sal died, the poor old bird just hasn't been the same."

I didn't know who Uncle Sal was, but his death certainly put the bird's misbehavior in perspective. Sort of.

"Let's go into my office. It's quieter in there." Bella paused and then used the most motherly voice I'd heard in a while. "Tres, be a good boy and let Mommy work. Would you like to watch a movie?"

"*Buddy the Warrior!*" He ran in circles, making me dizzy. Who had that kind of energy?

Bella's brows drew downward in a frown. "No, Son. I don't care what Uncle Lazarro lets you watch when Mommy's not around, I don't approve of wrestling shows. They're not good for you."

The toddler let out a squall and plopped down onto the floor, dissolving into a tantrum that involved tears and kicking.

This, naturally, made the baby cry even louder. Bella drew her close, nuzzled her nose against the little one's cheek, and hollered above the noise from the chaos, "I think Rosa-Earline is cutting teeth. She was a little feverish this morning. And you should have seen the fit she threw in the middle of the night. I've hardly had any sleep."

"Ah." I had to wonder how Bella got anything done around here with these two underfoot.

Bella's eyes narrowed. "I'm sorry. What were we talking about?"

"Wrestling shows?" I tried.

"Before that." She held tight to the baby with her left arm and scooped up the toddler with her right, amazing me with her ability to hang on to both with such precision.

"Um, birds?"

Bella shook her head. "No, before Guido, I mean."

"Video chats?"

"Right."

She continued to talk as she made her way through the foyer and into her office. Once inside, Bella put Tres down on the floor and set the baby in some sort of a swing-like contraption in the corner, then inserted a DVD into the player. Minutes later an animated movie filled the tiny television screen in the corner. Not that Tres paid it any mind. Instead, he scrambled up onto the desk and grabbed the cup that held his mother's pens and pencils. They plinked and plunked to the floor below, a couple of them landing under my chair.

I couldn't help myself. My hand slipped into my bag and came out with my camera. Just as Tres reached to spin one of the pencils, I snagged the perfect shot of him. Close-up, of course. I caught the sneaky little smile. The wrinkled nose. The mischievous eyes. Caught it all. He turned long enough to catch my eye, then offered a sly grin meant just for me.

You precious, naughty thing, you!

Bella didn't seem to notice I'd slipped into photographer mode. She scolded her son, lifted him down from the desk, then turned my way and sighed. "Do you mind if I call D.J.? He should be here by now."

Just as she reached for the phone, a sound from outside caught my attention. I glanced out the window at a large, black Dodge 4x4. It screeched to a halt, and a man—no, make that a strikingly handsome Texas cowboy—stepped out.

"Saints preserve us," I whispered under my breath as I took in his broad shoulders and lanky gait. *Who is that?*

"Finally." Bella rose and gestured for Tres to clean up his mess. "Son, your daddy's here."

Ack. Should've seen the resemblance between the father and the children. Bella ushered her husband into the room moments later and introduced him as D.J.—Dwayne Neeley Jr. The thick Texas drawl held me under its spell for a moment as the handsome blond cowboy laid out his plan for the evening—taking Tres to visit his grandparents in Splendora, about an hour north of Houston up Highway 59. I'd never been to Splendora myself, but listening to D.J.'s deep twang made me want to grab my cowgirl boots and scurry on up there as quickly as I could, especially if it meant finding a fella like this.

Do you have a brother, perhaps? A distant cousin?

Turned out he did have a brother. A happily married one named Bubba.

Why, Lord? Why?

By the time D.J. left, my nerves had dissipated. And when Bella finally got our video chat going, I felt my confidence return.

Until Sierra Caswell's face came into view on the screen. Then I felt a little shaky once again. Why did this girl have that effect on me? The petite blonde with the big Texas hair dove right in, her words coming at us a mile a minute. I found the tiny dimples on either side of her mouth fascinating. They would photograph well. And those big blue eyes would be great in print too. Just for grins, I squinted to see if I could find any wrinkles around them. Nope. Not a one.

Bella kicked off the conversation, making light chatter about the ceremony—a country-western extravaganza, of course. She and Sierra talked with big smiles about the food, the decor, the order of events . . . everything. Well, everything but the photography.

By the time they got around to talking about the photographs, Sierra's smile had disappeared. *Now* I saw the crinkles around her eyes. Hmm. Well, thank God for Photoshop.

Sierra's eyelashes took to fluttering as she spoke. "I won't lie, Hannah. When I got the call from Drew Kincaid a few weeks back, I was really tempted to go with him. He shot Brock Benson's wedding, you know. Brock's getting more famous by the day. And he's on *Dancing with the Stars* this season. You know what that does for a person's career. So I would have to say that Drew is very well connected, while you're . . ."

Her words drifted off, taking all of the air from my lungs. "Well, yes, but . . ." I began.

If you knew our clan's history, you would know that I win in the end. So there.

"Well, I went with you because I liked your portfolio better." She sighed. "Especially that one picture of the bride from the Irish wedding."

"Thank you. She's my sister Deidre. She—"

"Anyway, I'm counting on you to do your very best, which means you need to stay focused."

"I—I am."

"You should be studying my photos on my website and looking at the angles."

"What?"

"Prep work. Getting ready. It's important that you study the photo links I sent you so that you know my best angles."

What makes you think I haven't looked over those photos?

"George says he hasn't heard from you."

"I called him yesterday. And a couple of days before that. And responded to an email from him this morning." Suddenly I felt like a suspect in a whodunit. Hated that feeling.

"Well, he's really busy right now. But we're taking this photo thing very seriously. Just be aware that I've got to approve all of the photos before any are leaked to the media. You know that's kind of the reason for the great photo angles, right?" Her cheeks flamed pink. "George plans to slip them to the national media, then create a scandal, saying they were leaked against my wishes."

"Wait." My heart fluttered into my throat. "You're not going to pin that leak on me, are you?" A thousand thoughts shot through my head at once, none of them good.

"Oh. Hmm." She shrugged, and a little giggle escaped. "I don't think so, silly. I'm sure he has a plan of action for all that. You know George."

Yes. I knew George, all right. And I trusted him about as far as I trusted my younger sister's so-called potty-trained Pekingese on our mother's carpet.

"I'm not sure about all of that, Sierra." Bella's brow wrinkled, my first sign that she didn't care for the idea either. "Let's talk it through the next time we meet, okay?"

"I guess." Sierra rambled on, oblivious to my ponderings, and ended with, "I just know George is super picky about the shots you take."

"Well, I got his email this morning and—"

"I'm sure everything will work out fine." Off she went on a tangent, talking about her preferences for the photographs.

Nothing terribly unusual, unless you counted the whole "don't shoot me from the left side because my nose is crooked" thing.

I'd just opened my mouth to respond when Bella shot a warning glance my way. I clamped my lips shut.

"No worries, Sierra." Bella turned toward the screen with a confident smile. "Your wedding will come off without a hitch. I haven't lost a bride yet."

I paused to think about the confidence in her voice. After years in the business, she could actually say that and mean it. Me? I still trembled when I thought of using the words "come off without a hitch" to my brides. Not that I'd ever used those words, necessarily. But one day I would. And I would mean them too.

"Awesome." Sierra's face lit in a relaxed smile, and she brushed some of that big hair over her shoulder. "You should hear the song I've co-written to sing to David just before we say our 'I do's.' George is going to have a video team there, so they're going to catch the whole thing and use it for an upcoming music video."

I bit my tongue, in part because I couldn't imagine her publicist playing that large a role in her wedding, and in part because her poor groom must feel like quite a sucker, knowing his wedding was being used as a shoot for a music video. I could almost envision him now, just about to say "I do," with a video camera swooping down to capture a close-up of his face. What a joke.

"Hannah? You still with us?"

"Hmm?" I startled to attention as Bella gave me another warning look.

I noticed the door easing open in the distance. Seconds later, the most delicious aroma permeated the room. What was that—garlic? An older woman eased her way into the room with a tray of food. Holy cow. Not just food . . . the most delicious-looking, tantalizing-smelling tray of Italian food I'd ever seen in my life. Ravioli, red sauce, melted cheese—yum! At once my mouth began to water.

I glanced back and forth between the tray of food and the familiar-looking woman. Where did I know her from?

"Bella!" the older woman called out as she shuffled our way. "Time to eat. You need to keep up your strength while you're nursing that little bambina! Breast-feeding takes a lot out of a new mama. You don't want little Rosie to suffer."

Bella paled. She looked back and forth between the older woman and the computer screen, clearly unable to speak.

"It's okay, Bella." Sierra gave a little wave. "You go on and eat. I'm headed into a recording session, anyway. Might be better to finish up another time."

She clicked off, not even answering the ten or twelve questions I'd planned to ask. Still, with the distraction of—what was that to the right of the ravioli? manicotti?—staring me in the face, who cared about Sierra Caswell? No, she could wait. And so could the wrinkles around her eyes.

4

When Irish Eyes Are Smiling

Bless your little Irish heart and every other Irish part.

Irish blessing

With a belly full of manicotti and ravioli, I relaxed a bit. Until Bella's baby girl awoke in a fretful mood. I happened to catch a couple of funny shots of her throwing a little fit, shots that Bella happened to love.

She snatched the camera from my hand and stared at her favorite photo, then turned my way with tears in her eyes. "Oh, Hannah, you're the best!"

Can I get that in writing?

A squeal followed on Bella's end as she gave the photo another look. "See how you've captured Rosie's little dimples? No one's been able to get a good shot of those yet." She paused, then snapped her fingers, her dark eyes flashing with delight. "Ooh, perfect idea."

"What's that?"

Bella passed the camera back to me and shifted the baby to her other arm. "You've got to photograph my babies. Here. Soon."

"Here, at Club Wed?" My heart raced as I realized how important this could prove to be to my career.

Bella's eyes sparkled as she continued. "Well, Club Wed and my parents' place next door. There's a great vegetable garden behind their house, and a hothouse too. Maybe you've seen glimpses of the garden on the Food Network. The executives just love it. They say it's the most colorful in the country, and they should know."

"Wait . . . the Food Network?" Now she'd lost me completely.

Bella gave me a funny look. "Yes. My aunt Rosa and uncle Laz have a weekly show on the Food Network—*The Italian Kitchen*."

I almost choked at this news. "Oh my goodness."

No wonder Rosa looked familiar. She hosted one of my mother's favorite cooking shows, one where manicotti, garlic twists, and ravioli were daily fare. Yum.

Bella kept going, oblivious to my whirling thoughts. "Might be fun, since my babies have an Italian heritage, to get some shots of them with the tomatoes. Maybe a few photos of D.J. and me too."

"Wow. Sure. Of course."

"Oh, and my parents. And Uncle Lazarro and Aunt Rosa." She went off on a tangent, one that led to her brothers and their children. And her pregnant sister. And her ex-boyfriend, who happened to be married to her pregnant sister. Before long she had me photographing a couple dozen people, both at their home and Parma John's, a local pizzeria owned by her uncle Laz.

I swallowed hard, thinking it through. I'd asked the Lord for an opportunity to impress Bella. Was this his answer, perhaps? Did I have it in me to corral such a large group, especially with so many small children involved?

Oh. Help.

My father's words ricocheted through my brain: *A McDermott fights to the finish.*

Yes. I had it in me. I would conquer this beast, children or not. Chaos or not.

"Our family is long overdue for a photo shoot." Bella's face lit in the most glorious smile. "We need it for personal reasons, of course, but could stand to have photos done for advertising purposes as well. Club Wed is a family-run business, you know."

I glanced down at the baby in her arms and nodded. "Right."

"People always seem to gravitate to us because of the family atmosphere." She shifted the baby to her other hip. "I think they pick up on the fact that we really love one another, in spite of the craziness." She offered a grin. "There's nothing better than people who stick together in good times and bad."

"Ah."

Did I dare tell her about my family? Nah. If she figured out that all three of my younger sisters had married and left me in the lurch, she'd likely feel sorry for me. One thing I'd discovered about married women, especially those in their twenties and thirties—they lived to marry off their single friends. No thank you. After my high-seas fiasco with Jon, that blond, blue-eyed Swedish traitor, I'd tossed the idea of marriage overboard. Well, mostly, anyway.

By the time I left Club Wed, I'd committed to photograph the whole Rossi clan. Not that Italians called themselves a clan, but whatever. We hadn't talked price yet, but I could see dollar signs everywhere I turned. A shoot like this could cover my rent for a month. Or two.

Okay, so my parents didn't charge me rent. My mother had broached the subject once, but my father's swift reaction made me too nervous to offer the suggestion again. I'd taken to slipping Mama cash for groceries and utilities. If this photo shoot came off, I could add to that. I might even be able to afford to send my parents on a vacation or something. Though I doubted my father would break from his daily routine long enough to go on a vacation.

A sigh followed as I thought about how set in his ways Dad had become. I could almost hear him lilting, "*Níl aon tintéan mar do thintéan féin*, Hannah."

"I know, Dad, I know," I whispered to no one but myself. "There's no place like home. But even the most committed homebody sees the benefit of getting out of the house once in a while."

A couple of blocks away from Club Wed, my thoughts shifted back to marriage. Maybe I'd been a bit hasty in claiming I didn't want to find Mr. Right. Perhaps—à la Jerry Maguire—the right guy would complete me. He would have to understand my passion for the new business. And he would definitely have to be willing to live on Galveston Island. That much went without question.

I contemplated Bella Neeley's seemingly ideal life. What would it be like to have a handsome husband like D.J.? Someone who swept the babies into his arms with a broad smile on his face and contentment in his eyes? Someone who looked at me with such love and affection that I felt safe and secure on every front?

I sighed as the tick-tocking of my biological clock started again.

Think about something else, Hannah. Anything.

As I rounded the corner from Broadway to Rosenberg, I saw Kincaid Photography on my right. The snazzy front window display drew my eye at once. I slowed my car and stared at all of the brilliantly placed photos. So many wonderful, happy couples, eyes shimmering with love for one another.

I hated them all.

Well, not really hated, but strongly disliked.

Okay, I didn't really dislike them. I envied them. Like Bella and D.J. Neeley, they had their relationships—their picture-perfect relationships. No flaws. No imperfections. Nothing to Photoshop out.

And what did I have? My boring, predictable life. A life where I stood on the outside with a camera in hand, snapping moderately good shots of other people's lives while mine slipped by. Dull. Uninviting.

Tick-tock, tick-tock.

I stared at a photo of a young couple and noticed the way they gazed at one another. Classic pose, but slightly over-staged. If I'd photographed them, I would have suggested a slightly different angle with more focus on the expressions in their eyes. Then again, Drew always seemed to capitalize on shoulder and chin positions.

Not that I'd been paying particular attention to his technique, of course.

Okay, so I had been paying attention, but that didn't mean anything.

My gaze shifted to a large sign in Drew's front window: WELCOME TO KINCAID PHOTOGRAPHY—BELLA NEELEY'S TOP PICK FOR GALVESTON ISLAND. I almost drove the car into a fire hydrant as those words sank in. I tried to fight them off. Hadn't I just come from a great meeting with Bella? Weren't we becoming friends? Hadn't she chosen me to photograph the family? That had to count for something.

As I drove, the strangest sensation came over me. In spite of my joy at being asked to photograph Sierra's wedding, a niggling fear crept up my spine. Would this turn out to be another "almost" in my life? Would this opportunity morph into another disappointment? Would Drew somehow manage to slip into my place, stealing my thunder and my business?

In that moment one of Grandpa Aengus's proverbs flitted through my mind: "A scholar's ink lasts longer than a martyr's blood."

Got it, Grandpa.

No point in playing the role of a martyr here, even if things grew difficult. I needed to be smart. Savvy. Professional.

All of this deep thinking must've slowed my pace. Behind me, a woman in a baby-blue Volkswagen tooted her horn, and I picked up speed, headed down Rosenberg toward my studio. When I hit the red light at Mechanic Street, my imagination kicked into overdrive. I envisioned the article in *Texas Bride* magazine, the one capitalizing on my mismatched shoes and coffee faux pas. I could almost picture Drew Kincaid laughing as he read it. Handsome, hunky Drew Kincaid, doubled over, chuckling at my missed opportunity—the one he'd snagged from my outstretched hand.

My life flashed before my eyes. Well, not really my whole life, but crazy, minuscule snatches of it. I saw the many times

I'd come a quarter-inch shy of succeeding. Well, no more. Not this time.

I pushed a button on the dash to call my best friend. Scarlet answered after the third ring with a chipper, "Hey, Hannah. I was just thinking about you. What's up?"

"Jacquie Goldfarb." I spoke the words with a tremor.

Silence followed on the other end of the phone, followed by, "Who's that, again?"

"Jacquie Goldfarb." A sigh resonated from my end. "Don't you remember? I've told you about her. She was my archnemesis in high school. Voted most popular our senior year."

"O-okay."

"Everything I wanted, she got. The position on the drill team. First chair in choir. The guy I wanted to date. She got it all. I always came in second to Jacquie Goldfarb." I paused, my thoughts whirling as memories overtook me. "And now Drew Kincaid is my Jacquie Goldfarb. He gets the clients. He gets the accolades. He gets Bella's nod for top wedding photographer on the island. He gets . . ." Deep sigh. "Everything."

"He gets the guy you wanted to date? Ew."

"No. You're missing my point. He's going to come out on top, and I'm going to fail. Again. And it's all because of Sierra Caswell. I've never worked with such a diva before. She's a real prima donna."

"Ah. I see."

"You've seen those bridezilla shows, right?"

"Yeah. A few. You know me—it's cake decorating shows day in and day out. Most of the other stuff out there eludes me. But I know what a bridezilla is. I've worked with a couple."

"Right. But don't you see? Bella Neeley holds my future

in her hands. So this wedding we're doing together is critical to the equation. But the bride is awful."

"So this Sierra Caswell is making your life miserable?"

"You have no idea. She's hard to please, overly vocal, rude, and ridiculously picky. And above all that . . . I think she's out to get me."

"Out to get you?" The tone of Scarlet's voice changed. Now she was all business. I could almost picture her tossing those messy auburn curls over her shoulder and placing balled-up fists on her ample hips. "Where are you, Hannah?"

"On my way to the studio. Almost there, actually."

"Perfect. I'll meet you there." With a click, she was gone.

"O-okay." I spoke to the now-dead phone.

The next couple of minutes were spent in reflection. Well, first angst and then reflection. By the time I arrived at my studio on the Strand, I felt foolish for involving Scarlet. She might just think I'd lost my mind. Maybe I'd get a lecture on jealousy, a "you should know better than to give in to fear" speech. Scarlet was pretty good at those, her daddy being a preacher and all. Likely whatever advice she gave would be coupled with illustrations from an *I Love Lucy* episode. The girl always managed to attribute most of her sage advice to Lucille Ball.

I walked into my studio, my home away from home, and felt more at ease than before. Well, until my gaze traveled to the sign I'd taped to my computer desk—WARNING: DATES IN CALENDAR ARE CLOSER THAN THEY APPEAR.

This place usually had a calming effect on me. Might have had something to do with the architecture. The 1900 redbrick charm. The wood floors. The high ceilings. Or it might have had more to do with the fact that I'd somehow managed to start a business on my own and grow it into something I was proud of.

As I wandered from the front office to the studio, currently set up for a shoot, my heart sailed to my throat. Oh, how I longed to keep this place afloat. If I closed my eyes, I could see clients coming in droves. I could see myself converting the cluttered back room into a second studio, perhaps even hiring someone to help me with the overflow crowd. How fun would that be?

Right now, eyes opening to reality, all I saw was an empty studio. Quiet. Still.

Dusty.

I grabbed a rag and some furniture polish and took out my frustrations on the desk. Then I got busy downloading the photos I'd taken at Club Wed, cropping and adjusting the lighting on a few. I smiled when the photo of baby Rosie's dimples filled my computer screen. She captivated me with her smile.

In that moment it occurred to me that all of life is more precious when viewed close-up, like this. Seeing someone in person, you scarcely notice the minute details. But in a photograph—if the photographer has done his or her job—you always notice the details. Like the pink cherub cheeks, the wisps of hair that should've been smoothed down, the tiny bit of slobber on the lower lip that caught the light.

The front bell rang, offering the perfect distraction. I rose to wait on a couple of tourists who'd stopped by to ask for prices. They booked a shooting for a birthday party, which lifted my morale on several levels. Just what I needed. By the time Scarlet arrived, I felt over-the-top foolish for calling her in the first place. Then again, she knew me better than anyone, so she would probably sense my embarrassment.

She rushed into the studio, dressed as always in her messy Let Them Eat Cake apron and carrying a large tray. Through the clear glass dome lid I could see cake samples . . . lots and lots of cake samples. I felt my mouth water just looking at them.

Before I could say a word, she began to gush, her words passionate, her double chin quivering. "Why do you keep saying that Bella Neeley holds your future in her hands?"

"W-what?" I took a few steps toward my desk, hoping Scarlet would follow. She did.

"On the phone." Scarlet paused for a breath. "You said that Bella holds your future in her hands." She shifted the tray of cake samples to her other hand, nearly losing her grip on it in the process.

"Ah." I gave my answer careful thought. "Bella's the one who can make or break my career. You of all people know that." I took a seat and offered a weak smile.

"I know she's the top wedding planner on the island." Scarlet plopped herself into the chair across from the desk and set the tray down well within my reach. I eyed the tantalizing bites in their various colors and started salivating again. Maybe one wouldn't hurt. Or two.

"In the state," I corrected.

"Whatever." Her eyes narrowed, and I felt a story coming. "You know what Lucy would do, don't you?"

No, but I'm sure you're going to tell me.

I did my best not to sigh aloud as she lit into an example from a particular episode of *I Love Lucy* where Lucy went to work at a chocolate factory. On and on Scarlet rambled, her explanation making no sense to my situation.

I reached for a dark-colored cake ball, which I stuffed in my mouth. *Mmm. Chocolate.* Speaking around it, I said, "No offense to Lucy, but if you were paying attention, you'd know that Club Wed has ties to the Food Network, so this could eventually be good—or bad—for your business too."

At this news, Scarlet began to choke. She managed to get control of herself, thank goodness. I'd never been very good at the Heimlich maneuver. And with Scarlet being a little wide around the midsection, I honestly wondered if my arms would wrap all the way around her.

"What?" she said at last.

"Yep." I swallowed and reached for another cake ball, this one red velvet. "Bella's aunt Rosa and uncle Laz host a show on the Food Network. I just put that together today."

"Wait. *The Italian Kitchen*—that's the show you're talking about?"

"Yes."

Scarlet's eyes widened. She brushed a loose strand of hair behind her shoulders, and crinkles appeared around her eyes. Hmm. Maybe women in their twenties really did have wrinkles.

"I knew they lived on the island, of course. Everyone knows that."

Not me.

"And I knew they had the best vegetable garden in the world. But I had no idea they were connected to Bella Neeley or the wedding facility." A deep sigh followed on her end. "I love that show."

"Mama does too. But you get my point, right? These are powerful people with great connections. Life-changing connections."

"Still, you and I both know that Bella Neeley, powerful as she might be, doesn't hold the key to your future." Scarlet leaned forward and grabbed a piece of vanilla cake. "She can't make or break you. Or me, for that matter. Only God can do that."

"Well, yes, but . . ."

Popping the cake in her mouth, Scarlet leaned back in the chair, a look of contentment on her face. "I, for one, am getting really tired of hearing that she has all of this power over you when in fact she doesn't. That was the point of my *I Love Lucy* story, by the way. Lucy always felt like Ricky had all the talent when she had none. It was never true in the first place. Lucy always had the goods, just didn't realize it due to her insecurities."

Conviction set in, but I chose to ignore it, focusing instead on my passionate response. "I'm just saying that I can't take the chance of letting Bella down. I'll fight till the finish. I'll prove myself. I'll—"

"You'll wield your bloody sword." She sighed and brushed her hands on her apron. "I've heard that one before, you know. Several times, in fact."

"Oh?"

"Yeah. When you gave up your job on the *Clarity*. When you opened your studio. When you realized Drew Kincaid was opening his studio. When your mother suggested you stop wearing pink because it clashes with your hair."

"Hey now. That's a low blow."

"Looks like you won that battle." She pointed to my pink blouse. "And remember, you're talking to another redhead here."

Please. Yours is from a bottle. And it's auburn. There's a difference.

I sighed as I fingered the hem of my blouse. "Go on."

Scarlet leaned back in her chair and gave me a motherly look. "Hannah, that article in *Texas Bride* is going to come out soon. You're going to be a superstar. An icon. People on and off the island will flock to this studio to have their pictures taken."

"If you had any idea how badly I botched that interview, you would know better."

"Still, I don't think you realize just how blessed you are. It's got to be a huge boost to have such a great opportunity. Things like that don't come along every day."

"And when they do, I usually mess them up. You know me better than almost anyone. Don't you see that I'm the queen of missed opportunities?"

She rose and paced my office, her eyes now flashing with excitement. "Girl, when that article releases, this studio is going to be full, sunup to sundown. I can see it. In faith, I mean."

"Sure hope so. I'd like to eventually get my own place. Move out."

Scarlet's eyes narrowed, and she crossed her arms over her 42DDs. "Hmm. Doubtful."

"W-what do you mean?"

"I'm of the firm conviction that your parents are trying to hang on to you. They're not willing to let go. Now that all of your sisters are married . . ."

I must've flinched because she paused, a look of chagrin on her face. "Sorry. Didn't mean to rub salt in an open wound."

"It's not a wound." I reached for another piece of cake.

"Okay, well, anyway, I think you're afraid to move on."

This certainly got my attention. "What do you mean?"

"I mean, you're avoiding men because you're scared. After what happened with that Jon guy on the cruise ship . . ."

The piece of cake nearly slipped out of my hand. "For your information, that was a total fluke. I had no way of knowing he was playing me."

"Whatever. I'm just saying that you're giving off bad vibes. Guys avoid you because you've got walls up."

For whatever reason, my gaze shifted to the bricked walls of my studio. Had I really built up a barricade meant to keep others out?

"It's just my . . . situation." I spoke the word like a death sentence.

"Your situation? What do you mean?"

"I mean I'm nearly twenty-seven and I still live at home with my parents. All of my sisters are married—and I hear every intimate detail of their lives whenever we're together. They all have stories. I just have the same old, same old, day in and day out. Nothing ever really changes."

"For Pete's sake, you worked on a cruise ship. You saw ports all over the world. Traveled to places the rest of us only dream about."

I hated to debate her on this point, but it wasn't exactly like that. "Mostly I just saw the inside of the ship. And not to discount the great experience, but our rooms on the ship weren't like what you see in pictures. They were really small. Think cracker box." I hesitated, unsure of how to redeem this. "I'm just saying that I sometimes look at my life—factoring in my age, my singleness, my codependent relationship with my parents—and wonder if things will always be the same."

"Ready for a change?"

I nodded. "I think so. Not an abrupt, move-to-Australia sort of shift, but something on a smaller scale."

"You want to fall in love and get married and have babies."

As the sigh inside of me released, I felt like a balloon deflating. She'd just summed up in one sentence everything I currently longed for. I would add only one thing to her list—a flourishing career where I actually came out on top instead of playing second fiddle to Drew Kincaid. But how could I have any of those things with walls up?

"See my dilemma?" I asked. "I'm avoiding the very thing I know I want."

"Why?"

"Because." I swallowed hard, ready to admit the truth. "I just know myself. I can't be trusted."

"Can't be trusted?" Her thinly plucked brows arched, showing off her over-the-top teal eye shadow, which she'd applied to match her apron. "Dying to know what you mean by that."

"I mean, so few guys hit on me that when they do, I crater. What's wrong with me?" I hung my head in shame. "I'm a sucker for a handsome face."

And Drew Kincaid has the handsomest face on Galveston Island.

Where that thought came from, I had no idea.

"What do you mean?" Now Scarlet really looked nervous.

"I mean, every time a great-looking guy glances my way, I melt like buttercream on an overheated cupcake. I lose all control of my senses. He could be an ax murderer for all I know, but my discernment goes out the window because I'm so flattered a guy—any guy—would give me the time of day."

Scarlet clucked her tongue. "Oh, girl, you really are in bad shape, aren't you?"

"Yeah." I reached for a square of carrot cake and took a bite, then spoke around it. "But I don't know what to do about it. I'm a hopeless case."

The stillness of my empty studio haunted me as I spoke those words. I looked around, thinking of all the hopes and dreams I'd invested in this place. And here it sat, empty. Well, empty except for the two of us.

"There's no such thing as a hopeless case." Scarlet's eyes grew misty. "I guess some people would say it's a self-image problem, but I don't really look at it that way. You're created in God's image, Hannah."

"I know that."

Sort of.

"Hmm. Well then, if you know it, you have to know that he sees everyone as beautiful, whether they're young, old, chubby, thin, have freckles, warts—you name it." She pointed at herself. "Look at me. I'm a good thirty pounds overweight."

Hmm . . .

"Okay, fifty. But do I beat myself up? No, I do not. And you shouldn't either. It's time to change the way you see yourself. You're beautiful, Hannah, inside and out. And I'm not just saying that. I've never been one for condescension. I get enough of that from my aunt Wilhelmina."

"I know, but you're not going to get me to say I think I'm pretty, so forget about it. I've known a lot of girls over the years who've bragged about their gorgeousness." *Gorgeousness? Is that a word?* "I've never been one of them and don't care to be."

Scarlet shook her head. "I'm not talking about vanity. Nothing like that. Just the self-assurance that God created you exactly like you are and loves you just the way you are. You don't have to pretend to be something you're not around guys." She took another nibble of cake. "You know how it is just before you go out on a date? You spend all of those hours primping to make sure you look your best?"

I released a slow breath, realizing that I hadn't been on a date since the fiasco with Jon. Thank goodness she jumped back into the conversation.

"You don't have to primp for God. He thinks you're gorgeous, even on the bad hair days." Scarlet pointed at her unruly auburn mop, which she'd pulled back in a sloppy ponytail. "And trust me, he's got a guy out there for you who will love you just like you are too. You'll be able to relax around him. Be yourself."

Easy for her to say. She had a boyfriend. Well, a sort-of boyfriend. Kenny, her beatnik assistant, had been hanging on her apron strings from the time she'd started baking cakes. Then again, he didn't seem to be in any hurry to pop the question. Still, Scarlet had options. I had nothing.

Well, nothing but a fabulous photography studio, an article in *Texas Bride* magazine, and connections to the greatest wedding planner in the history of mankind.

Oh, and a great family.

And a wonderful church.

And a prepaid, yearlong membership to the best gym in town.

And an upcoming job with one of country music's top celebrities.

Suddenly I felt stupid for whining. I gave Scarlet a weak smile, reached for another piece of cake, and swallowed it down whole. She responded by easing herself up from the chair and offering me a hug that made everything all right again.

Melting into my best friend's sympathetic arms, I realized I really did have just about everything a girl could ever want.

Almost.

5

Wrap Your Troubles in Dreams

An elderly man called Keith
Mislaid his set of false teeth—
They'd been laid on a chair,
He'd forgot they were there,
Sat down, and was bitten beneath.

Irish limerick

After Scarlet left, I felt a little better about life. Well, unless you counted the stomachache I'd acquired from all of the cake samples I'd consumed.

My mind now freed up, I went back to work, editing the pictures I'd taken at Club Wed and putting together a marketing brochure for Galveston's upcoming Christmas extravaganza, Dickens on the Strand. The afternoon flew by at lightning speed. I paused as the clock rang out the hour. Five o'clock. No way. Had the whole day slipped right by me?

I'd need to keep an eye on things if I wanted to be home in time for dinner.

One thing about the McDermott clan—we were predictable. Every day at 6:01 my father would pull his chair up to the table, where my mother would serve a meal he'd seen hundreds, if not thousands, of times before. Every meal had to incorporate potatoes or cabbage, of course, and either corned beef, roast beef, or stewed beef. Sometimes chicken. No exotic side dishes. No unusual desserts. Just the same fare, day in and day out. One time, my mama—I shiver to remember—made the mistake of serving up homemade enchiladas. The result was not pretty.

And so, at 5:56, I entered the house—the same house we'd lived in all of my life, with the same furniture, the same carpets, the same pictures hanging on the wall. I smelled the usual smells coming from the kitchen, heard the usual sound—my father turning off the news channel—and waited for the usual words, the same words I heard every day: "Shutter Speed, you're home! Thought you'd never get here."

I couldn't help but smile as I clapped eyes on my father. Except for a few wrinkles and his graying temples, Dad looked pretty much the same as I remembered from my childhood. Funny how nothing ever seemed to change.

"How was your day?" he asked, slipping an arm over my shoulder and pulling me close.

"Long, but my appointment with Bella went all right. I think everything's going to turn out okay with Sierra's wedding. I hope so, anyway."

"Glad to hear it. You know what your grandpa Aengus would say right now, don't you, Shutter Speed?"

Um, no. But I have a feeling you're about to tell me.

"As you slide down the banisters of life, may the splinters

never point the wrong way." My dad grinned and gave me a kiss on the cheek. "Remember, darlin', some banisters are slipperier than others. Just hang on for the ride, even if you do come in contact with a few splinters."

"I've seen more than my share already. When it rains, it pours."

His brow furrowed. "Speaking of which, I saw on the news there's a tropical disturbance in the gulf."

Yikes. Hopefully it wouldn't interfere with my photo shoot this coming Saturday. Galveston's weather could be pretty unpredictable.

I followed on my father's heels into the dining room, where we would take our usual places at the massive table and eat from the same dishes I'd eaten off of since childhood. Nothing had changed, even after my youngest sister's wedding, though not for lack of trying on my part. Mama and I had both done our best to convince Dad to eat in the living room in front of the television now that we were down to three, but he wouldn't hear of it. No way, no how. And so we dined— the three of us—at a table that once seated six. Before my sisters abandoned me.

Instead of taking my seat, I popped my head in the kitchen to say hello to Mama. I found her watching the tail end of a show on the Food Network. Nothing new there, though she only watched "my TV shows," as she called them, when Dad was working his shift at the post office or in the other room. I would have to remember to tell her about Bella's aunt and uncle later, when he wasn't listening. She would flip when she realized two of her favorite TV stars lived close by.

I walked across the linoleum floor and leaned against the tiled counter. "How are things?"

"Good. I had a call from Deidre today," Mama said as she

served up the sliced beef. "She and Corbin are coming down for a visit in early December for Dickens on the Strand."

"Oh, when is that, again?"

When my mother gave the same date as Sierra's wedding, I almost choked. "W-what? You know I have the event of a lifetime that weekend, don't you?"

"Oh?" Mama's brow wrinkled. "Something going on?"

"Yes, I told you all about it. The big wedding at Club Wed. Sierra Caswell. The country singer."

"Oh . . ." With a wave of her hand, my mother dismissed any concerns. "Just a wedding."

"Just a wedding?" I fought the temptation to enter into an argument. "It's the opportunity of a lifetime."

"That's what you said about the interview with *Texas Bride*." She placed thick slices of beef on a platter, the same platter she used every Monday night.

"Well, it was."

"And if memory serves me correctly, you said the same thing when Bella Neeley called you the first time."

"I've been blessed with a lot of opportunities lately."

Most of which I end up botching, but that's a story for another day.

Mama reached for a pot holder, then pulled a loaf of soda bread from the oven. "Well, hopefully you can spend a little time with your sister and her husband, in spite of this wedding of yours."

Strange that she phrased it "this wedding of yours." I didn't have time to respond, though, because the clock in the dining room chimed six times, and my dad coughed, his usual sign that Mama had better get the food on the table—quick.

We ate our usual dinner, had our usual conversation, nibbled at the usual dessert, then headed into the living room to watch our usual Monday night fare—one of Dad's pre-recorded true crime shows. Still, I felt something stirring deep inside me and couldn't let it go. I'm not sure how I garnered the courage to do it, but I managed to spit out the most shocking thing I'd suggested to my father in years.

"Can we watch something different tonight, Dad?"

"W-what?" From his worn recliner, he glanced my way, his jaw dropping.

"*Dancing with the Stars* is starting up again tonight," I explained. "It's a new season."

He pulled the handle on the side of his recliner, and his feet shot up in the air. "*Dancing with the Stars*?" Creases formed in his brow. I could almost hear the thoughts clicking in his head.

I used my most persuasive voice. "Brock Benson is going to be on it this season. You know who he is, right? He plays a talent scout on *Stars Collide*. You like that show, don't you?"

"Well, yes, I tolerate it. But I do not—repeat, do not—like dancing shows. And nothing will change that. So I would rather not, thank you."

"Michael McDermott, don't be so stubborn." My mother's voice rang out in scolding fashion as she entered the room, coffee cup in hand.

My father looked stunned. "But I recorded my show. You know I always watch the same thing on Monday night."

Mama settled into her usual spot on the sofa and clucked her tongue. "Let your daughter have her way for a change. She rarely asks for anything. It won't kill you to switch things up every now and again."

"But I . . ." He couldn't seem to manage the rest.

"She's the last remaining child at home." My mother's

brow furrowed and her voice intensified. "We don't want to drive her away because of your stubbornness. Do as she asks."

I swallowed hard at this statement, unsure of which bothered me more—the fact that she called me a child, or the idea that leaving them, whether sooner or later, would cause pain of the empty-nest variety.

Mama waggled her finger. "If you've recorded your true crime show, we can watch it after *Dancing with the Stars*. I, for one, want to see Brock Benson do the cha-cha." A dreamy-eyed look came over her, and she appeared to be lost in her thoughts, judging from the winsome smile that now tipped up the edges of her lips. "That man is so captivating. I tell you, he could charm a snake right out of its venom."

My father rolled his eyes and muttered something I couldn't quite make out.

"Brock is dancing with Cheryl Burke," I added.

"And this should be important to me because . . . ?" My father crossed his arms and settled back into his chair.

"Because she's one of the best. I think you'll really like her. And because he's Brock Benson."

Handsome, dashing, hotter-than-life Brock Benson.

Mama changed the channel on the TV, and the show started. I watched as the host introduced the new dance pros, along with this season's guest stars. My heart pitter-pattered as Brock descended the stairs with Cheryl Burke on his arm. Oy. Was it getting hot in here, or what?

"Saints preserve us." Mama fanned herself as she watched the television screen. "Look at that, will you? That man is handsomer than ever in a tuxedo. If he can actually dance, it might just send me into heart palpitations." Her cheeks flushed, and tiny beads of sweat emerged on her brow.

"Should I get the nitroglycerin tablets, just in case?" My

father grunted, then reached for his newspaper, which he used to shield himself from the TV.

"If those girl dancers don't put on more clothes, maybe." My mother wrinkled her nose. "I'm always so concerned there's going to be a wardrobe malfunction."

At this proclamation, my father lowered his newspaper, gave the TV screen a quick glance, grunted, then lifted his paper once again.

Mama and I enjoyed the show from start to finish. Well, all but the part where that one gawky speed skater—what was his name again?—fell in the middle of the dance floor. We found ourselves captivated when Brock took the floor. I did my best not to sigh aloud as he cha-cha-cha'd across the dance floor with Cheryl, but I couldn't hold back the squeal when the judges gave him high marks. I felt like doing a little dance myself but showed significant restraint by remaining in the chair. No point in alarming my father more than necessary.

Behind his newspaper, he continued to grumble. Mama eventually pacified him with his favorite evening diversion— Irish coffee. When *Dancing with the Stars* ended, she turned on his true crime show and he settled down in a hurry. Still, the whole thing threw his schedule off by not just one hour but two, and the man never handled change well.

I slipped out of the room unnoticed when my father started snoring in his easy chair. Mama disappeared into the kitchen to finish up the dishes, and I headed upstairs to call Bella. Maybe she could answer some lingering questions about this coming Saturday's photo shoot, particularly the big one about what time I should arrive.

From the comfort of my bedroom—the same room I'd slept in for twenty-six years—I made the call.

Bella answered on the third ring. "Hannah! I was just

telling D.J. about our plans. The date works for everyone, and we're so excited."

"Me too." I plopped down on the floral bedspread, my gaze traveling to the matching curtains, the same curtains I'd looked at thousands of times before.

"Hey, speaking of excited, I just watched *Dancing with the Stars*. Did you see it?"

"Yep. Amazing."

She giggled. "Priceless. Brock has always been a great actor, but who knew he could dance? I've never seen such a fun cha-cha. Even D.J. loved it, and he's not really into dancing."

"Want to bring D.J. over here next Monday night? Maybe he could influence my dad."

"Ha! Well, he's not that into it. But he knows I am. And he's a friend of Brock's, so that helps."

"Brock is great. Do you think he has a brother?" I gave a nervous laugh.

"No, but I do." Bella sounded suspiciously happy about this. I couldn't help but wonder what she was up to. "And speaking of which, I've had the most delectable idea." She released a girlish giggle. "Armando is coming back to the island on Saturday for the photo shoot. He's been living in Houston and hardly ever comes home, so thank you for serving as inspiration."

"Happy to be of service." *I think.*

"You're a lifesaver," Bella added, the lilt in her voice sounding a little too rehearsed.

Still, I couldn't help but smile at that proclamation. If she saw me as a lifesaver, she would call on me more often. Hopefully.

Bella's next words caught my attention. "So, I can't help

thinking you and Armando will fall hopelessly in love with each other. Wouldn't that be great?"

"I . . . what?"

"You two would be a great match. He's such a sweetie, and really handsome too. And he could use a good woman to . . ."

"To what?"

"Well, to calm him down." Her tone stiffened a bit. "He's lived on the edge for a while. Faced a few challenges. But see, that's why I think you'd be perfect. You seem really . . . settled."

Gee, thanks.

"Armando's got his issues," she continued, "but he's a great guy."

"Issues?"

"Yeah." She sighed. "He has a hard time holding down a job. Mama always says he does the work of three men: Larry, Moe, and Curly."

Okay, that got a laugh out of me. Still, what kind of a goober-like brother was she trying to set me up with?

"You want me to date your brother to calm him down?" *Not in a million years, even if it means getting on your good side!*

"Well, I'm just asking you to consider the possibilities. After you meet him, of course."

A significant amount of noise on the other end of the line told me that Bella's attention had shifted.

"Tres Neeley, what are you doing out of bed? I've told you a thousand times not to get up after we've said our nighttime prayers. It wakes up the angels."

He must've responded with something naughty, because she now referred to him as Dwayne Neeley the Third. Uh-oh. Poor kid must really be in trouble, to get his real name.

Her words faded away, but it was clear she was no longer talking to me. I could hear more chaos and confusion on her end. After a minute or two, she returned. "Sorry, Hannah, but I've got to go. This little monster is struggling to get to sleep tonight, and now the baby's crying too."

"No problem." I rolled over on the bed and sat up. "See you Saturday."

"At ten," she added. "If that works for you."

"Perfect. See you then. I'm excited."

"Me too." She went back to scolding Tres, and the call ended.

I headed downstairs to grab a glass of water and say good night to my parents. I found Mama in the kitchen, standing—shirt unbuttoned—in front of the open freezer.

"Um, Mama?"

She turned, her face red. "Oh, hey, Hannah."

"What are you doing?"

She made quick work of buttoning her blouse, then took to fanning herself. "Melting."

The only thing melting right now was the Blue Bell homemade vanilla ice cream in the freezer, and we couldn't risk that. I reached through the open door and grabbed the container.

"I hate menopause." Mama groaned. "It's going to be the death of me yet."

"I hope not." Watching my mother go through "the change" made me wonder what she might do next. Still, it was rather refreshing to see something changing around here.

"Well, you know what I mean. Hot. Cold. Hot. Cold." She closed the freezer and shivered as if to prove her point. I leaned back against the counter and took a bite of ice cream.

Not that I needed the calories after all the cake I'd consumed today, but oh well.

Mama untied her apron and hung it on the hook on the back of the kitchen door. "I keep forgetting to remind you about our shopping date this coming Saturday."

Yikes.

"We're going to the mainland, remember?" She grabbed a spoon and stuck it in the open container of Blue Bell.

I paused to look her way. "Mama, I've been asked to photograph Bella Neeley's family on Saturday."

Mama's smile twisted into a frown. "But we talked about this a couple of weeks back, remember? You said you would go. I like to do my holiday shopping early, and you know I hate to drive off the island by myself."

Another bite of the creamy ice cream went into my mouth. Yum. "Get Dad to go with you."

She rolled her eyes. "You know he won't do that. Besides, you promised. You even said we could go out to lunch at Dixie's. You know how much I love that place."

Ack. Yes, I'd promised. And a McDermott never went back on a promise unless, perchance, the earth tilted off its axis.

"I'll make you a deal," Mama said with a wink. "You come with me this Saturday, and I'll spring for the last season of *Stars Collide* on Blu-ray. That way you can see Brock Benson as much and as often as you like." She placed the lid back on the Blue Bell and put it in the freezer.

"But . . ."

My thoughts shifted to Brock in his tuxedo with Cheryl on his arm. Thinking about Brock—for some reason—got me to thinking about Drew Kincaid. Though I found both strikingly handsome, I'd stick with the television hero, not the real-life pain-in-the-neck adversary.

Okay, so maybe he wasn't really my adversary. Maybe he just kept showing up at the wrong times and stealing my thunder.

An insane thought suddenly crossed my mind: I could get Drew to cover for me with Bella's family this coming Saturday so that Mama wouldn't have to shop by herself.

No, that would never work. The ultimate goal here was to impress Bella Neeley. She wouldn't be very impressed if I turned down the opportunity to photograph her family. Maybe she would be willing to change the date to accommodate Mama.

No, that wouldn't work either. I'd made a commitment to be with her this coming Saturday at ten.

I heard my father's voice ring out his usual "*Oíche mhaith*," his nightly indicator that he was headed to bed.

Mama and I both responded with our usual "Good night to you too," followed by a promise from my mother that she would join him shortly.

As he walked up the stairs to bed, my father broke into his usual nightly song, "Irish Lullaby." But I didn't feel very "too-ra-loo-ra-loo-ral-ish" tonight. In fact, I felt plenty down in the dumps as I looked in my mother's somber face. No matter what decision I made regarding this Saturday, someone would be disappointed.

Five words flitted through my brain at that very moment: *What would Grandpa Aengus do?*

I knew the answer. He would figure out a way to make everyone happy. Now if only I could do the same.

6

Fancy Meeting You Here

A family of Irish birth
Will argue and fight,
But let a shout come from without,
And see them all unite.

Irish saying

At some point late Monday night I came up with the perfect solution to my problem du jour. I would photograph Bella's family on Saturday morning and shop with my mother in the afternoon. That way I really could have my cake and eat it too. Barring a hurricane, of course.

Thank goodness the disturbance in the gulf dissipated and life went on as usual as the week progressed. I breathed a sigh of relief when Brock made it through the elimination process on *Dancing with the Stars*. Praise the Lord for small favors. He had lived to dance another week. I felt as if I had too. I managed to advertise a new special at my studio and even took on a couple of new clients as a result.

Yes, things were definitely looking up. Well, until Friday night. Somewhere in the wee hours of the night, I had the weirdest dream. I was dancing the cha-cha with Brock Benson. But when the music came to a halt, I gazed into his eyes and realized it wasn't Brock at all . . . it was Drew Kincaid. Weird. Then Drew morphed into a horrific-looking sea creature that bore an uncanny resemblance to Jacquie Goldfarb. The sea creature chased me around my studio, eventually crawling up the high brick walls and slithering into the attic space above. Creepy.

I awoke Saturday morning feeling confused yet, at the same time, strangely invigorated about the day ahead. I slipped on a pair of jeans and a lightweight green sweater and pulled my hair back into a ponytail. Wearing tennis shoes made perfect sense. No point in ruining a good pair of heels for an outdoor shoot in a garden.

Deciding to forego too much makeup, I applied a little lipstick and mascara and I stepped back to examine my reflection in the mirror. As always, I fought the desire to sigh as I took in the freckles. Who had freckles at twenty-six? My reddish-blonde ponytail was a little lopsided, but it didn't really matter. I'd been through enough of these photo shoots to know that the family members wouldn't be focused on the appearance of the photographer. Likely the parents would be far too preoccupied scolding the children.

Another quick glance in the mirror reminded me to stand up straight. I could almost hear Grandpa Aengus calling me his little pixie. Sure, I was petite. Five feet two if I stretched. And yeah, my size 6 jeans were a little loose. Still, pixie hardly described me. Besides, I packed a lot of punch in this tiny little frame. I would show the competition what was what. I would fight to the death, wield my bloody sword, and—

Hmm. Well, I'd keep my eye on the prize, anyway.

I bounded down the stairs, my grandfather's words flitting through my mind: "As you ramble through life, whatever be your goal, keep your eye upon the doughnut, and not upon the hole."

"I'll do it, Grandpa Aengus. I'll do it."

Thinking of doughnuts made me hungry. I headed into the kitchen to grab a breakfast bar, all the while humming a happy tune.

As I passed through the living room, my father looked up from his morning paper. "You're chipper this morning." His gaze narrowed. "Very suspicious."

"Nothing suspicious about it. Just have a feeling this is going to be an amazing day."

"Carpe diem, Shutter Speed."

"Seize the day!" we said in unison.

I felt like dancing, so I did a little jig down the hallway, stopping only when I landed in the kitchen.

Mama looked up from the soapsuds in the sink and stared at me as if I'd grown a second head. "Hannah?"

"Yes?"

"You're dancing? Practicing your cha-cha in case Cheryl Burke sprains her ankle or something?"

"Nah." I giggled. "Just in a great mood today, that's all. I'd dance on the moon but don't have time to get there. I'm excited about the photo shoot at the Rossis' house. I think it's going to be good for my business."

"Ah, that's right. Well, wrap it up as quick as you can, honey. I'm dying to hit the malls."

"I'll do my best, but I can't rush, okay? I need to do a good job." I turned to grab a breakfast bar from the pantry, but something on the countertop caught my eye. "Mama, what's this?" I pointed to a stack of mail shoved under an empty oatmeal bowl.

She turned to face me and shrugged. "Yesterday's junk mail, I think. Grocery store fliers and such. Meant to toss it."

Something in my gut told me to go through it. I scrambled through the stash until I landed on a familiar magazine. My heart went into a tailspin, then roller-coastered up into my throat as I clapped eyes on *Texas Bride*.

"I . . . I . . . I . . ."

My father walked into the kitchen, a perplexed look on his face. "Hannah, you're as white as a ghost. Never knew ad sheets had that effect on you."

"This isn't an ad sheet. It's—it's my article!"

And Mama almost threw it in the trash!

I released a slow breath and peeled dried oatmeal off the cover. Straightening out the wrinkle on the first page, I ran my finger down the table of contents until I came to "Photo I Do's." My heart almost came to a stop as I turned to page 46 and skimmed the article, eyes darting this way and that to take in as much as I could.

Strangely, much of the piece was about Bella. Not that I really minded. And the reporter had plenty to say about Drew Kincaid's business too. Still, she'd given me a fair shake, and she hadn't even mentioned my mismatched shoes or the faux pas with the coffee. Praise God for small favors! She'd even mentioned my business by name, along with the appropriate address and website information. Yes and amen!

"Can I see it?" My mother stepped next to me and wiped her sticky hands on her apron.

"Sure. Of course." Still beaming, I handed her the magazine.

Mama pulled it close as she looked at my head shot. She backed away a tiny bit and squinted. "Wow, that's a close-up photo of your face."

"Yeah, I can almost see the fillings in your teeth." My father's voice sounded over my shoulder. He opened the refrigerator, came out with a gallon of milk, and took a swig.

I groaned as I took in my head shot. "Wish I'd opted for a different photo of myself. Have you ever seen so many freckles?"

"Hey now, don't despise the freckles." My father took another drink of milk, then closed the jug and put it away. A couple of seconds later he opened the freezer and grabbed a carton of ice cream. "You come from a long line of freckles, darlin'." He pulled the top off the ice cream carton and grabbed a spoon from the drawer. My mother groaned.

"I know, I know." Still, I'd hoped my portfolio photographs would make up for the head shot. Sure enough, I found three of the pictures I'd shot at recent weddings beautifully inserted into the story.

Unfortunately, I also found a few of Drew Kincaid's. I should have expected that.

"Ooh, I love that one." Mama pointed to one of Drew's pictures. "Hey, look! It's Brock Benson . . . again." She gave a drawn-out sigh, a blissful expression on her face. "Every time I turn around, there he is."

Oh, if only life were like that.

Mama gazed at Drew's photo of Brock all gussied up in his "I'm getting married" tux. "That man's quite a looker."

From across the kitchen, my father let out a belch, then muttered, "Why, thank you. I've often been told I'm a looker." He ambled out of the kitchen, ice cream carton in hand.

Under ordinary circumstances, Mama would've scolded him for eating ice cream for breakfast. This time, however, she couldn't seem to take her eyes off Brock. "I don't remember you showing me the photo of Brock Benson before, Hannah." She pressed the magazine back into my hands. "But it's wonderful. Great angle. A lot better than that one." She pointed down to a photo I'd taken at a wedding last spring.

I released a sigh. "Mama, I didn't shoot Brock's wedding. Drew Kincaid did. That's his photo, not mine." I pointed to the one I'd shot. "*This* is mine."

Her eyes widened. "Oops. Sorry."

I pointed to Drew's slick, perfectly aligned head shot and winced. "That's him. That's the competition. Drew Kincaid."

Again, Mama pulled the magazine from my hand. She let out a slow whistle. "*That's* the competition?"

"Yep."

"Can we just concede right now?" She looked up at me with a twinkle in her eyes.

"Mama!" I grabbed the magazine back from her, wanting to savor the article, but I found my gaze riveted on Drew's handsome face. Those captivating eyes held me spellbound, as if he'd stepped into the room alongside me. And—perhaps for the first time—I noticed a teensy-tiny splattering of freckles along the edge of his nose.

Looks like we have more in common than photography, Jacquie Goldfarb.

Er, Drew.

I couldn't help but give him another look. His light hair stood in stark contrast to his deep tan, and the expression on his face spoke of contentment. Happiness.

Then again, why wouldn't the guy be happy? He got all the breaks.

"Well, one thing's for sure, Hannah Grace," Mama said as she faced the sink full of dirty dishes. "We McDermotts might fight to the finish, but with competitors like that, it'll be a lovely fight."

"A lovely fight?" I let out an unladylike snort. "I somehow doubt it. According to Dad, the Kincaids and McDermotts don't get along. I guess this is no time to sign a peace treaty."

"Oh, I don't know about that." Mama glanced over her shoulder at the picture, and a girlish smile turned up the edges of her lips. "I might be willing to sign."

"Mama!"

She giggled and went back to work, her hands now deep in suds. "I'm sorry I almost threw away your article. Guess I should pay more attention to the mail."

"I guess so." I finally ripped open the breakfast bar and took a little nibble. "I have to go. Not quite sure when I'll be back, exactly. Kind of depends on how much work is involved. The Rossis have a big family, so pray for me. It's going to be a challenge to get this done."

She turned toward me once again, and her face lit in a smile. "Hey, I have an idea. Why don't I come with you? That way we'll already be together. We can go on from there. And maybe I could help you in some way. You know? Doesn't that sound like fun?" Her expression told me it sounded fun to her.

"Hmm." I paused to think this through. Might not hurt to have someone else there to assist.

At once my pride kicked in. What would it look like to Bella? I didn't want her to think that I couldn't handle things on my own.

"I'm not sure," I said after a moment.

Mama sighed and reached for a dish towel to dry the bowl in her hands. "I understand. You're a grown woman. You don't need your mama tagging along."

"It's not that. I just don't want you to be bored." I offered what I hoped would look like a convincing smile. "And it's going to be really chaotic. They've got kids. Lots and lots of kids."

"I love children. You know that." She gave me that same "why don't you get married and have a few?" look I'd seen so many times.

Good grief. How would I get around this?

"I'll tell you what." I grabbed my mother's hand, an idea taking hold. "You come by Club Wed around noon, okay? We should be wrapping up by then. There's someone I want you to meet before we head out for the day."

"Bella Neeley?"

"Well, Bella, yes, but someone else too." I filled her in on the Food Network connection, and for a minute there, I thought she might faint.

Mama could barely get a word out. "You're—you're— you're telling me that Rosa—the very Rosa who makes all of that great Italian cuisine—lives here, on the island?"

"Yes. She's Bella's aunt. It took me awhile to figure it out too, because Rosa's last name is Rossi. Bella's is Neeley, but that's her married name."

"I—I—I see." Mama began to pace. "And I get to meet her? And Laz too?"

I nodded, praying Bella would go along with the idea. Had I spoken too soon?

"There is a God, and he loves me!"

Her joyous outburst surprised me. "Well, of course, Mama. We've always known that."

"Oh, honey, you don't understand." My mother's eyes filled with tears. "I watch every episode of *The Italian Kitchen*. I record it and watch while your father's at work. He would never understand my passion for Italian food. I've been sneaking around for months, wishing, hoping, dreaming about manicotti. And ravioli. And garlic twists. And tiramisu."

"Ah." I smiled. "I've actually eaten Rosa's manicotti. It's wonderful."

"You—you have? I'm so jealous."

I gave my mother a detailed description, which had my mouth watering in short order. Mama began to gush—now in Gaelic—about how much she would love to cook Italian food. About how my father, God bless him, had the dullest digestion in the world. About how, if it were up to her, we would eat a wide variety of foods from around the globe, starting with Aunt Rosa's famous garlic twists.

I had to admit, this whole thing was making me hungry. Hopefully Bella wouldn't mind if my mother stopped by for a quick hello. Surely not.

Off Mama went in Gaelic once more, her words flowing like honey. I couldn't make out all of it, but I did catch something about her desperate need to spice up her life. After a couple of minutes, she went into hot-flash mode and opened the freezer, waving the door back and forth to cool herself down.

Finally she paused and smiled at me. "How can I ever thank you?"

"Oh, no need."

Please, dear God, let Bella go along with this.

"This is going to be the best day of my life." Mama tugged at her apron strings, finally pulling them loose. "I must get ready. I want to make a good impression."

"Well, you have several hours. No rush."

"This is a day I will never forget. Bless you, sweet girl. Bless you." Mama dried her hands, gave me a huge hug, then sashayed out of the room, humming "Oh Happy Day!"

Heart, don't fail me now.

I ushered up several pellet-gun prayers, begging God for help. Why oh why had I promised Mama something so huge without asking Bella first? Would I live to regret this?

Deep breath, Hannah. This will work out fine.

I somehow managed to calm down, and my thoughts eventually returned to the article in *Texas Bride*. I flipped the pages of the magazine back to read the article in its entirety as I headed out to my car. In spite of the weird head shot, the rest of the article proved to be amazing. I couldn't have asked for better advertising for Picture This. Oh, and what perfect timing! I could hardly wait to get a copy of this article into Bella Neeley's hands. Once she saw how many times I'd credited her, the deal would be sealed. I would move to the number-one slot on her list, no problem.

I just had to keep endearing myself to her in the meantime. That meant pulling off the photo shoot of a lifetime this morning with her family. Oh well, no big deal. I'd done family shoots before. Dozens of them. I'd never lost a family member.

Yet.

I drove down the seawall, noticing the lazy gulf waves as they lapped the shore. In so many ways that poor shoreline, speckled with seaweed and sand dunes, reminded me of myself. It seemed I always took a beating from life. Well, not today. Nope. Today, like my ancestral clan, I would fight back and win. I might even make a little cash along the way.

I arrived at Bella's house at ten o'clock, as planned. The massive Victorian home loomed ahead of me, its gingerbread trim exquisite and its veranda inviting. What would it be like to live in one of these old restored homes? Likely I'd never know. Still, visiting one was almost as nice.

After checking my appearance in the rearview mirror, I bounded from my car, camera bag slung over one shoulder and magazine pressed underneath my arm, ready to share it with Bella. Oddly, I found Drew Kincaid arriving at the same time. It didn't take long to figure out he had a copy of the magazine on hand too.

Oh no you don't. I've got this one covered, buddy. Bella's going to read my copy. My oatmeal-encrusted, bent-page copy.

"Well, hello." His face melted into a buttery smile. He folded the magazine in half and shoved it under his arm. "Are you following me or something?" A lock of wavy hair fell casually on his forehead, and he brushed it away with the back of his hand.

"Um, no." *Don't flatter yourself.* I kept walking toward the house.

"I've got an appointment with Bella to talk about an upcoming, um . . ." He appeared to be stumbling over the word. "Actually, I don't know what she wants to talk to me about. She just told me to get here at ten o'clock. You?"

A niggling suspicion ran through me. How dare Bella kick the confidence out from under me by inviting Drew Kincaid? *Why did you bring him here today of all days, girl?*

"I, um, I'm here to shoot the family," I managed at last.

"Shoot the family, eh?" He leaned in close and whispered, "What did they do to deserve *that*, I ask you?"

It took me a minute, but I finally caught on just as I reached the veranda. "I meant a photo shoot, obviously." The eye roll that followed shared my thoughts on his attempt at humor.

Before I could rap on the door, it swung open and Aunt Rosa came bounding out, shaking her fist at an unfamiliar boy and hollering something in Italian. I couldn't make out much of it, but she looked plenty mad.

Well, until she saw me. Then her scowl morphed into a smile. She took me by the hand and grinned. "Come. I'll feed you breakfast."

"Oh, no thanks. I've already had—" My near-empty stomach growled, and I realized I'd left the rest of my breakfast bar sitting on the kitchen counter at home.

"I made frittata." She gave me a little wink and pulled me inside.

Okay, so maybe a little breakfast was in order.

Drew trailed along behind me, and soon we were both inside Rosa's kitchen, where the smells wafted up to tempt my senses like nothing I'd ever experienced. Boy oh boy. If only Mama could get a glimpse of this! She would totally flip. After gushing all over Rosa, of course.

Minutes later, the room filled with the sounds of dishes clanging, silverware clinking, and voices overlapping.

Tres came rushing into the kitchen with Bella hot on his heels. She stopped and looked at Drew. Then me. Then Drew. Then me. Finally, she clamped a hand over her mouth. "Oh no." Bella pulled her hand back. "I can't believe I did this. I double booked the morning, didn't I?"

Yes, and this would be a good point in the conversation to send Drew packing, don't you think?

She gave him a winsome smile. "Drew, would you mind hanging around until we're done? Hannah's going to photograph our family."

"Sure." He spoke to Bella, but his gaze never left Rosa and the food. "Sounds yummy. Er, good."

Great. Now I'd have to photograph the family with Jacquie Goldfarb looking on. Just what I'd always dreamed of.

Tres took off running out of the kitchen, and before long I heard the voices of several children in the next room.

I pulled the magazine out from under my arm and put it on the counter. I could hardly contain my joy as I spoke. "Bella, did you see that the latest issue of *Texas Bride* is out?"

"I did." She reached over and ran her finger across the sticky cover. "Just got my copy this morning. I'm so excited that—"

"That all of Texas now knows how great Club Wed is," Drew said with a sweep of his hand. "That reporter really sang your praises, Bella. Great promotion for the wedding facility. It's going to be wonderful for your business, I'm sure."

"Well, I daresay you two added to the excitement with your kind words about us." She flashed a smile Drew's way. "For that, we're very thankful."

Grandpa Aengus's words "*Níor bhris focal maith fiacal riamh*" flitted through my mind. I knew the literal translation: "A good word never broke a tooth." Of course, Grandpa's version made a bit more sense: "A compliment never hurts."

Yep, Grandpa. This is the perfect time to compliment her. If only I could come up with something brilliant to say.

Drew waggled a brow. "You're becoming a phenomenon, Bella. You really are. Before you know it, people will be coming to Galveston from coast to coast. From other countries, even."

"That would be so cool." She giggled. "I think it will be great for your studio too."

Say something, Hannah. Anything.

"Well, I, um . . ." I began.

"You think?" A boyish grin turned up the corners of Drew's mouth. "Well, if my business takes off, I'll give you the credit.

I really can't thank you enough, Bella. You've been such a door opener, and I'm so grateful. First Brock Benson's wedding, and now the piece in *Texas Bride*." He bowed gallantly at the waist and then rose. "My career and I thank you."

Shoot me now. Why didn't I say that?

"You're welcome, Drew." Bella gave him an encouraging nod, then turned my way. "I'm sorry. What were you saying, Hannah?"

I'd just opened my mouth to say something sure to impress when Tres came running in the room, being chased by an older boy. "Mama! Mama! Deany-boy hit me."

The older boy, chubby and looking a little rough around the edges, took to shoving the littler ones around. I wanted to intervene but didn't. Beside me, Drew cleared his throat. I half expected him to reach out and grab the kid in the blue shirt by the back of the collar.

The boys ended up in a squabble, the noise level rising substantially. Since no one intervened, I pulled out my camera, zooming in on the older boy, who scowled at Tres. Through the eye of the camera, he almost looked like a prizefighter. Almost. Half devil child, half mama's boy. Typical Italian male child, right?

Stop it, Hannah. Don't judge.

Still, I couldn't help but think of Grandpa Aengus's words regarding kiddos, especially naughty ones: "If you have a headache, do what it says on the aspirin bottle: take two, and keep away from children." Surely even he would've run for the hills right about now, McDermott or not.

Finally Bella caught the bigger boy by the shirtsleeve and held him in place, then gestured with her head toward the door. "Hannah, meet my brother Armando."

I shifted the camera a bit until the cocoa-brown eyes of

one of the most handsome men I'd ever seen came into view. Pulling the camera down, I stammered, "H-hello."

His eyes appeared to sweep over me, and those lips—those gorgeous, sexy lips—curled up in a delicious smile. Oy. Now *here* was a typical Italian male. A fine specimen, to be sure. His thick, dark hair tapered neatly to the collar of his shirt, and dark tendrils of hair curled on his forehead.

Oh, mama mia!

I didn't mean to stare, but who could look away from such a magnificent creature? His arresting good looks compelled me to focus on him.

"Well now." His dark eyes flashed with interest. "Hello to you too. Guess it's a good thing I decided to come back home for this photo shoot." He took my hand and gave it a kiss, then released it with a wink.

Saints preserve us.

As Armando headed to the other side of the kitchen to greet Rosa, Drew stepped behind me and leaned down so close I could feel his breath on the back of my neck. "Watch your back, McDermott."

"W-what?"

"Just guard yourself around this guy," he whispered. "I've met him a time or two before, and I can tell you he's trouble. Not at all who he makes himself out to be."

Anger rose up inside of me. "I'm pretty sure I can take care of myself, Drew." As I stared into his eyes—his beautiful blue eyes—I was less sure by the moment. And while I wanted to look over at Armando, the only face holding me captive right now was Drew's.

Armando came close once again. I felt the heat rush to my cheeks as he gave me another sweep with his eyes. Rarely did a man look at me with such interest. I hardly knew what to make of it. Still, it felt mighty good to have a handsome man's attention, especially with Drew Kincaid looking on.

But why do I care what Drew thinks?

Still, I did. Maybe a little too much. I glanced his way and noticed the warning look in his eyes. I chose to ignore it, shifting my attention back to Bella's brother.

As Armando quirked a brow and gave me a teasing "come hither" look, I thought about my words to Scarlet less than a week ago: "Every time a great-looking guy glances my way, I melt like buttercream on an overheated cupcake. I lose all control of my senses. He could be an ax murderer for all I know, but my discernment goes out the window because I'm so flattered a guy—any guy—would give me the time of day."

Except now, with those words dancing through my brain, the only handsome man to draw my eye was the hunky, broad-shouldered photographer reaching for his Nikon, with a "watch your back" look in his eyes.

7

It Could Happen to You

May your blessings outnumber
The shamrocks that grow.
And may trouble avoid you
Wherever you go.

Irish blessing

I kept an eye on my watch during breakfast. Clearly, a 10:00 photo shoot with an Italian family didn't really mean 10:00. If it involved food—which this one did—it meant 10:30. Okay, 10:40.

At exactly 10:43 I managed to gather the troops on the veranda for the first photo. The children, God bless them, were in rare form. I'd never seen such craziness. They chased each other, slapping, slugging, and hollering at the top of their lungs. In fact, the only one louder than the boys was

Rosa. She shook a broom at them and threatened to sweep them under the rug if they didn't hush. Not that they paid her much mind. The more amped up they got, the nuttier her reactions.

Bella seemed to take it all in stride. So did D.J., who looked on with a lopsided grin. Even the grandparents found Rosa's somewhat erratic behavior laughable. I'd hoped to get a handle on things quickly, but how could I get these kids calmed down?

Grandpa Aengus's words came to mind: "Praise the child and you praise the mother."

I fought to think of something clever to say about the boys, finally settling on, "They're very fast, aren't they?"

Brushing a loose hair out of her face, Bella grinned. "You have no idea." She let out a piercing whistle, and soon the boys calmed down.

I faced the Rossi family and clapped my hands to get their attention. "Okay, let's get this show on the road," I said, offering a confident smile.

The family members spent the better part of the next ten minutes getting situated. Now, I'd worked with large groups before, but rarely so many children all at once. And knowing that Drew was standing behind me—likely analyzing my methods, style, and demeanor—caused me to break out in a sweat comparable to one of Mama's infamous hot flashes. So much for coming across as a professional.

Jacquie Goldfarb, you will not bring me down! I will slay this dragon. Watch and see!

Not that the Rossi children were dragons, of course. Still, they did unsettle my nerves.

Just about the time I got everyone situated to my liking, the baby began to cry. One of the older boys—the one called

Deany-boy—slugged his brother in the shoulder, which resulted in an all-out fistfight on the steps, one that could have ended in bloodshed if not for the long string of Italian words from Bella's uncle Lazarro. Thanks to his commanding manner, the boys finally settled down. Bella also managed to get the baby to stop crying and used a tissue to dab the little one's eyes and runny nose.

"Okay, folks, let's try that again." I managed a forced smile.

Eventually they stood in a semblance of order. Well, sort of. A couple of them remained hidden behind the others. Figured. Just about the time I thought I had a handle on things.

"Here, try it this way." Drew stepped beside me and gave me a quick glance, as if to ask, "Do you mind?" Before I could respond—what would I have said, anyway? "Go away"? "Leave me alone"? "Let me do my work"?—he walked up the steps, shuffled a few people around, and basically got everyone in the perfect order.

I should have thanked him. Really, that's what a better person would have done. Still, the only thing I could think to do was catch a few shots while the kids were behaving and pray Bella didn't see me as a complete idiot.

Deep breath, Hannah. This is going to be fine. Just relax and enjoy the moment. This is the opportunity of a lifetime.

I did my best to remain calm, but a clicking noise to my right piqued my curiosity. What in the world? I looked over to see Drew kneeling about ten feet to my right . . . taking pictures. Anger gripped me, and I shot him a warning look, one he couldn't possibly misinterpret.

"Ah." He rose, brushed the dust from his jeans with his free hand, and shrugged. "Sorry. I just couldn't resist. From this angle, there's a great shot of Bella holding the baby."

Do not say a word. Do not say a word.

"Drew, you're so sweet." Bella's voice rang out from the porch. "And I think this is the perfect idea. While Hannah's getting the wide shots, you do some random close-ups. We'll merge both of your pictures in the end."

Great. Just what I needed. Go ahead and put the knife in my back, Jacquie. Pretend to be my friend one minute and then stab me in the back the next. And while you're at it, why not give that knife an extra twist?

The clicking of cameras continued as new opportunities presented themselves. Before long I forgot to be angry with Drew. We wrapped up on the front porch, and I led the crew to the backyard to Rosa and Laz's vegetable garden. I couldn't help but watch the family dynamics as the children, parents, grandparents, aunts, and uncles all played and laughed together. Rosa looked so happy with her arm looped through her husband's. And Bella's parents—what were their names again? Cosmo and something . . . Anyway, they were an odd but blissful pair, him with his near-balding head and her with all of her finely tuned makeup.

Who has pores like that in her late fifties?

My gaze shifted to Bella and her husband, D.J. They stopped just short of the back garden for a quick kiss—one that almost drew a sigh out of me—and then brushed some dirt from Tres's cheek.

I walked toward the hothouse, hoping for a glimpse inside.

"Cute kid." Drew's pace matched mine, and he gestured to the little boy. "Reminds me of myself when I was that age."

"You had brown eyes and spoke with a Tex-Italian accent?"

"No." He laughed. "Didn't mean that. He's just so rambunctious. My mother always said I kept her on the edge of her seat at all times. I've spent the last few years trying to make it up to her."

"How so?"

He shrugged. "By making her proud. Ever since my father died, she . . ." His words drifted off, and I saw a look in his eye I'd never seen before.

Wow. Maybe I'd better reconsider my former thoughts about this guy. He was a mama's boy with a soft heart? Who knew?

Drew shook his head. "Well, she's had a rough time of it."

After a moment's pause, I managed a weak "I'm sorry." I wanted to say more, but nothing came to mind.

We stopped at the edge of the hothouse, and I glanced inside, amazed to find it just as colorful as the garden. More so, perhaps.

"You come from a big family?" he asked as he swung his camera over his shoulder.

My response—"I'm Irish"—got a laugh out of him.

"Don't be so quick to judge based on the gene pool," he said. "I'm Irish too, and I'm an only child. It happens."

Well, this certainly answered my question about his heritage, but something in his expression caused my heart to twist as he mentioned being an only child. How would I have survived without my three younger sisters?

I didn't have much time to think about this, however. The perfect photo op caught my eye. Tres leaned down to pluck a tomato from the vine. Ideal angle, sunlight . . . everything. How could I resist?

Drew reached for his camera and pointed it at Bella and D.J., who remained in a tight embrace, the garden making a lovely backdrop behind them. I did my best not to sigh at the beauty of the moment. Would I ever know such love?

We spent the next hour getting shots of the kids, first in the Roma tomatoes and then among the brilliant red Costolutos.

I'd been in a handful of gardens in my day, but nothing like this one. Apparently, Laz and Rosa had worked with precision to plant and cultivate this colorful wonderland. Tomatoes by the gazillions lined the area to my right. To the left, carrots, onions, and peppers. On the south end of the property, an herb garden. The pungent scents of basil and oregano drew me in. In spite of our larger-than-life breakfast, seeing and smelling this wonderful garden made me hungry—so hungry, in fact, that my stomach rumbled.

Bella's aunt Rosa approached as I continued to catch one luscious photo after another. "You stay after and I'll give you a little taste of gravy from this garden," she said.

"Gravy?"

"She means sauce," Drew whispered in my ear. "*Gravy* is her word for tomato sauce."

My mouth watered. I almost responded with "You've got a deal," but then remembered my shopping plans with Mama.

I didn't have time to answer, anyway. I found the perfect opportunity to get some shots of little Rosa-Earline curled up on a blanket among the eggplants. The contrast of colors—the deep purple next to her soft, white skin—made for an adorable, albeit staged, photo op.

Next I caught the boys playing among the radicchios. Perfect. After that I located Rosa and Laz kissing next to a trellis lined with ivy. Primo. From there I caught a glimpse of Bella's sister and brother-in-law kneeling to play with the children among vibrant green heads of lettuce.

On and on the photo ops went. I'd never known such joy or freedom as in those moments. I felt more at home working my way through Rosa and Laz's garden than I'd felt in years.

We wrapped up a couple of minutes before noon. Rosa and Laz headed inside to cook, and Armando approached—or should I say, he strolled my way with a devilish grin on his face.

"So, Hannah . . ." His right eyebrow elevated.

My heart took to pitter-pattering, half in fear and half in intrigue. "Y-yes?"

"Inquiring minds want to know—why did you call your business Picture This?"

I paused to think through my answer. "It just sort of came to me. Divinely inspired, I guess."

"Interesting." Armando leaned in close. Maybe a little too close. "When I hear the words *picture this*, I really hear *imagine this*," he whispered, then gave me a little wink. "That's what I'm doing right now, imagining the two of us. You. Me. Us."

Ew.

From several yards away Drew caught my eye, and his gaze narrowed as he took a few quick steps in my direction.

Armando, clearly undaunted, kept going. Those thick, dark brows of his got to waggling as he leaned so close that our shoulders touched. "So, tell me more about this business of yours. Maybe I could use some head shots for my deejay business."

"Oh? You're a deejay?" Interesting.

"Sure am. Well, part time. When the opportunities present themselves."

Okay, now the shoulder action was getting a little creepy. I did my best to ease away from him without being too noticeable.

"Surprised Bella didn't tell you. I've been working at a high-end club in Houston. Pretty swanky place. You should come see me in action sometime."

I was seeing him in action right now, and I didn't care for

it one little bit, though the chocolate-brown eyes did hold me spellbound. Well, mostly.

Don't do it, Hannah. Don't lose control of your senses just because he's g-g-gorgeous.

Speaking of gorgeous . . . out of the corner of my eye, I noticed Drew moving next to me. Part of me breathed a sigh of relief, the other part felt swallowed up by testosterone.

To my right, Armando said something, but I missed it.

"I'm sorry, what?" I turned to face him.

"What are you doing this afternoon?" he repeated. "Got a hot date?"

"Oh, I . . ." If I told him that I planned to go shopping with my mama, would he find me boring? Probably.

"Actually, she does have plans." Drew slipped his arm through mine and gave it a gentle squeeze. "Sorry."

Armando's eyes narrowed to accusing slits. "You two are a couple?"

A muscle tensed along the edge of Drew's jaw. He shrugged, then slipped his arm over my shoulder.

Armando wandered off, and I could almost feel the anger that coiled inside of him as he muttered, "Someone should've told me."

I glared at Drew, temper flaring. "What do you think you're doing?"

His tightened jaw appeared to relax. "Saving your neck. You can thank me later."

"I doubt it. First you interrupt my photo shoot, then you pretend you're my . . . my . . ." I couldn't make myself say the word.

"Your boyfriend?" He gave my shoulder a squeeze as Armando spoke a few words to Bella, and they both looked my way.

"Drew. Don't." I clenched my teeth. "Bella's going to think—"

I couldn't finish the sentence, what with her heading my way, a perplexed look on her face.

"Um, Hannah?" She glanced at Drew. "Drew? Something you two want to tell us?"

"No. Definitely not." I tried to shrug my way out of Drew's embrace, but he held tight.

"We're not ready to talk about it yet," he said with a smile.

Armando drew close, his gaze narrowing as he gave me one last glance. Then he turned to Bella. "Tell Rosa I can't stay for lunch, okay? I've got a hot date in Houston tonight and need to get back." He lit into a detailed conversation about the woman he planned to meet at some bar near downtown, and I suddenly felt a little nauseous.

In that moment I realized Drew had been right . . . about everything. I couldn't really fault him for trying to save my neck. He wasn't kidding when he said he knew Armando, now was he?

With Drew's arm still slung over my shoulder, we made our way to the front of the house . . . just in time to see Mama pulling her car into the driveway at Club Wed next door. She got out of the car and came bounding my way. I cringed a little when I noticed she was wearing her favorite Irish Lass T-shirt, circa 1996.

Mama's eyes flashed with merriment as she saw Drew's arm around me. "Well, hello there." She looked back and forth between us, clearly intrigued.

"Hi, Mama. I, well . . . we were just finishing."

"Finishing what?" She giggled.

"The photo shoot, of course." I shrugged off Drew's arm and cast a warning look at Armando, who took off for his car.

"Mama, this is Drew Kincaid." I fidgeted with my necklace and smiled weakly.

"Is this the enemy?" Mama whispered in my ear a little too loudly. "The handsome fella who took the pictures at Brock's wedding?"

Drew must've overheard because he gave me a "why would you call me your enemy?" look. I shrugged, then turned back to Mama and tried to convince her—with my eyes, not my voice—to can it.

Mama looked away from me and scrutinized Drew, her face lighting in a smile. "Well now . . ."

Please, Mama, watch what you say.

She turned back to me and shrugged. "Color me confused."

"Beg your pardon?" His brow wrinkled.

"Oh, just thinking out loud. Nice to meet you, Drew. I've heard so much about your work. We're all fans."

I glared at her, in part because I didn't happen to be a fan, and in part because she shouldn't be conspiring with the enemy.

From behind us, Bella's voice rang out. "Hannah, I know we'd planned to get some shots at Parma John's, but I don't think we'll have time today."

"Oh, that's fine. Really. I have so many great shots already. Plenty to choose from."

"I'm sure. Can't wait to see them. I hope you can stay for lunch. I know Aunt Rosa would love that."

Before I could respond, Mama turned to face Bella and began stammering. "Oh! Oh, oh, oh!"

Time to make introductions. "Bella, this is my mama—"

"You have to introduce me to your aunt," my mother interrupted before I could even finish giving her name.

"My aunt?" Bella shifted the baby to her other hip. Tres

chose that moment to start crying. Bella passed the baby off to me, then gazed at my mother. "You want to meet my aunt Rosa?"

"Do I ever!" Mama clasped her hands together. "You have no idea what an honor this is. Is she home?"

"Yes, she just went inside to start cooking lunch. It's Saturday. She and Laz always cook for the whole family on Saturdays. You would be welcome to join us, of course."

Mama gave me a little wink. "This was meant to be. Your father has his bowling league on Saturdays."

Mama. Tell me you did not just agree to have lunch at the Rossi home.

"You want to come inside and meet her?" Bella asked. "She's always happy for company. And she could probably use your help since the whole crew is here today."

My mother's cheeks flamed red. "Oh. No. I. Couldn't. I'm. No. Cook." Her stammered words caught me off guard.

"Well of course you are," I threw in. "You're an expert at all sorts of things." I began to list her credentials as if she were applying for a job as chief cook and bottle washer.

"I mean, I'm not an Italian cook." Mama's eyelashes fluttered.

"You will be in no time if you hang out with Rosa." Bella grinned. "To be honest, I couldn't cook a thing when D.J. and I got married, but Rosa has turned me into a gourmet. You should taste my ravioli."

"I'd love to." Mama and I spoke in unison and then laughed.

"Perfect. Because I've agreed to make some for this afternoon's get-together. C'mon in and we'll put you to work."

Mama gazed my way, a near-frantic look on her face. "You . . . you won't tell your father?"

"I hate that you feel you have to hide your cooking passion from him, but no, I won't tell him."

"He wouldn't understand." She sighed. "If it's not his familiar meat and potatoes, he won't eat it."

"But what about our shopping spree?" I reminded her. "You were supposed to be Christmas shopping today, remember? What about that list of gifts you made?"

"I can order your father's gifts online. He'll never know the difference." She winked. "Same for your sisters and the babies. It's easier to order online, anyway. And look on the bright side—I'll save money on gas." She offered a smile meant to convince me, no doubt. Not that I needed convincing. Sticking around sounded like a lot of fun.

Apparently Drew liked the idea too. When Bella offered the invitation to stay for lunch, he practically sprinted indoors.

Mama and I followed Bella into the house. In the spacious kitchen, we found Rosa standing at the island, kneading dough, and Laz nearby, stirring a pot on the stove. The most luscious aroma filled the room. Mama, usually not one to shy away from a situation, froze up the moment she saw Rosa. I could read the rapt awe in her expression—Mama's, not Rosa's—and wondered if she would ever be the same.

Thank goodness Bella made the introductions. My mother found her tongue and sprinted into a glowing conversation about Rosa and Laz, singing their praises like a television advertiser. Then Drew joined in, adding his two bits about cooking. Like the guy knew anything about cooking.

Okay, after hearing his detailed recipe for soda bread, I had to wonder if maybe I'd judged him too soon. Sounded like he knew his stuff, both with photography and with cooking. Figured.

The ladies worked together to make homemade garlic

twists, and I looked on alongside Drew, who turned to give me a friendly smile.

"Next time we all get together for a meal, we should add some Irish food to the mix," he said. "I make a mean corned beef and cabbage. My mom says it's better than hers, and that's really saying something."

"Ooh." Rosa looked at Drew, a smile turning up the edges of her lips as she waved a large spoon in his direction. "Say that again, young man."

He repeated himself and shrugged.

Rosa's eyes sparkled, and she clasped her hands together. "The Food Network has asked me to branch out and add a few other items to my springtime season. It's mostly Italian food, of course, but we've already covered most of the favorites, so I'm looking at ways to incorporate foods from other cultures."

"Then you should ask my mom to make her sausage and potato coddle," I said.

Where those words came from, I couldn't say. I could no more picture my mother making a guest appearance on the Food Network than I could imagine her whipping up a tiramisu for dessert. And if my father ever found out . . . I shuddered just thinking about it.

"That's it!" Rosa clasped her hands together and giggled. "We'll do an Irish-Italian segment, merging both worlds." She turned to Lazarro. "What do you think?"

"I think we'll end up with some of the best food this side of the Mediterranean." He grinned. "Or the English Channel."

The two of them dove into a lengthy chat about the various foods they would feature. Mama and Drew joined right in, adding their voices and opinions to the fray. Mama promised to wear her Irish Lass T-shirt on the episode. Perfect.

"We're only missing one thing," Rosa said, her brow wrinkling in concern. "Some sort of dessert."

"Hannah makes wonderful buttermilk scones," Mama said. "She makes them every holiday season. They're a real hit with the rest of the family and with my husband's lodge buddies." She went on singing my praises, as if I'd somehow earned a spot on the Food Network because I could bake a scone.

I shook my head as they all looked my way. "Oh no. No. No. No." Another firm shake of my head should convince them they'd better not broach this subject. Sure, I could make buttermilk scones, but on television? No way.

"I think it's a great idea." Rosa grinned. "In fact, we'll focus the segment on people your age, since you and Drew will be featured. Bella and D.J. can come along for the ride. And we'll fill the audience with several other young folks. It'll be so much fun. A springtime food extravaganza!"

Off she went again, talking about the episode as if I'd agreed to do it. Which I hadn't. And never would.

Drew kept looking at me with those pouty, puppy-dog eyes of his. Who could resist that? Even the toughest McDermott in the history of all McDermotts would melt under such an intense gaze, sword or no sword.

"Okay, okay, I'll do it." I had no idea where those words came from. Still, I couldn't very well take them back now, could I?

"Perfect!" Rosa beamed with obvious delight. "I always say the family that cooks together stays together." She gave Mama a little wink. "I also say that a good marriage is like a good lasagna: only those involved actually know what goes into it."

This got a nervous chuckle out of my mother, who no

doubt wondered if my father would know a lasagna if it jumped up and bit him..

Thank goodness the conversation shifted and Rosa invited Drew to help her make the manicotti. He agreed and went to work without question. I looked on, wondering how in the world I'd landed in the kitchen of an Italian master chef with Jacquie Goldfarb—okay, Drew Kincaid—so close by.

Not that I really minded. Something about being here, surrounded by Bella's amazing family members, made me wonder if perhaps the leprechauns had cast some sort of strange spell over me. Might have something to do with the tantalizing aromas wafting up from the stove.

Oh well. I couldn't really argue with bliss, now could I? And, judging from the look in Drew's eyes as he gave me a little wink, neither could he.

8

Be Honest with Me

May your thoughts be as glad as the shamrocks,
May your heart be as light as a song.
May each day bring you bright, happy hours
That stay with you all the year long.

Irish blessing

Sharing a midafternoon feast with the happiest Italian family on Galveston Island proved to be pure delight. Not only did I get to know Bella and her husband better, I truly felt as if I'd bonded with Rosa as well. And Bella's mother, Imelda, went out of her way to make me feel welcome in her home. She also fell head over heels for my mother, and all the more when she figured out we lived just a couple of miles away.

"I can feel it," she said as she gripped Mama's hand. "We're going to be fast friends."

In our world, nothing moved fast. Well, unless my dad happened to be taking his fiber pills. Still, I had to wonder if these two women could really survive a lasting relationship, their lives being so busy and all.

Mama responded with a smile and a hint of tears. "I would love that," she whispered. "I really would."

I pondered my mother's reaction, realizing the truth. Her very predictable life didn't leave much time or room for real friendships. Sure, she belonged to the ladies' group at church, but beyond that, her entire world revolved around Dad. And me.

Imelda, my mother's polar opposite in both appearance and posture, offered a broad smile. "Well, I don't know if you're interested in the Grand Opera, Marie, but I'm on the board and would love to get your take on a script we're looking at for St. Patrick's Day. It has an Irish-American theme."

"Perfect." Mama's cheeks flamed pink. "Thank you for thinking of me."

I could hardly believe my good fortune. Who knew these women would sweep in and make my sweet mother feel so at home? And the icing on the cake? Bella's in-laws arrived just in time to join us. Interestingly enough, they rode in on Harleys.

Dwayne and Earline Neeley were introduced, and Mama took to Earline like a cat to cream. D.J.'s mama was a little older, but she had the energy of three women. And who could top that I've-been-out-in-the-wind-on-my-Harley hairdo? She laughed and shared the stories about their day, filling us in on their motorcycle ministry, which explained the leather jackets with the Kingdom Riders logo on the back.

Drew looked on, laughing and talking as if he somehow

fit right into this fascinating bunch. Maybe he did. Maybe he came to the Rossi home on a regular basis. From the way he got along with D.J. and Bella's oldest brother, I had to wonder.

As we settled into our spots around the huge dining table, I stared at the feast in front of us. From across the table I caught a glimpse of Mama's face. I'd never seen her look so happy. In fact, I was pretty sure I saw tears in her eyes. Who could blame her? This happy-go-lucky environment probably put her in mind of our own family . . . a few years back. If I closed my eyes, I could almost hear my sisters' voices ringing out.

Okay, my sisters didn't squabble in Italian, and we never had the scent of garlic permeate our dining room—ever—but the ambience was the same, regardless.

Family.

As I glanced around the table, I had the intense feeling of belonging that came only when one was surrounded on every side by family. I hadn't realized just how much I'd missed feeling like this till now.

If I closed my eyes, I could envision the table at my house. Three people seated at a table for six. Minimal foods. Minimal plates. Minimal conversation. I couldn't help but contrast that with Bella's family table. Loaded down with foods. Tantalizing aromas of garlic and oregano. Chatter in abundance. Swirling conversations in both Italian and English. Kids laughing. People hugging and kissing. Voices raised in sheer delight, mixed with just the right amount of squabbling to keep it all in balance.

Bella, you are one lucky girl.

Not that I believed in luck. Still, she was blessed, no doubt about it. And as Drew—seated to my right—passed the large serving platter of eggplant Parmesan, I had a twinge of jealousy, realizing Bella was blessed by the colorful foods that greeted her each day too. Vibrant red tomato sauce. Brilliant green peppers. Deep purple eggplant. Then again, if I ate like this every day, I would have to invest in a new wardrobe. How Bella stayed slim and trim was beyond me. Of course, she worked harder than anyone on the planet and took care of two children to boot.

Boot—ha! I glanced down at her feet and smiled as I took in the sparkly cowgirl boots.

I tried to nibble on the various foods in ladylike fashion but found it difficult. Eating with abandon came more naturally, so I went for it. Drew did the same, pausing only to add funny tidbits to the conversation. He glanced my way with a smile, and I relaxed, realizing that he probably didn't mind if I enjoyed my food. From the way he shoveled down the manicotti, I could tell he wasn't holding back. Why should I?

Several times during the meal I noticed Bella looking back and forth between Drew and me as if to ask, "What's up with you two? Are you really a couple?"

I'd have to fill her in later. Oh, wait. I couldn't. If I told her why Drew had come to my rescue, then she would know that her brother had hit on me. I couldn't risk upsetting her, could I?

Over the next several minutes, I swallowed down more than the food. The photographer in me took note of several details that most people would have overlooked: Tres passing nibbles of his eggplant to the yappy little dog under his chair. Marcella, Bella's sister-in-law, the quiet observer, taking in the faces and voices of those at the table. D.J., the loving father, cradling baby Rosie in his arms when she started fussing. Rosa, the energetic one, making dozens of trips back and forth to the kitchen. Laz, the entertainer, telling stories about the old country. And Bella—sweet, loving Bella—caring for all of the young ones at the table, never flinching once when they made a mess or too much noise.

At one point I caught Laz rolling his eyes at the antics of the older boys. Just as quickly, though, he had them laughing with a funny story. Then Drew added his two bits to the story, and before long the boys were howling with laughter. Who knew the guy was a comedian?

Imelda, Bella's mama, observed all of this with a quiet smile, a look of pure satisfaction on her face. In fact, my own mama looked pretty content as well. No doubt she missed these chaotic scenes around our much-too-large-for-the-three-of-us dining table.

Rosa must've picked up on Mama's expression. She placed a tray of garlic twists in front of her and smiled. "So, Marie, tell us about your family."

Mama pulled away the napkin she'd tucked into the neckline of her T-shirt, revealing the Irish Lass logo beneath. "Well, let's see now." She dabbed her mouth with the napkin, then looked my way as if asking for permission to share. "I have four daughters."

"Four girls? Wow." Drew chuckled.

"Yes, four girls." Mama smiled. "Close in age too. Grew up as best friends."

Please don't tell them I'm the oldest.

"Hannah here is my oldest, and the others are stair steps, each a year apart."

Rosa reached for the bowl of grated Parmesan and passed it to Laz. "My goodness, you must've had your hands full."

"Oh, you have no idea." Mama's girlish laughter rang out. "But I came up with ways to make things easier, trust me. Little tricks of the trade. I've been thinking about writing them down to help young mothers with their little ones."

"Tricks?" Laz gave Mama a funny look, then passed the Parmesan my way. "Like what?"

"Well, for instance, getting four little girls dressed for church every Sunday morning can be quite a challenge. So I would remedy that by dressing them on Saturday night."

Drew let out a snort. I elbowed him, and he went back to eating in silence.

"Yes. I'd bathe and dress them on Saturday night." Mama grinned. "That was my secret weapon for arriving at church on time on Sunday mornings."

"She's leaving out the part about the lecture we would all get every Saturday night as she tucked us in," I added, sprinkling excessive amounts of grated Parmesan on my food. "'No tossing and turning. You'll wrinkle your pretty dress.' 'No water before bed. You might have an accident.'"

"My youngest, Deidre, ignored that last one." Mama grinned. "Oh, but I had a thousand other shortcuts too. Maybe I'll list them all one day. If I can remember them."

"I've only got two little ones, but I could use a list like that, trust me." Bella gave her son a winsome look. "Thank God I've got D.J. He's such a huge help with the kids." She looked at her husband with such affection that it actually caused my heart to skip a beat.

Mama's gaze swept across the table to D.J., who held a now-sleeping Rosie in his arms. "You're very blessed. My husband never really helped with the children. But then, we're from a different generation, I suppose. Back then men left the tending of the babies to the women."

"Times are definitely changing," Bella said with a nod. "But I appreciate a man who can change a diaper. Trust me."

"I'm not saying that diaper changing is my favorite thing in the world," D.J. threw in. "But someone's got to do it, and it just doesn't make sense that the task should always fall to the same person." He gave Bella a comfortable smile. "We both hold down full-time jobs and raise the kids together."

"Well, I think that's just wonderful," my mother said. "I wish there were more men like you in the world."

"There are," he said with a nod.

Mama gave him an admiring look, then went off on a tangent, talking about some of her other tricks of the trade. Soon all of the ladies were chiming in.

I stayed out of the conversation until Rosa and Laz lit into a funny story about Frank Sinatra and Dean Martin, one that got everyone at the table talking. I had my favorite, but it was neither of the ones they mentioned. How could they talk about the greats without bringing up Bing Crosby? Grandpa Aengus would turn over in his grave at the suggestion that either singer outshone Bing.

"I have a great idea." My words stopped their chatter midstream.

Rosa glanced my way. "What is it, Hannah?"

"My dad always hosts a Bing and Bob party to kick off the holiday season."

"Bing and Bob?" Laz's brow creased.

"You know, Bing Crosby and Bob Hope. Dad invites a ton of his buddies to come to the house. They have to dress like Bing or Bob, and they perform some song or scene from one of their movies. We play Bing Crosby music and sometimes watch a movie together before the night's over. It's a blast."

"What about the ladies?" Rosa asked. "Surely they don't dress up like Bing Crosby or Bob Hope."

"No, no. We have to dress up like someone who starred opposite Bing or Bob."

Drew gave me a funny smile. "And you're coming as . . . ?"

I paused to consider it. "Pretty sure I'm coming as Grace Kelly this year."

"I'm coming as Rosemary Clooney," Mama chimed in.

The whole table came alive as folks added their two cents' worth. Rosa loved Mama's idea of coming as Rosemary. Imelda felt sure she would choose Dorothy Lamour. Bella's sister wasn't sure who Bing and Bob were, and Marcella— sweet, quiet Marcella—listened without commenting. Still, the smile never left her face.

"So, who all comes to this party?" Bella's father asked. "Just your dad's friends?"

"Sometimes family too, but I'm not sure my sisters will make it this year, now that they've got babies to look after. So you guys should come in their place. The party is the first Saturday night in November."

What are you saying, Hannah? You won't be able to fit all of these people in your house.

I looked at Mama, hoping she wouldn't panic. No, she seemed relaxed and even excited by the idea.

"Oh, yes. I think you'll love it," she said. "We always have Irish food on Bing's side of the room and English food on Bob's side. Bob was born in England, you know."

"I had no idea." Bella reached for her napkin to wipe Tres's face.

"It's true," I said. "We'll play lots of games and music and even have prizes."

Rosa's eyes lit up. "I like this idea very much. Laz and I did something similar on the show once with Dino and Ol' Blue Eyes. I cooked Frankie's favorite foods and Laz cooked Dino's. It got a little competitive."

"My aunt and uncle have always had a competitive thing going over Dean Martin and Frank Sinatra," Bella explained as she refolded her napkin. "But they've resolved that dispute."

"I wouldn't say we've resolved it." Rosa's eyes narrowed. "There's no one like Sinatra."

"Unless you count Dino at his finest," Laz threw in. "But we've agreed to lay this argument down because it was putting up a wall of separation between us, and we can't have that." He leaned over and gave Rosa a peck on the cheek. Her face reddened.

"Well, our Bing and Bob party gets a little competitive too," I said. "My grandpa Aengus was nuts about Bing Crosby, but my dad is a Bob Hope fan. So every time we would watch *Road to Singapore*, there would always be this banter going back and forth."

Drew shook his head. "I still say no one can top Bing Crosby's voice. I grew up listening to his music. Even have it on my phone." He pulled out the device, and seconds later the strains of "White Christmas" filled the room.

"I've always loved that song." Mama sighed and leaned back in her chair. "Really puts me in the mood for Christmas."

The conversation shifted to our holiday plans. On the heels of that, Laz served up a tiramisu that made my head swim. I could feel my cholesterol rising as I nibbled. Imelda made some remark about gaining weight, which sent the ladies into a lengthy conversation about how hard it was to keep their weight in check during the holidays. This, of course, bored the men to tears, so they eased their way into a conversation about football. I couldn't help but notice that Drew didn't have much to add to the football conversation. Then again, as he reached for a second piece of tiramisu, I had to conclude the boy was slightly distracted. He probably didn't get this kind of meal very often either.

Just about the time the conversation wound down, I glanced at my watch—4:05. Yikes. Mama and I would have to head home soon.

Or not.

Rosa pushed back her chair, flashed a winning smile, and invited my mama to join her in the garden. "Come, Marie." She extended her hand. "You must see my Romas."

"Ooh, I want to come too." Earline rose and brushed her hands against her slacks. "I've been dying to figure out how you keep them growing year-round."

"That's my little secret." Rosa gave her a wink and chuckled.

The three ladies made quick work of clearing the table. Minutes later the room emptied out. Well, mostly. D.J. took the kids to the other room for a nap, but Bella lingered behind. I could tell she had something on her mind. I'd just started to get out of my chair when she looked at me.

"Hey, can you hang around a minute? There's something I need to tell you." She glanced at Drew, who remained seated next to me. "Both of you, really."

"Sure." I settled back into my chair, curiosity setting in.

Bella looked Drew's way again and sighed. "Drew, I'm sorry you got stuck here all day. Pretty good of you, since you didn't even know why I'd asked you to stop by in the first place." She eased her way down into an empty seat. I could read the exhaustion in her eyes.

"It's been a great day." His smile seemed genuine enough. "Had a blast with your family, Bella. They're great."

"Thanks. But it's time to tell you why I wanted to meet with you. I've got some news to share. I hadn't really planned to let anyone else know, but since you're both together . . ." She gave me a strange look, as if analyzing the word *together*.

"News to share?" Drew asked. "What do you mean?"

She hesitated. "Well, what I'm about to tell you may come as a shock. And you have to keep it to yourself, okay? Brock will kill me if this gets leaked to the media."

"B-Brock? Brock Benson?" I couldn't help the words. They just slipped out.

"Yes." She grinned and put a finger to her lips. "But we really have to keep this quiet, okay? My family doesn't know. Yet. They'll flip when they find out. They love Brock, so this is going to mean the world to them."

"You asked me to come over because of something to do with Brock?" Drew looked confused. "Something to do with his wedding photos?"

"No. Nothing like that." Her smile now lit her face. "He's been asked to serve as the grand marshal for the Christmas parade at Dickens on the Strand the weekend of Sierra's wedding."

"No way." My breath caught in my throat. "Are you serious?" I felt the room spinning. Brock Benson, my favorite actor in the history of movies, was coming back to Galveston Island?

"Yes." She nodded. "His wife is from Texas, you know."

"No, I didn't."

"Yeah, Erin's from Austin," Drew said.

"Her grandfather lives here on the island, though, and he's a bigwig with the Dickens project," Bella added. "So of course he thought Brock would be the perfect choice."

"Wow."

Bella turned to Drew. "And that's where you come in. Because you've worked with Brock before, he felt you would be the perfect candidate to capture some shots of him leading the parade."

"Wow. That's great." Drew grinned, and I could read the look of satisfaction in his eyes.

Ouch. Once again Drew Kincaid swept in behind me to steal my thunder.

Bella now looked at me, her eyes twinkling mischievously. "But wait—there's more."

"O-oh?" I managed.

"Yes." She quirked a brow. "See, there's a little teensy-tiny thing I haven't told you, Hannah. One very important thing."

I felt my nerves kick in. "More than this, you mean?"

Bella nodded and gave a sly grin. "Yep. See, Brock is also in Sierra Caswell's wedding on the day after the parade."

"He—he—what?" I could hardly believe my ears. Suddenly I had that weird out-of-body sensation. Surely I was dreaming this. Bella did not just say that Brock Benson—hunky, gorgeous Brock Benson—was going to be in the wedding I'd been hired to shoot.

Oh. Help.

"Sure. Think about it, Hannah. Sierra wrote the theme song for *Stars Collide*."

"Right." I knew that. But what did one thing have to do with the other?

Bella rose and paced the room, then turned to give me a pensive look. "Brock set all of that up. He met Sierra through his wife. Erin and Sierra went to high school together in Austin."

"Oh. Wow." I could hardly manage those two words, let alone anything else.

I'm going to take pictures of Brock Benson. Just like Drew.

"Now you see one reason why Sierra's been so keen on keeping things perfect for her wedding," Bella said. "She's carrying the stress of making things right not just for herself but for Brock and Erin too."

Suddenly it all made sense. The high-pressure emails from

George. The tension in Sierra's voice. The insistence that I only capture certain shots, certain angles.

"But if he's been asked to be in the parade, everyone will figure out he's here." Drew's words gave away his confusion about the matter.

"Right. They'll know he's here for the parade, but they won't have a clue about his participation in the wedding the next day. The timing works out perfectly. Parade on Saturday. Wedding on Sunday afternoon." She looked my way again. "So you see, Hannah? You see why I needed you to know? I didn't want you to show up at the wedding and find out in the moment. Might've been too much of a shock."

Too much of a shock? Well, yeah! Brock Benson was coming here? Not just coming to Galveston for Dickens on the Strand, but coming to be in the very wedding I happened to be photographing? My mind reeled as the reality set in. Every nerve in my body felt exposed. A mixture of excitement and sheer terror overtook me. How could I manage photographing not only Sierra Caswell but Brock Benson as well? I couldn't even pick out matching shoes.

A quick glance down at my matching tennis shoes should've convinced me otherwise, but then I realized that I happened to be wearing one pink sock and one white one. Go figure.

Every ounce of confidence slithered right out of me as I stared at my feet. What sort of fool was I, anyway? I couldn't do this. I couldn't shoot Sierra Caswell's wedding if Brock Benson was involved. I would find some way—likely some very public, excruciating way—to prove that I didn't have the goods. And no matter how many Irish proverbs I quoted, no matter how many swords I wielded, I would come out looking like a fool in the end.

9

I've Got a Pocketful of Dreams

May you get all your wishes but one,
So you always have something to strive for.

Irish blessing

It took me all of five minutes to shake off my fears regarding the whole Brock Benson thing and then readjust my thinking. I would photograph Sierra Caswell's wedding and would do so with confidence and grace. I would not show up in mismatched shoes, nor would I humiliate the McDermott clan in any form or fashion. Instead, my business would grow into a thing of beauty as a result of this opportunity.

I hoped.

Bella forged ahead, giving us particulars about the upcoming events, her words now soaring. I got a little confused somewhere in the middle of the whole "grand marshal for the parade" part. Not that Drew appeared to be terribly focused on her story either. At one point—probably in a sugar-induced state from the tiramisu—he let out what sounded like a little snore.

"Looks like we've lost him." Bella chuckled as she gestured his way. "I guess we can wrap this up another time when he's not comatose."

He stirred a few seconds later, then gave us a sheepish look. "Sorry." A yawn and stretch followed. "Guess the food got to me."

"Yeah, Rosa's pasta is pretty intoxicating."

"No kidding. Not to mention all of that sugar in the dessert." He rose and yawned again. "Maybe I should hit the road. Might make more sense to nap at my own house."

Bella gave him a sympathetic look. "Thanks for coming by. Hope the news about Brock Benson didn't throw you for a loop."

"Nah, I can handle it. He's a pretty normal guy. Puts his socks on one foot at a time, just like the rest of us."

I couldn't help but glance down at my feet.

Drew gave Bella a confident smile, then said his goodbyes and staggered out of the room, still looking a little loopy. I couldn't help but notice when he turned back to give me one last glance. Sizing up the competition, maybe? I couldn't be sure. As long as he didn't notice my socks, I would be okay.

After he left, Bella rose and sighed. "It's been quite a day."

"Perfect, really." I rose as well and stretched as a wave of exhaustion settled over me. "You have an awesome family. I'm a little jealous."

"Aw, thanks. They're a little crazy, but I love 'em." She

flashed a winning smile and stepped toward me. "Speaking of people I love, have I mentioned how much I'm enjoying getting to know you?"

My heart warmed as she gave me a sisterly smile. "Thanks. I feel the same way."

"I feel like . . ." Here she paused. "I feel like we're kindred spirits. You know?"

Offering up a lame nod, I managed, "I do."

It felt really good, in fact. To think I'd been worried about impressing her. Turned out she was as normal as the rest of us.

Her gaze narrowed as she looked my way. "Since we're so close and all . . . one of these days you're going to have to tell me what's going on with you and Drew. It kind of surprised me to see the two of you as a couple."

"We're not." I sighed. "Trust me. He's a great guy . . ."

"He is, isn't he?" She laughed, then gave my hand a squeeze. "He's no Armando, but he'll do."

I couldn't help but laugh aloud at that proclamation.

"I don't blame you where Armando's concerned. He's a piece of work. We all know it." She rolled her eyes in dramatic fashion. "Anyway, we can talk about that later. Guess I'd better get to work in the kitchen. I usually do the dishes when Rosa and Mama do most of the cooking. The longer I stay here, the less I feel like working."

"I'll help." In fact, I didn't mind a bit. And I wasn't just offering to win her favor either. I really enjoyed hanging out with her.

I trudged along behind Bella into the kitchen, stunned to find it empty. Well, empty except for the dozens and dozens of dirty plates, bowls, cups, and silverware. She rolled up her sleeves and went to work, rinsing dishes and placing them in the dishwasher. I did my best to help, but my thoughts were elsewhere.

She gave me an inquisitive look. "Can we go back to the conversation about Drew? I promise to leave it alone if you don't want to talk about it."

"No, it's okay." I grabbed a dirty plate and passed it her way.

"He made it look like you two were a couple, but you're not."

"Right."

"But you look really natural together, and it's obvious you've got good chemistry."

"Seriously?" I shrugged. "Well, he's a nice guy. But he *is* my competition, you know."

I could have slapped myself silly for saying that out loud. Bella glanced my way, clearly confused. "What do you mean?"

"Well, we're in the same business. I'm trying to grow my studio and he's trying to grow his." I hesitated. "Maybe it was wrong to say we're in competition, but it feels like it. You know?"

"But you're both so good at what you do," she said with a smile. "I think you'll be equally successful. If you don't spend too much time worrying about it." She gave me a pensive look. "Are you worried about it?"

Please don't sigh out loud.

I sighed aloud. "Yeah." A lengthy silence followed as I thought through my next words. Might as well come clean. She would figure this out sooner or later. Besides, the sooner I got this off my chest, the better. "I have this . . . this . . . flaw."

"Flaw?" Bella paused from her work, clearly troubled by this statement. "What do you mean?"

"I always come up short."

"Come up short? How?" She gazed at me with such intensity that vulnerability slipped over me like an ill-fitting garment, one I would like to discard as soon as possible.

I shrugged. "I sometimes think the headstone on my grave will read, 'Good but not great.'"

Bella looked aghast at this idea and responded with, "Are you kidding?"

"No. I really mean it."

"Whose standard are you measuring yourself by?"

"What do you mean?"

"I mean, are you comparing yourself to other people, or to yourself? Has someone put you in a position where you feel like you have to measure up or something? Maybe one of your parents?"

"No, it's not my parents." I gave a deep sigh. "Neither of my parents has a competitive bone in their body. My dad makes out like he does by talking about the McDermott clan's glory days, but he just loves a good story."

"So, where did this come from?"

"From my grandpa Aengus, I guess. He always wanted the best for me. He said that being an Irish American was a privilege, and not one to be taken lightly. So he really thought I would go places. Make a name for myself."

"You have made a name for yourself. You own your own business, for Pete's sake. And you're only twenty-seven."

"Twenty-six." I offered a weak smile.

"See there? That makes you even more accomplished. You don't have to be good enough or prove yourself to anyone."

Shame washed over me afresh. "See, that's the real problem right there."

"What?"

"I have been trying to prove myself to everyone."

"Well, stop. Seriously. You're awesome, and so are your photos. Just rest easy in that, Hannah. You're going to go a long way. I know a pro when I see one."

"Thank you so much." I really meant those words. She'd extended a hand of kindness in spite of my stupidity. "To be honest, it's just kind of weird to see my sisters all married and living in other cities while I'm still in the same bedroom I grew up in. Ya know?"

"You're describing my life before I married D.J." Bella grinned. "Only, add about twenty relatives to the mix, plus several extended family members and a host of friends and business associates."

"How did you handle it?" I asked.

She sighed. "Honestly, I just focused on my work. A lot. Tried to stay busy. Didn't really want to push any buttons with my parents because I knew they were worried about that whole empty-nest thing."

"I get it. Everything stays so busy, and yet . . ." I couldn't finish the sentence because unexpected tears sprang to my eyes.

Bella stopped working and gave me a sympathetic look. "See now? I'll bet I know just what you're thinking. Something you probably didn't even realize until now." Her eyes filled with compassion and her next words were whispered. "You're lonely, aren't you?"

Before I could stop it, the word "Yeah" slipped out. I hadn't realized it, but she was right. Loneliness had enveloped me, and I'd given myself over to it.

"Is it really possible to be lonely when you live in a house with your father who hardly gives you a minute to yourself and your mother folding your clothes?"

"It's possible. In fact, it's possible to be surrounded on every side by noisy, crazy people and still feel like you're all alone in the world. Ask me how I know." She grinned and gestured to the mounds of dirty dishes.

Suddenly I felt like a real heel for using Bella to advance my career. What a jerk I'd been, looking after my own interests. Ugh. It was likely—*brace yourself, Hannah*—the real reason for meeting her had nothing to do with business at all. Maybe the Lord had something else in mind.

Watching her today—with the kids, with her family members—put my behavior over the past few weeks in perspective. Had I really been taking advantage of her without truly getting to know her? What sort of person was I?

After a couple of minutes of pondering, feeling ashamed, I couldn't stand it any longer. I had to say something . . . or bust.

"Bella, I . . . well, I owe you an apology."

"An apology?" She looked up from the dishes, her brow wrinkled. "Why?"

A deep sigh escaped before I could stop it. "Because it turns out you're a really nice person."

"Well, thank you." She leaned down to put a plate in the dishwasher. "But why are you apologizing? Don't you want me to be nice?" The edges of her lips turned up.

That got a much-needed smile out of me and lifted the tension a bit. I handed her a dirty bowl. "It's just that I think I've had the wrong opinion of you all along. I saw you as this powerful force to be reckoned with, someone who could make or break my career, and there's so much more to you than that."

"Wait . . . make or break your career?" She shook her head, then placed the dirty dish on the counter. "How so?"

Was she kidding?

"C'mon, you have to know how important your word is in the wedding biz. People take what you have to say very seriously. And I have this little fledgling business—"

"Little fledgling business?" She laughed and leaned against the counter. "Are you serious? You're one of the best photographers I know. And Picture This is an entity. Everyone knows about it, and your work. You're amazing, Hannah. Not to mention you have the coolest studio on the island. Love that old-world style. And to capture a place on the Strand? Primo!"

"Thank you." I paused to think through my next response. "But don't you see? I wanted to get close to you because I thought it would help my career. Initially, anyway."

"Ah." Her smile faded a bit, but she didn't say anything else.

Time to admit my full shame. "But then I got to know you—your whole family, in fact—and fell in love with all of you. At that point I realized that maybe I'd been using you." I let out another deep sigh and gazed into her eyes. "Can you forgive me for that? I wouldn't blame you if you stopped recommending me to your brides."

She chuckled, then went right back to work loading the dishwasher. "You're so funny."

"I am?"

"Yes. I've walked a mile in your shoes, trust me. And you can't begin to know how nervous I was when my dad handed over the wedding facility to me. I was basically clueless. I'd never even done a themed wedding before and certainly wasn't manager material. I leaned on anyone and everyone I could think of."

"But you turned things around."

"God turned them around. Once I got out of the way. But

we had a zillion calamities along the way. Surely you've heard some of the stories."

I shook my head.

"You don't know about the time Guido—Sal's parrot— stole a toupee right off the head of one of our guests?"

"I . . . I think I would've remembered that."

"And you don't know about the time D.J.'s brother, Bubba, was barbecuing for a wedding and ended up with no eyebrows? Uncle Laz added fuel to the fire at just the wrong time, and it took off every bit of facial hair the boy had."

"Um, pretty sure I would've remembered that one too."

"Girl, I made a royal mess of things. I accidentally bought eighty cowboy boots off eBay for my first country-western-themed wedding when I only needed a dozen. I even got arrested once because of a misunderstanding."

"Actually, I do remember that. You and Brock both ended up in jail, right?"

"Yes, but it was all a big mistake. Still, you can imagine how embarrassed my parents were. I didn't set out to make a mockery of Club Wed, but I managed to do it anyway. Trust me, it's only by the grace of God that I managed to survive."

"Not just survive," I added. "You've thrived. And look what God has done."

"Yes." She grinned, then placed another plate in the dishwasher. "Look what he's done. He's given me a husband, two children, a business I love, and more family members than a girl could shake a fist at."

"You're very . . . blessed."

"I am. But I also know the value of hard work, just like you. It takes a lot of blood, sweat, and tears to grow a business. You're in the sweat cycle." She laughed and I joined her.

"That's about right."

"Just remember not to sweat the small stuff, okay? If you've got to perspire, save it for the stuff that really counts."

Ugh. She would have to go there.

"See, that's the problem. None of it is small stuff to me. It's all huge. And it always seems like I have to work harder than anyone I know to accomplish anything at all." Visions of Jacquie Goldfarb danced in my head. "Because I work for myself, I carry so much responsibility. How do I get past feeling like the ship could go down at any moment?"

"Girl, I get it. I totally and completely get it." Bella gazed at me with pure compassion emanating from her eyes. "It's going to sound so cliché, but you've got to stop trying to fix everything." She put a hand up. "I know, I know—this coming from the fix-it queen. But you were never meant to hold all things together. Only God can do that."

I sighed.

"Here's another little tidbit—one I learned from an awesome trio of godly ladies from Splendora. There's no storm too big to praise your way through. You might not feel like it, but praising God in the middle of the tough times is really the best way to shift your focus and to build your faith."

"Praise." I chewed on the word, deep in thought.

What I could never admit to Bella—or anyone, for that matter—was that praising God didn't come as naturally to me as it once had. Oh, there had been a time just a few years ago when I could keep my praise pom-poms bouncing up and down with youthful enthusiasm. These days, however, I just felt tired. I'd packed my pom-poms and replaced them with a more jaded view of life.

"I know what you're thinking, girl," Bella said. "Remember, I said I've walked a mile in your shoes. You're thinking that praising God takes energy and you don't have a lot of it."

"You're pretty good at seeing inside my head."

"Told you, we're two peas in a pod. Been there, done that. But if you want change, whether it's in your personal life or your business, there's really only one way—you have to start thanking God for it now, before you ever see a thing. In all things give thanks." She grinned.

"In all things? When my parents are putting me through a guilt trip or when the rent is due on the studio?"

"All things, girl. Oh, speaking of your rent, don't let me forget to pay you for today's photo shoot."

I'd just put up my hand to argue that point with her when she shut me down. "Anyway, let's get real, Hannah. We really need to be praising even more during the rough times. That's probably why the Bible calls it a *sacrifice* of praise."

"Ah, sacrifice. A word I know well." I chuckled.

I thought about how ironic it was that Bella and I had both lived here on the island for so many years, but we hadn't really known each other until today. Of course, she was a few years my senior, so we hadn't been schoolmates. Still, how had so much time lapsed without us meeting and becoming friends?

We didn't get a chance to wrap up the conversation because Rosa and Mama entered through the back door with Earline close behind. Minutes later, D. J. swept into the room, planted a kiss on Bella's forehead, and banished her to the living room, taking her spot at the dishwasher.

Really? Are you sure you don't have an unmarried brother somewhere?

Maybe not. But now I understood the point of Bella's passionate conversation. She'd put in the hours building her business and had trusted God with the details. As a result, he had blessed her with a husband who adored her and complemented her in every way.

Seeing it all in perspective made me want to try all the harder so that my story would have the same happily-ever-after ending. Now all I had to learn to do was praise my way through it.

10

After Sundown

Both your friend and your enemy think you will never die.

Irish proverb

I had to practically tear Mama and Earline apart around 5:30. We had to get home—and quickly. Dad would be waiting for his dinner at 6:01. No veering from the usual plan.

As we prepared to leave, Mama offered tearful hugs all around, her voice emanating with joy. "I feel like my whole life has changed in a day," she said. "Promise me we'll do this again."

"Of course we're doing it again," Rosa said. "Hannah invited us to your Bing and Bob party. And you'll have to come back over here soon so we can talk about your upcoming episode on the Food Network."

"I still can't believe it." Mama's eyes glazed over. "I'm going to be on television." She gave me a "what will your father say about this?" look, and I just grinned. Likely he would flip out—at first—then get used to the idea. Surely Mama worried in vain.

We arrived home in record time, and she reached into the refrigerator to pull out some leftovers, which she quickly crafted into a typical McDermott meal. "After what we've eaten today, it doesn't look like much, does it?" Mama grinned. "But that's our little secret." Her eyes widened. "You will keep it secret, won't you, Hannah? The part about me cooking Italian food, I mean."

"I think it's silly that you don't want me to mention it. He's going to have to know before that television episode hits the air. But I'll keep it to myself . . . for now."

"Thank you. I just don't want to stir the waters. Yet. My day will come. I know it will."

No doubt it would. In front of millions of television viewers, no less. The idea made me giddy and nervous all at the same time, especially when I remembered that—heaven help me—I'd agreed to do the show too.

Dad arrived home at 5:58, and we were seated around the table at the usual time, having our usual conversation and sharing in our usual fare. Afterward we settled in to watch our usual Saturday night television show, *Stars Collide*.

The opening song kicked in—the new one, with Sierra Caswell's voice strong and steady—and I managed to calm down. The show began, and I laughed right away as my favorite characters—Angie, Jack, and Basil, the Greek talent scout we all loved to hate, played by Brock Benson—swept me away to worlds unknown. Laughter ruled the day.

My father dozed off in his recliner after the show ended,

and I headed upstairs to call Scarlet. With so much brewing, I had to fill her in. She answered on the third ring, and I dove right in, telling her all about my day. I shared the part about Armando—handsome, conceited Armando. I told her about Drew coming to my rescue. I even told her about my heartfelt conversation with Bella Neeley.

"Wow. Sounds like quite a day." She chuckled. "And to think I spent the whole day in the kitchen baking." Off she went on a tangent, telling me about a new recipe she'd concocted for Italian cream cake.

Ordinarily I zoned out during her recipe-a-thons, but I was intrigued by this one. Likely it had something to do with the fact that I would soon appear on the Food Network.

"I've never been much for time in the kitchen, but after today I can see the appeal," I said.

"And you're over this whole 'I have to prove myself to Bella Neeley because she holds my future in her hands' thing?"

"Yeah." A sigh followed my words. "I feel like a real goober."

"And all of this competition stuff with Drew." She paused. "He's a nice guy after all?"

"Yeah." I couldn't deny it, could I? He was a nice guy. Maybe a little too nice.

"Are you still worried that he's your Jacquie Goldfarb?"

"Oh. Hmm. Not sure."

After my whole coming-clean-with-Bella speech, I'd kind of forgotten that he was supposed to be my archnemesis. And every time I thought about Brock Benson coming to town, I realized that Drew and I now had something in common. Something big. I did my best to relax and think more clearly about all of this. Why see him as my competitor? Why not just view him as someone who understood my business and had similar goals?

Oblivious to my whirling thoughts, Scarlet continued to gab. "Hey, do you ever wonder what became of the real Jacquie Goldfarb? I mean, do you keep up with her on social networking sites or anything?"

"Keep up with her?" To be honest, I hadn't. In fact, I'd gone out of my way to avoid finding out what had become of her. "I just know that she left for college and then moved away somewhere."

"No idea where?"

"Nope." I shrugged. "Never really cared to know."

"You should try to track her down. Find her on Facebook."

"Why? So I can see with my own eyes that she's living in a mini mansion in Beverly Hills with the perfect husband and 2.5 kids?"

Scarlet chuckled. "I'd like to see a photo of 2.5 kids. Can't imagine what that would look like."

"It would look kind of like the family I spent the day with—pretty ideal. And I'm not sure I need to see just how perfect Jacquie's life is." A dark cloud hovered over me, casting its shadows on what had, until this moment, been a pretty blissful day.

Thanks, Scarlet, for bringing this up. I owe you.

"Still, seeing her again might help you jump this hurdle. You could talk through your feelings. Get it all out in the open."

"Please." My frustrations mounted. "You don't know me very well if you think I would actually do that. I'd probably just end up making small talk or wishing I hadn't found her in the first place."

"C'mon now. Surely you'd come up with something to say to her, wouldn't you?"

I paused to give my answer careful thought. "I'm not sure.

It's not really her fault she always beat me out at everything. I'd probably just say, 'Hope you're having a great life.'"

"What if you found out she's a supermodel, living a life of big money and high fashion?"

I shrugged. "Wouldn't really matter, I guess. I never aspired to be a supermodel. I would just wish her well and go on with my life. No problem."

Scarlet's voice tightened. "What if you found out she had her own photography studio in Houston and just made *Texas Bride*'s top ten list of photographers in the state?"

Alarm bells sounded. My heart suddenly felt like lead. "Is that true, or are you speaking theoretically?"

"Speaking theoretically."

I felt as if I'd lost a hundred pounds in an instant. Man. "Scarlet, I really don't think we need to be having this conversation. I mean, honestly, what difference—"

"Let's be gut honest. What if you found out she'd married some guy who treated her bad, and as a result of her sad, defeated life, she'd packed on eighty pounds?"

"No way."

"Use your imagination."

I would have to, to imagine Jacquie as anything other than slim, trim, and fit. Still, who ever knew?

"I saw this once in an *I Love Lucy* episode."

Of course you did.

"Lucy was jealous of Ricky's old girlfriend. She pictured all sorts of things about the woman in her mind. In the end, the old girlfriend showed up in town and she was . . . well, let's just say she was no beauty queen, okay?"

"Ah." Maybe I could learn a few lessons from Lucy, after all.

"The point is, I think you need to try to contact Jacquie just to lay this to rest. It doesn't matter what happened yesterday.

You can't let who or what she turned out to be rule what you do. We weren't designed to worry about what others think. There's only one opinion that matters, and I have it on good authority that he thinks you're pretty swell."

"Swell?" I grinned. "Who says *swell*?"

"God does. He told me you're swell and I believe him. So there."

"I see."

"No you don't. That's the point." The emotion in her voice intensified. "It's pretty clear you don't see just how swell you are or you wouldn't always bring up Jacquie Goldfarb when you're feeling down."

"Hey, you brought her up this time."

"I just beat you to the punch, that's all. I knew it was coming. It's inevitable."

"Hmm."

"Look, Hannah, here's what I think. You might not be able to turn back the clock, but you can always wind it up again."

"Huh?"

"Start fresh. If you can get past this, we can spend our days talking about that great business you've built and the number of clients you're getting, now that the article in *Texas Bride* is out. We can also talk about how great it is that you have the opportunity of a lifetime shooting Sierra Caswell's wedding, and how you go to bed at night thinking about the various camera angles and lighting problems."

"How did you know that?"

"How did I know that?" She laughed. "You're so funny, Hannah. I'm your best friend. It's my job to know all of that, in the same way that you know I go to sleep thinking up cake recipes and decorating tips. We're two peas in a pod. Only, not."

"Oh."

"So, promise me you'll pray about trying to find Jacquie so you can put this behind you. Okay?"

After an exaggerated hesitation, I finally managed a quiet "Yeah."

We ended the call, and I changed into my nightgown, wondering how my happy-go-lucky mood could have so easily shifted. Several minutes later I climbed into bed, snuggled under the covers, and reached for my laptop on the bedside table. Scarlet's words bounced around in my head. Did it really make sense to look for Jacquie on Facebook? Of course not. Only a glutton for punishment would go looking for her archnemesis from the past. Right?

I paused to think it through before making a move. If I could talk to Jacquie Goldfarb again, what would I say? What would I secretly be hoping for? A chill ran through me as I contemplated my motives. The devilish side of me would hope for the worst, while the angelic side of me would wish her the best.

Likely she'd married a wealthy man, lived in a mega mansion in Houston, and spent her days at the country club or on the tennis court. Or maybe she had achieved fame or stardom in her field—whatever that happened to be. Yes, surely she had made something big of her life. She'd always been larger-than-life.

Then again, why would I want to know? It's not like we could possibly have anything in common. And after years of battling the knots in my stomach every time her name was mentioned, resolution just seemed impossible. Not that contacting her would resolve anything, anyway. It would probably open a Pandora's box and fill me with even more angst than before.

Yet something inside of me propelled me forward. I just couldn't seem to help myself. After signing onto Facebook, I hesitantly typed in her name. A handful of names came up, most with slightly different spellings. Scrolling all the way down to the bottom of the page, I came across a match. To the left, the photo of a woman's face—a familiar face—greeted me. There she was, in all of her glory—as beautiful and perfect as ever. Jacquie Goldfarb.

I read her profile information and tried to make sense of it, but it didn't seem to compute. *She's a realtor?* Odd. I'd never pictured her in that line of work. Stranger still, I'd never imagined her to be single. Last thing I heard, she and Matt Hudson—my near-miss prom date—were engaged. Weird.

I looked at Jacquie's photo, wondering what her life in Houston was like. My imagination took off sprinting as I stared at the screen.

And stared at the screen.

And stared at the screen.

Until my curiosity got the better of me.

It took about three minutes to work up the courage, but I finally did the unthinkable.

I sent her a friend request.

11

Top o' the Mornin'

May there always be work for your hands to do.
May your purse always hold a coin or two.
May the sun always shine on your windowpane.
May a rainbow be certain to follow each rain.

Irish blessing

I've always loved the color green, and not just because I'm Irish. There's something so invigorating about a field of green grass, or the vibrant green leaves on Galveston's palm trees as they sway in the breeze.

Grandpa Aengus used to say it was no coincidence that dollar bills are green, the same color as shamrocks. I'm inclined to agree. I'm not overly partial to money, mind you. I know that falling in love with the stuff can land you in all sorts of trouble. Still, having enough to pay the bills, particularly the bills related to my studio, has always been important. That's why, when I saw the heads-up email from Sierra Caswell's publicist in my box on the second Monday morning in October, I sensed trouble coming. Trouble that would eventually spell m-o-n-e-y. Or the lack of it, rather.

Reading the note didn't calm me down any. In fact, it tied my nerves in tighter knots than before. Attached to the email, which had been sent on Saturday, was an addendum to our original contract, awaiting my signature. According to the note, I must sign it and fax it back within thirty days or they would look for another photographer.

I thought about Grandpa Aengus's words: "Confidence is the feeling you have before you understand the situation."

With fingers fumbling all over the place, I opened the document and skimmed it.

In addition to all matters previously agreed upon in the original contract, vendor agrees:

- *To provide photographs of the highest quality that not only meet but exceed the standards of the industry.*
- *To work within the confines of the bride's specialized requests, shooting only photographs from the front, back, or right side when possible.*
- *To remove any visible surface flaws, including the small scar on the right side of the bride's lip and any or all wrinkles around the eyes, lips, or chin. To adjust, as possible, any abnormalities in the structure of the bride's nose.*
- *To hold private all details of the ceremony, sharing no information—in the affirmative or the negative—about the event with anyone who could potentially bring the parties harm.*

- *To maintain the privacy of all parties involved in the wedding (vendors, participants, and/or guests), sharing no information that could be deemed personal and/or private with members of the media and/or others outside of the event.*
- *To seek no personal gain from any of the photographs, other than the amount agreed upon in the original contract.*
- *To accept all liability—financially, legally, and otherwise—should the photographs fall into the hands of any undesirable entities.*

At first glance the addendum looked completely doable. So they wanted a few touch-ups of Sierra's face. Big deal. I'd been down that road before and knew how to Photoshop with the best of 'em.

Just about the time I thought I could breathe a sigh of relief, however, I went back and read the last clause one more time.

- *To accept all liability—financially, legally, and otherwise—should the photographs fall into the hands of any undesirable entities.*

As the sentence rooted itself in my brain, my thoughts began to spin. I remembered Sierra's words during our Skype conversation: "I've got to approve all of the photos before any are leaked to the media. You know that's kind of the reason for the great photo angles, right? My publicist plans to slip them to the national media, then create a scandal, saying they were leaked against my wishes."

Oy. He planned to leak them . . . and then hold me responsible, financially, legally, and otherwise? No way!

Now what?

My initial reaction? Figure out some way to make this okay. Justify it. Sign the document and forge ahead.

My second, more realistic reaction? Give way to fear. Maybe he didn't have a significant amount of power over me or my career, but at this moment it certainly felt as if he did.

My final reaction? Call Scarlet. She would talk me through this and lend clarity to the situation. No doubt she would encourage me to go with my gut, which in this case was churning like cottage cheese. If I went with my gut and didn't sign, all bets were off. The opportunity with Sierra—and, for that matter, Brock Benson—would pass . . . likely into the hands of Drew Kincaid.

In the flash of an eye, as I punched in Scarlet's number, I saw my career ending. Off in the distance, Jacquie Goldfarb, that weasel of a woman, roared with laughter and proclaimed on my Facebook wall that I was an undeniable failure.

"Hey, Hannah. I was just thinking about you." Scarlet's happy-go-lucky voice caught me off guard as she answered. I'd half expected her to sound as frantic as I felt. "I just got off the phone with my aunt Wilhelmina, and she's going to fund my new bakery."

"Oh? That's great." It was, only I didn't have time to talk about bakeries right now, not with so much brewing.

"Yeah, I need your help finding a place. Working out of my home is getting old."

"Okay. Maybe one day later this week."

She dove into a lengthy chat about her business but finally paused for breath. I managed to sneak in a few words.

"Houston, we have a problem." I rose and paced the front room of my studio, praying no one would pick this time to stop by.

"What's happened?" Scarlet's tone changed immediately, and I could sense her concern.

I filled her in on George's email, and she flew into best friend mode at once. "Who do they think they are? They can't ask this of you, knowing full well that they plan to leak the photos on their end once this is done. There's got to be some legal precedent here."

"I know, right? They've got to know that. But they're acting like I'm some sort of amateur, like I'm just going to go along with whatever they say because I'm naive." Fear snaked through me as I spoke those words.

Maybe that's why they hired me instead of Drew, because they thought I looked like a sucker.

Ugh! The very idea made me ill. Yes, surely they had chosen me because they believed I'd go along with their crazy plan.

"They're going to let me shoot the wedding, pay me, have me turn in the photos, and then release them to the paparazzi as if I'd leaked them." I did my best to calm my nerves by releasing a breath. "And they want me to sign off on it all so that I'll be held liable for any legal fees when the lawsuits start rolling in. I won't do it."

"Of course not."

"This could ruin my business. I can't even believe they're asking this of me. I mean, to talk about leaking the photos is one thing. But to actually do it and hold me liable? Not only will it ruin me financially, it will take down my business." I picked up a pen from my desk and rolled it around in my fingers like a twirler with a baton. A nervous twirler with a very slippery baton.

"Right, right. Well, let's don't go there, girl. Don't get discouraged."

"I'm not doing it deliberately, trust me. But no one will trust me with their business if they hear I've created a scandal. I can't even imagine the lawsuits that could come out of this. Maybe Sierra will end up suing me personally." I kept the pen rolling, now gaining momentum. Even Jacquie Goldfarb would've been impressed.

"Yikes."

"And Brock too. I mean, can you even imagine?"

"Brock?"

A dead silence filled the gap between us over the phone line. I swallowed hard, my heart now sailing to my throat. The pen slid out of my hand and plunked as it hit the floor.

Oh, Lord. Help.

With my heart pounding in my ears, I whispered, "Scarlet. You. Never. Heard. That."

"O-okay." She giggled, now sounding giddy. "But girl, we're going to have to talk this through."

"No, that's the point. Don't you see? We can't talk it through. I'm not supposed to give any details of the wedding to anyone. Nothing that could be deemed personal or private."

And I've just proven that I can't even trust myself.

"Right." She sighed. "But only if you sign the addendum. Which you're not going to do . . . right?"

"If I don't sign it, I don't shoot the wedding."

"But that's crazy. You can't sign it. Don't sign it."

The trembling in my extremities continued. "He's given me thirty days from this past Saturday—then all bets are off. The job goes to Drew Kincaid."

"Did the email say that?"

"No, but it might as well have. Sierra already told me that she wishes she'd chosen him." Well, that wasn't exactly what she'd said, but close. "The email said they would look for another photographer."

*And if Brock Benson weighs in, I know they're going to
go with Drew. He's already worked with him.*

"That's terrible."

"Not that I would really mind losing this gig, if we're being
completely honest. Sierra's the biggest bridezilla I've ever
worked with. Or, rather, her publicist is. It's been a nightmare
from the beginning." One I hoped to wake up from. Soon.

"So, maybe you're better off not signing and just forgetting
the whole thing?"

"I just don't want to run the risk of putting too much on
Bella's shoulders. You know? It's a lot for her to get stuck
with."

"Surely she won't go along with this. And it's somewhat
likely Drew Kincaid won't either."

"So what do I do?" Another cleansing breath calmed down
the shaking in my hands.

"Beat Sierra at her own game?"

"How do you beat a bridezilla at her own game?" I reached
for a piece of candy from the jar on my desk. "It can't be
done."

"Sure it can. You just have to be quick on your feet. Didn't
you already sign some sort of contract with them weeks ago?"

"Yes. What they sent today was an addendum to the original."

"Okay, well, take a close look at the original. Do you have
an attorney? Maybe he can help you figure this out."

"No." A deep sigh followed. Mama had suggested getting
an attorney before opening the business. Had I listened? Of
course not.

"You need someone with some street smarts—someone
who knows how to turn this back on them. But whatever you
do, don't sign the document."

"I won't, I—" I didn't get a chance to finish because another call came through. I pulled the phone away from my ear and glanced at the number. Not one I recognized. Still, with a local area code it could be an incoming client. Or, saints preserve us, Bella Neeley, calling from her house phone or something. "Scarlet, let me put you on hold. I have a call."

"Okay, I—"

Before she could finish, I clicked over to the other line. The voice that greeted me was familiar but surprising.

"Hannah, this is Drew Kincaid."

A mixture of emotions washed over me—fear that he somehow knew my plight with Sierra, and relief that it wasn't Bella Neeley calling.

"Hey, what's up?" I said, doing my best to sound calm and normal.

"I wanted to come by and bring a disc with the photos I took at Bella's place the other day. Thought maybe you could drop them off when you give her yours." He paused. "I'm not too late, am I? Have you already sent her the pictures you took?"

"No." I shook my head. Not that he could see my head, but whatever.

"Great. Is this a good time? I've got an hour free and thought maybe I could—"

"Sure, that would be great. See you in a bit."

I switched the line back to Scarlet, my fingers fumbling, a true sign that my nerves hadn't completely dissipated.

"Hey, you'll never believe who that was." My words shot out, breathless. "Drew Kincaid. I can only pray he won't find out about the mess with Sierra. I swear, Jacquie Goldfarb is following me!" I let out an exaggerated groan for effect.

"Jacquie Goldfarb?" Drew's voice sounded from the other end of the phone.

My heart skipped a beat as I realized what I'd done.

Oh. No.

"Someone is following you, Hannah?" His tone changed at once. "And what mess with Sierra? What are you talking about?"

"Oh, I . . . Oops. Wrong number." I ended the call, then tossed the phone—that venomous serpent—on my desk. For a moment, anyway. I needed to call Scarlet back to fill her in, after all.

"Okay, so Drew's on his way," she said when I told her about my phone faux pas. "And now he knows something's up with Sierra."

"Yeah." I sighed. "Why oh why do I always mess up everything?"

"I think you're just nervous. But I don't blame you. What Sierra's publicist is asking you to do is wrong. W-r-o-n-g. Got it?"

"Yeah."

"Okay, well, get through this meeting with Drew as best you can without giving anything away, and do not sign that addendum, no matter what."

"I won't."

"Oh, and just for the record . . ." She paused. "I plan to be a bridezilla when it's my turn to get married."

"No way." I managed a halfhearted chuckle. "You're so easygoing."

"No I'm not. Have you seen me in the kitchen? I'm ruthless. No one gets the better of me. Just like you are when it comes to photography."

"Wait. You're calling me ruthless?"

"If the shoe—er, camera—fits." She laughed. "Aw, c'mon, Hannah. When it comes to your business, you're one tough mama. Nothing gets the better of you. Not Jacquie Goldfarb. Not Sierra Caswell. Not her publicist. Not Bella Neeley. Not even your toughest competitor."

"Speaking of which, he's on his way, so I'd better go."

"Okay. I'm praying, girl. Keep a stiff upper lip."

"I'll do my best."

I ended the call and scurried around the office, making the place as tidy as possible and hiding all evidence of any conversations with or about Sierra Caswell. What I would say about her, should he ask, I had no idea. Hopefully he wouldn't broach the subject. If he did . . . well, I'd just smile and remind him that all matters between a photographer and her subject were to be kept private and confidential.

My thoughts reeled as I thought back through the addendum awaiting my signature. If I did decide to sign it, I could always ask Scarlet to bake me a cake—one with a nail file inside so that I could scrape my way out of this predicament once Sierra Caswell threw my tail in jail.

In the meantime, I would remain calm, cool, and collected. I hoped.

12

You Belong to Me

The longest road out
Is the shortest road home.

Irish proverb

When Drew arrived, he found me seated at the front desk, hair brushed, shoes matching, blouse properly buttoned, looking as cool as a cucumber. Well, if you didn't count the ribbon of sweat trickling down my back. But he couldn't see that. Unless he stood behind me, anyway.

"Drew. Nice of you to come." I extended my hand for a shake.

He gave me a curious look, then shook my outstretched hand and placed the CD in my open palm. "Great studio,

Hannah. I've only seen it from the outside, but I love the back-in-time feel inside. Very turn-of-the-century."

"Oh, this little old place?" I gestured around the now-tidy studio and smiled. "Thanks. I like it. So do my clients."

"It's kind of like visiting Galveston a hundred years ago, before the big storm, I mean."

"Right." If only I could actually take a few steps back in time, I'd forget all about Sierra Caswell and her wedding.

I gestured for Drew to take the seat across from my desk, which he did. His gaze, however, traveled the walls, taking in every photo. I could almost hear the wheels clicking in his head as he analyzed my style, my technique.

Finally he turned my way. "So, who's this Jacquie Goldfarb, and what does she have to do with Sierra Caswell?"

I couldn't help but notice the inherent strength in his face as he posed the question. The confidence in his squared shoulders and the set of his jaw. For a moment it put me at ease. But just as quickly, his strength made me feel weak in comparison.

"Ah." A delicate pause followed. "She's an old friend. Really, that was just a mix-up. What I said on the phone, I mean. You know me, always tripping over my tongue."

"Hmm."

"All is well." I gave him a weak smile.

"Good. You had me a little confused."

"I've been told I have that effect on people." A light bulb went on in my head as I thought about a great segue into a normal conversation. "Hey, speaking of confused, what did you think about the chaos over at Bella's parents' place on Saturday? Nuts, right? But a lot of fun. I had the time of my life. And that food!"

"Yes." He leaned back in his chair and appeared to relax.

"I love going to the Rossis' house, but man . . . lots of noise and confusion with all of those kids involved."

"I'm used to family chaos. Or at least I was, growing up. These days, not so much."

His gaze shifted to a photograph of a mother and son. "Well, I live a pretty quiet life. I think I mentioned that I'm an only child."

"Ah. That's right."

"With no brothers and sisters in the picture, things were very . . . settled. Just my parents and me."

"You've pretty much just described my current existence. But things didn't start out that way. I grew up with a houseful. Chaos all around and no privacy whatsoever."

"Oh, that's right. You have three sisters? Isn't that what your mom said?"

"Yes."

Please don't ask me again if they're married.

"They still live at home?"

I did my best not to sigh aloud. "No, they're all married."

Please, please, please don't comment. I don't think I can take it.

And yet he persisted. "Do you have your own place?"

If I were prone to lying, this would be a good time to come up with something great: "Yes, I have a lovely condo on the seawall" or "I purchased my own home last year with the proceeds from my new business."

Instead, I told the truth. "I live with my parents. That's what I meant about my current existence."

"Ah." He grinned. "One more thing we have in common."

"You still live at home?"

He shrugged, and a smile lit his face. "Well, my dad passed away a few years ago, but I live in the house with my mom because I don't like the idea of her being alone right now. She's been through a lot and needs my support."

"Oh, wow." I laid aside my acting skills for a genuine response. "I'm so sorry to hear that. So I'm guessing she turns to you for just about everything."

"Mostly." He shrugged. "Interesting how life turns out."

"What do you mean?"

"Well, I'm adopted. Didn't come to live with the Kincaids until I was five. So I can't help but think about how lonely she would've been if I hadn't come into the picture."

"What?" The strangest sensations shot through me. "You mean you're not really a Kincaid?" Visions of swords being wielded on both sides of the McDermott-Kincaid feud rushed through my mind.

"Of course I'm a Kincaid."

The expression on his face sent a wave of guilt through me. "Oh, I didn't mean—"

Why, Hannah? Why do you say such stupid things?

"Sorry." He grimaced. "Kind of a sensitive subject. I guess, from a biological standpoint, I'm not a Kincaid. But I'm as much a Kincaid as anyone else in the clan, trust me."

"Of course you are. I really am sorry. I was just trying to figure out the whole Irish thing. Are you really . . . I mean, were you born . . ."

"Irish?" His nose wrinkled. "Guess I'll never know. I haven't searched for my biological mother. Don't really care to, at least not at this point in my life."

"I see."

"Anyway, I'm as Irish as they come. I sing 'Danny Boy.' I look great in green. I have every U2 CD ever recorded."

"I'm really sorry for what I said. I didn't mean—"

"When you're Irish from the inside out, you don't have

to drum it up or make it more or less than it is. It's already a huge part of you." He pointed at me. "Take you, for instance. You didn't even have to tell me that you're Irish. It's totally obvious, and not just because your mom has the right T-shirt." He leaned forward. "My mom has the same shirt, by the way. She said it dates back to some event here on the island in the nineties."

"Interesting. Maybe our mothers have met at some point along the way."

"Maybe. But to answer your question, I am Irish. Or, as my dad would've said, 'I'm Oirish.' And thanks to him, I've learned to share the blarney as well as the next guy."

"That, we've established." I offered him a cockeyed grin, and he laughed.

I couldn't get past the fact that he wasn't a biological Kincaid—and certainly not the warring kind. Not that it really mattered, but knowing the history between the McDermotts and Kincaids had relieved me a little.

Immediately the angel on my right shoulder scolded me. *Why are you so hard on him? He's a great guy.* Just as quickly, the demon on my left shoulder chimed in. *Because he's the competition, stupid.*

From outside the window, a young woman probably in her twenties caught my eye. She paused in front of the studio window, and for a moment I thought she might come inside and interrupt our conversation. On one level, I wanted her to. Garnering a new client in front of Drew would boost my confidence.

The woman waddled by, her weight on her heels. I took a second look, noticing her feet. She wore those funny little rubbery shoe-like things you get at the nail salon after a pedicure. Must've come from Nail Tropics next door.

Drew smiled. "You know what I find funny?"

"What's that?"

He pointed at the woman, who continued to waddle toward her fancy car, now fishing around in her large designer handbag. "That's a woman with money."

"You can tell that from looking at her feet? My goodness, you are good. Very discerning."

"Well, look at her. Driving a BMW. Carrying a designer handbag. Wearing great clothes. Probably wouldn't be caught checking the mail without a face full of makeup."

"True." I scrutinized the woman, who'd located her keys and was trying to make it from the sidewalk to the driver's-side door in her flip-floppy shoes.

"And here she is, waddling like a platypus in front of dozens of people, without a care in the world." He gestured to Parma John's, the restaurant on the opposite side of the street. "See all of those people looking at her through the window? Do you think she has a clue? And would she be humiliated if she did?"

"Never thought of it before. I see people coming out of the nail salon wearing those things all the time—rich, poor, and otherwise."

"It's just something to ponder. Some women care too much about how they look. Give me someone who's more laid-back any day." Drew pulled out his camera, pointed it at the window, and began clicking.

"You're photographing her without permission," I argued.

"Only her feet. And I'm pretty sure there's nothing about those feet that would incriminate me, should she find out." He zoomed out and then chuckled. "Unless you count the little butterflies on the nail of her big toe."

"Still . . ."

He released the zoom and put the camera down, then glanced my way. "Hannah, can I ask a question?"

"Sure."

"You're pretty in the box, aren't you?"

"What do you mean?"

"I mean, you're really . . ."

Stiff? Pretentious? Stuck in my ways?

"Used to doing things one way." He shrugged, and a dimple appeared on his right cheek. "I've noticed that about you. You're . . . predictable."

He hadn't exactly spoken the word as a death sentence. Still, it felt like one.

"You can thank my father for that. You've never met a man more set in his ways. Guess maybe he's rubbed off on me."

"Oh, I'm not saying there's anything wrong with predictable." Drew shoved his camera back in its bag. "Predictable people get the job done. They're reliable, trustworthy, and always tell the truth."

"You make me sound like a Boy Scout."

"Oh no." He reached for my hand and gave it a squeeze, his eyes locking onto mine. "That would be *Girl* Scout. You're all girl, Hannah."

Any or all "predictable" comebacks flew out the window. Drew Kincaid had called me a girl.

There you go again, Hannah—melting like butter when a guy flatters you. What's wrong with you, anyway? And what's so flattering about being called a girl? You are one, you know.

Doing my best to still my racing heart, I glanced out the window once more, then started fidgeting with my necklace.

"You do that a lot," he said, his voice now lower than before.

"Do what?"

"Grab your cross when you're nervous."

"Oh? I—I do?" Instinctively, I released my hold on it.

"You do." A boyish smile lit his face. "I think it's cute. Just so you know."

Good gravy. He'd called me a girl and said I was cute, all in less than two minutes.

Is it warm in here? Did someone turn on the heater?

I picked up a brochure and began to fan myself.

"Well, I'd better get back to work." He rose and gave me a smile. "One of these days I'll figure out the whole Jacquie Goldfarb thing." A wink followed. "But I guess that's a mystery for another day."

"Yes. Well, I guess it is."

Not one I planned to reveal . . . ever. But he didn't have to know that, now did he?

13

Blue Skies

May God give you . . .
For every storm, a rainbow, for every tear, a smile.
For every care, a promise, and a blessing in each trial.
For every problem life sends, a faithful friend to share.
For every sigh, a sweet song, and an answer for each prayer.

Irish blessing

Just as Drew made it to the door of my studio, Scarlet
came barreling in, holding a tray of cake samples. She
almost knocked him over, then offered a rushed apology.
"Oh, I'm sorry, I'm—"

"Jacquie Goldfarb?" he tried.

"No." Scarlet giggled. "But that's funny. Really. Very funny."

"Wish I knew why." He shrugged. "Just one of life's little
mysteries that I'm not supposed to understand, apparently."

From across the room, I did my best not to groan.

"Are you . . ." Scarlet gripped the tray with her left hand and brushed her hair off her shoulders with her right. "Drew Kincaid?"

"The one and only."

She grinned and offered a nod. "Scarlet Lindsey. Let them eat cake."

"Beg your pardon?" He glanced at the tray in her hands, then back up again.

"Oh." She laughed again. "That's the name of my business—Let Them Eat Cake."

"Ah. Glad to hear. I thought maybe you were offering me a mandate."

"No, but I would like to offer you some of my cake samples." She batted her eyelashes and placed the tray on my desk. "Now that you bring it up."

Oh no you don't, girl. Tell me you're not using him to promote your business.

Then again, she had learned from the master, hadn't she?

With the tray now safely on the desk, Scarlet opened the dome lid, revealing over a dozen different types of cake in neat little bite-sized squares.

Drew took several confident strides toward it, a perplexed look on his face. "Someone getting married?"

"No. Unless that's a proposal." Scarlet released another one of those goofy giggles of hers, then fanned her ever-reddening face. "They're just samples. Have one." A pause followed as she set the dome lid down on top of some important papers. "Or two. Or three."

"Don't mind if I do." He grabbed a square of chocolate cake and popped it in his mouth. His eyes widened at once, and he looked back and forth between us. "Did you make this from scratch?"

"Of course." She grinned. "It's a brand-new recipe. Do you like it?"

"Best chocolate cake I've ever eaten. I need to pick up one for my mom's birthday. She loves chocolate. And she's got a lot of friends in the Grand Opera Society, so maybe she would spread the word about your business."

"Ooh, that would be divine." Scarlet's cheeks turned pink again. "I'll bake her birthday cake for free. It'll be good advertising for my new shop, which I hope to open in a few months. Right now I office out of my home." She reached into her purse and came out with a card.

Stop flirting with the enemy, girlfriend.

Only, he wasn't really the enemy, was he? No, he happened to be a great guy who had stopped by to drop off a CD. And she wasn't necessarily flirting, just promoting her business.

Scarlet glanced my way and mouthed, "Wowza! He's gorgeous!"

Okay, so maybe she was flirting.

I gave her a warning look. "Well, Drew was just leaving. Isn't that right, Drew?"

Scarlet's lips curled down in a pout. "Oh, that's a shame. I was hoping to see the photos you two took at Bella Neeley's place. Guess that's out of the question?"

"I've got a few minutes." Drew pulled up a chair. "If Hannah does."

"Sure."

I put his CD into my computer and did my best to still the trembling in my hands. Right away the email from Sierra's publicist popped up. I quickly minimized it and opened my photo app, and the photographs—dozens of them—appeared in glorious display. Wow. This guy was really good.

Keep your cool, Hannah. Don't let him see you sweat.

A photo of Tres appeared, his olive skin glistening and his cockeyed smile charming.

"Oh, Hannah, that's priceless!" Scarlet went on and on about the picture, talking about the angles, the curve of his cheekbone, the darling smile.

"Drew took that one," I muttered. I grabbed a tiny piece of Italian cream cake, which I popped in my mouth. I chased it down with a square of lemon. Then orange fudge. By the time we'd looked through all of Drew's photos, I'd wiped out nearly a quarter of Scarlet's cake samples.

Scarlet pointed to my lips, and I wiped away a bit of fudge frosting. Perfect.

"Wow." Drew's eyes widened. "I had no idea you liked cake so much, Hannah. That's pretty impressive."

"I don't." And it didn't like me very much either, from the rumbling in my stomach. Then again, I'd skipped breakfast. What I needed was real food.

After giving me a funny look, Scarlet turned back to the computer and began to rave about the photos all over again, her sentences loaded with adjectives.

Just what I needed—a bellyful of sugar and an earful of spice.

After that, though, Drew asked to see the pictures I'd taken. We spent the next several minutes going over them, and I breathed a sigh of relief when he gave them rave reviews.

By the time Drew left, I'd almost forgotten about my dilemma with Sierra Caswell. Almost. When the bell rang out as the door closed behind him, Scarlet looked my way. But I couldn't focus on her right now. My gaze shot to the window. I watched as Drew opened the door to his SUV and climbed inside, my eyes narrowing as he glanced back at me through the glass.

"Mm-hmm." Scarlet clucked her tongue as she took a few steps in my direction. "I had my suspicions, but you've just confirmed them."

"Suspicions?" I shut down my computer. "What do you mean?"

"I mean about the way you look at Drew Kincaid. Drew 'so hot you'd have to blow him out to keep the house from going up in flames' Kincaid."

Okay, so Drew was plenty hot. And yeah, he'd pretended to be my boyfriend so that Armando would leave me alone. But guys like Drew never really looked my way unless they wanted my take on something business or sports related. More likely he'd come to my studio today to scope out the place. Size up the competition.

"Girl, no wonder you've been keeping him all to yourself." Scarlet put the dome lid on the remaining cake samples. "He's gorgeous."

"I guess." I shrugged. "Never really paid much attention."

"Please. You'd have to be blind. And I happen to know you're not. You'd never make it as a photographer if you were." She grinned and pulled the tray of cake samples away from me. "So, what happens next?"

I rose and reached for my purse. "What happens next is I call Bella and tell her what's going on with Sierra Caswell's publicist. Tell her that I cannot under any circumstances sign that document, even if it means losing the gig."

"Oh, right. That." Scarlet released a sigh. "I was hoping you'd say, 'We're going to lunch.'"

"Well, maybe we can do that too."

Five minutes later, after a quick call to Bella, I turned back to my best friend, who'd taken to nibbling at her own cake samples. "She's across the street at Parma John's. Her uncle owns the place. She's there a lot." I paused, then asked, "Want to go to lunch?"

"I thought you'd never ask."

She traipsed along behind me as we crossed the Strand with its magnificent old buildings. The island-themed tourist shops advertised winter specials—hot chocolate and coffees, to be precise. I didn't blame them. Anyone with a business on the Strand realized that tourists were an essential part of the income equation.

Down the block, but well within view, I saw a family going into the local confectionery. My stomach grumbled, and I realized I'd better stay focused on real food for now.

Moments later I led the way inside Parma John's, pausing as the fragrant smells of pizza sauce, garlic, and sausage rose up to meet me. Mmm. The always-busy restaurant was jam-packed with customers, most laughing and talking over the strains of a familiar Dean Martin song playing overhead. I loved the ambience in Parma John's. Always had. But the smell . . . now that's what really got to me.

"So much for my diet." Scarlet laughed. "Want to split a pizza?"

"Sure. Why not. But I've got to talk to Bella first."

I walked up to the counter, where I discovered a very pregnant young woman about my own age manning the register. She wore a nametag that read Jenna.

"Welcome to Parma John's." Her voice rang out above the melody of "Mambo Italiano," which played through the restaurant's sound system. I started to say something, but she continued before I could get a word in edgewise. "Would you like to try our special of the day—a large Mambo Italiano pizza with two cappuccinos for only $17.95?"

"No thank you. I'm looking for Bella Neeley. She said she would be here."

"Ah. She's in the back, meeting with Laz. Hang on a minute." The young woman turned, revealing the girth of her belly, then disappeared into the kitchen. She returned a couple of minutes later with Bella on her heels.

Bella's brow wrinkled. "Hannah? Everything okay? You sounded kind of funny on the phone. A little stressed out?"

"Yeah. I mean, no. I mean . . . we really need to talk." Might as well get this over with.

Scarlet gave me an encouraging pat on the arm, followed by, "I'll get the pizza."

I nodded, then took a seat at an empty table. Bella joined me, and I did my best to fill her in on the email I'd received from George. I could tell from her countenance—her expression shifting to one of genuine concern—that the whole thing worried her. It worried me too.

"Oh, man." She drummed her fingertips on the table after hearing the whole story. "Are you serious?"

"Yes." I felt a lump in my stomach and nausea set in. Still, what could I do? Resting my elbows on the table, I leaned forward, ready to admit defeat. "Bella, I can't sign it. It would destroy my career. Surely you can see that."

"Yes. I get it, but . . ." She shook her head. "If we can't get this figured out, it messes up everything, especially with Brock coming. You know? And if it's a legal issue for you, it could end up being a legal issue for me too."

My breath caught in my throat. "Surely not. You've done nothing wrong."

"Neither have you."

"Yes, but they're still coming after me, regardless. And thank you for acknowledging that I've done nothing wrong, by the way. That helps." I drew in a breath. "I can't sign something that could take my business down. I've worked way too hard for that. And besides, we need to protect Brock's privacy too. If the wedding photos are leaked against his will, he could hire an attorney and come after me."

"I can't imagine Brock doing something like that."

"Still." Off I went on a tangent about how difficult my life was. About how hard I'd worked to prove myself. When I ended, I leaned forward, my forehead on the table, and groaned. "Jacquie Goldfarb is out to get me."

"Huh? Who's Jacquie Goldfarb?" Bella asked.

I looked up and said, "Never mind. I'm just a little freaked out."

"I can tell." She chuckled. This served to alleviate the tension, at least for a moment.

"Do you ever feel like all of your hard work is in vain?" I dabbed away the moisture from my eyes and sniffled.

"You're asking a woman who works from sunup till sundown if she feels like all of her hard work is in vain?" A dazzling smile replaced her near-frown. "Oh, girl! You have no idea. But then I look at D.J. and the kids—I see all that God has accomplished in our lives—and I know there's a bigger plan." Bella grabbed my hand and gazed at me with such intensity that I felt like a kid standing before a teacher after being caught cheating on a test. "God has a bigger plan for you, Hannah. He does."

"I know." But as I thought through her words, I realized they required a slightly different response. "I mean, I think I know. I say that I know. I tell people that I know. But in my heart I'm not sure that I really know. You know?" Leaning forward, I plopped my forehead down onto the table again and began to mumble.

"You are in bad shape." Scarlet's voice sounded as she took a seat next to me. "But pizza will help."

"W-what?" I looked up.

"Pizza. It'll cure whatever ails you. Trust me on this. I've used this prescription many a time with positive results." She rubbed her ample midsection and grinned, then turned to introduce herself to Bella. Within seconds the two were best friends. Go figure. Then again, Scarlet often had that effect on people.

A couple of minutes later, the young woman behind the register turned to the kitchen and hollered, "One Mambo Italiano, heavy on the cheese."

"Heavy on the cheese?" I shook my head. How cheese could solve my problem, I had no idea. Still, with my near-empty stomach grumbling, I was willing to give it a try.

"You're not lactose intolerant, are you?" Bella asked.

"Not to my knowledge."

"Good. You're going to love the Mambo Italiano special, trust me."

As we waited for the pizza, I did my best to reason things out with Bella without coming across sounding like a scared child. "I don't want you to think I panic easily," I explained.

Scarlet gave me a "sure you don't" look, but I plowed ahead. "I'm really easygoing. Or, at least I used to be. When I was a kid."

"Weren't we all?" Bella chuckled.

"Yeah." My thoughts tumbled backward in time. "I want to go back to the way I was when I was a little girl. Grandpa Aengus used to say that I had lilt."

"Lilt?"

"You know, a spring in my step." I reached for my necklace and started fidgeting. Until I remembered what Drew had said. "Maybe it's an Irish expression. I don't know. I just know that I was quirky and fun. Didn't care so much about things. I let them roll off me, not weigh me down. Somewhere along the way I lost my lilt. My resilience. My cheerfulness. My buoyancy. You know . . . my lilt."

"Where does one go to buy lilt?" Scarlet took a sip of her drink and leaned back in her chair.

"If I knew, I'd buy it." I closed my eyes and thought back to my childhood. "I wish you'd known me then. I was the classic fairy-tale heroine—cheerful, always singing a happy tune, skipping through the proverbial meadow, looking on the bright side of things."

For a moment I had a vision of Bella's parrot singing "Amazing Grace." Lighthearted. Carefree.

B.J.G. Before Jacquie Goldfarb.

"You're still like that." Bella gave my hand a squeeze. "At least that's how you come across to me."

"Thank you." Sure, I was glad I came across that way, but in my heart I knew it wasn't the same as before. "Just feels like I get my feet knocked out from under me a lot. Going all the way back to high school, actually, when the guy I thought I loved—emphasis on *thought*—told me that he planned to ask me to the prom, but he ended up going with my so-called friend instead."

"Wait, your dream date ended up taking your friend to the prom?"

"Jacquie Goldfarb." I sighed. "But I guess we should be calling her a frenemy, not a friend."

"Why do I keep hearing that name?" Bella's nose wrinkled.

"Just wait." Scarlet rolled her eyes. "You'll be hearing it a lot."

"She's a girl I knew in high school," I explained. "Cheerleader. Dated the quarterback."

"Ah, I know that girl." Bella grinned. "Well, maybe not Jacquie Goldfarb, but I definitely know her type."

You probably were *that girl. C'mon, Bella. You're the kind of girl everyone envies.*

I released the wistful sigh wriggling its way to the surface.

"So, were you real friends?" she asked. "With Jacquie, I mean."

"I always wanted to be. Guess I tried a little too hard to be like her. But I never came close."

"You've got to be joking." Scarlet's gaze narrowed. "You're not going to try to tell me that you were socially awkward as a kid, are you? Because frankly, you're one of the coolest girls I know."

"I was socially awkward."

"I don't believe it."

"Okay, not when I was a little girl. All of this started in high school. Before that I was pretty carefree. And I'd love to get back to that place. Not saying I want to be a kid again. Just saying I want my lilt back."

"Lost your lilt, eh?" An older woman's twangy voice rang out from behind me. "Sounds pretty tragic."

"Yes. Not sure what to advise," another woman countered, her voice even more countrified. "Maybe a trip to the beauty salon for a perm?"

"I once had a Lilt perm," a third voice sounded. "The derned thing like to fried my scalp."

What in the world?

I turned to see three unfamiliar ladies standing directly behind me. The first woman—a large, glitzy gal with a beehive hairdo—stared at me with such intensity that I felt as if she could see all the way into my soul. My bare, naked, writhing soul.

Oh. Help.

"Well, if you aren't the prettiest thing I've ever seen." She reached out to stroke my hair. "Gorgeous hair. And look at that peaches-and-cream complexion. You must know the secret of a great moisturizer."

"Oh, I . . ."

"Your pores are magnificent." The second one bent down—albeit arthritically—to have a closer look at my pores. "How do you do it?"

I fought the temptation to swat her hand as she touched my cheek. *Ew!*

"Easy," Scarlet chimed in. "She stays indoors all day."

"An island girl who stays indoors?" The third woman snorted, then rested her hand on my shoulder. "Scared of the sun?"

"My complexion is light. I burn too easily to go outdoors."

And why are you all touching me?

"Smart girl." The first woman leaned down—*Lord, help me look away from the boobs that are headed my way*—and I smelled the peach tea on her breath.

Bella rose from her chair, all smiles. She threw her arms around the largest of the three ladies and began to gush in Italian. After a couple of minutes of greeting them, she looked my way. "Hannah, what perfect timing! If anyone can advise you, these precious ladies can."

"O-oh?"

"Yes, I want you to meet three of my best friends in the world. These are the ladies I was telling you about, from Splendora."

She introduced them as Sister Twila, Sister Jolene, and

Sister Bonnie Sue from the piney woods of east Texas. And though she referred to the buxom trio as sisters, I had a feeling they weren't related. And they *definitely* weren't nuns. No way, no how. Not with those glittery blouses and froufrou hairdos. Turned out, in their neck of the woods, everyone was referred to as *brother* or *sister.*

I guess that would make me Sister Hannah. Perfect. Grandpa Aengus always wanted me to be a nun.

"Well, happy to meet you, sweet girl," Twila said with a grin. "You've got to be one of the prettiest little things ever."

"Th-thank you."

"Really, you're a true beauty queen. That gorgeous red hair . . ." She clucked her tongue. "Girl, I have to pay top dollar at the Cut 'n' Strut in Splendora to have my hair dyed red. God blessed you with that color naturally."

"I've never considered it a blessing, trust me." Once the words slipped out, I wished I could take them back. I didn't care to talk about my hair color. Or my freckles. Or my pale skin.

"You need to embrace what the good Lord gave you," Jolene said, her gaze narrowing. She turned to Scarlet and took her hand. "And if you aren't a soul sister, I don't know what you are!"

Oh dear. The only thing Scarlet appeared to have in common with these three was her fluffy size. Still, she didn't even flinch. In fact, she greeted them like long-lost sisters with a confident "Happy to meet you."

"We never come to Galveston without stopping in to see Bella and the kids," Bonne Sue said.

"And to have the Mambo Italiano special." Jolene nodded. "It's the perfect pick-me-up when you've had a hard day."

"Exactly why Hannah's here," Scarlet said. "She needed a pick-me-up today."

"Well then, we're just in time."

The ladies pulled up chairs, and our party of three morphed to six. Bella ordered more pizza, and it arrived shortly. The women instigated a fun conversation filled with lilt, and I found myself captivated by their funny, easygoing style. Their conversation bounced back and forth from hair and makeup to deep spiritual issues. In spite of our obvious differences, there was a certain quirkiness about them that resonated with me. Why?

Because you used to be like them, Hannah. You used to approach life from a carefree place.

"Don't recall ever praying for someone's lilt before." Sister Twila dabbed some pizza sauce from her lip, then reached over and took my hand. "But I'm open to the idea, so I commit to give it a go."

"I think her problem is a little deeper than that," Bella said.

"It's a matter of conscience," I added. "Well, conscience and money. And legalities. And a few other things." A wave of nausea passed over me, and I did my best not to let my emotions get the better of me in front of these ladies. They hardly knew me. Wouldn't be fair to total strangers to have a nervous breakdown in front of them.

"Something you can share?" Bonnie Sue gave me a pensive look. "It just so happens I specialize in praying for the personal needs of others, and I'm ready, willing, and able to bow the knee right here, right now."

I could hardly picture this plus-sized woman kneeling, let alone in the middle of a pizza parlor, but stranger things had happened.

"If there's anything we've learned," Jolene threw in, "it's how to stop right where we are and pray."

Interesting concept. I couldn't imagine being that bold, but I admired them for their dedication to prayer.

"So what's happening, honey?" Twila's eyes showed her concern. "Something you can share publicly?"

"Oh, well, I . . ." How much should I disclose? I barely knew these women. "I'm having a little trouble with a bridezilla. Or, rather, the bridezilla's publicist."

"A bridezilla, eh?" Jolene's beehive hairdo bounced as she turned my way. "I saw this once on television. Quite a pistol, if memory serves me correctly. Made things a nightmare for everyone. I daresay, if Bella's got a bride who treats her like that gal treated her wedding planner, she'll knock some sense into her. Won't you, Bella?"

For the first time ever, I got to hear Bella's take on the matter of one Sierra Caswell. Off she went, talking about what a rough time we were having with our bride-to-be's publicist.

"Oh, is this the wedding I read about in *Texas Bride* magazine?" Twila's eyes widened. "Isn't the bride that feisty country-western singing gal?"

I hesitated, not wanting to incriminate anyone. "Well, it's a bride whose name you might recognize. That's really all we can say."

Twila winked. "I understand, honey. Say no more. You're working double time to maintain her privacy."

"That's right."

"Good for you. That's admirable." She patted my hand. *Again with the touching?* "I like a girl who can be trusted."

"See?" I turned to Bella. "People count on me to be trustworthy. How trustworthy would I be if I agreed to sign that document? People would see me as a traitor. This is more than a matter of right and wrong, it's a matter of perception from my would-be clients."

"Well, you know what I always say," Twila interjected. "It's easy to be flexible when one is spineless." She leaned forward and gave me a pensive look. "Stiffen your spine, girlie. Don't let 'em get to you."

This, of course, led to a rebound conversation from the three Splendora sisters, who offered all sorts of advice, some of it usable, some not so much. The conversation rolled right past Bonnie Sue's tidbit: "When the devil starts messing, God starts blessing," and right on through to Jolene's sage advice: "When you're arguing with a fool, make sure the other person isn't doing the same thing."

I found their chatter to be wonderfully distracting. Just what I needed. Well, that and the pizza, which really hit the spot. As we nibbled on the cheesy goodness, drank our Diet Cokes, and basically unloaded our cares on one another, I found my spirits lifted. To think my attitude could change this drastically, and all in an extended two-hour lunch.

Two hours? I'd better get back to my studio. I had a three o'clock appointment with a new client.

Wrapping up with the Splendora trio was easier said than done. Another fifteen minutes of goodbyes transpired, followed by hugs all around, along with a promise from Scarlet to bake a cake for Jolene's upcoming birthday party. Go figure.

I left Parma John's feeling better than I had in weeks. Well, unless you counted that whole "what am I going to do about the obvious?" issue with Sierra Caswell's publicist. Still, that decision would wait for another day. And Bella trusted me to do the right thing. I could sense it. Right now I had to focus on my new client and try to get back to the business of photography.

As I bounded from the restaurant, my cell phone beeped. I looked down to discover a Facebook message had come through. No biggie.

Still, curiosity got the better of me, so I opened it. My heart sailed into my throat when I saw that Jacquie Goldfarb had accepted my friend request. Not only that, she'd sent me a private note, sort of a "long time, no see" bit.

Saints preserve us.

Now what?

14

Ac-Cent-Tchu-Ate the Positive

May you never forget what is worth remembering,
Nor ever remember what is best forgotten.

Irish proverb

After a long day, I arrived home anxious to have a quiet dinner and enjoy *Dancing with the Stars*. Knowing that Brock was coming to Galveston—*Really, Lord? I get to meet him in person?*—made me want to watch the show more than ever.

Unfortunately, my father had other ideas. He groaned as Mama and I introduced the idea of watching the show once again. "Are you serious?"

"Of course we're serious," my mother said as she served up our usual Monday night dinner. "This is going to be our new routine for the next several weeks."

"I cannot believe you're going to make me watch it again. Has my life really come to this?"

"Yes, it has." Mama wrinkled her nose. "Besides, you didn't really watch it last time. You read the paper. That hardly counts."

He rolled his eyes and reached for his plate.

"Brock made it through last week, and tonight he's dancing the tango," I explained. "The judges are merciless on the tango, especially that one judge."

"The older man?" My father took his fork and jabbed at his potatoes.

"Yes. I'm sure Brock will do well. But how did you know one of the judges was older if you weren't paying attention?"

And trust me, Dad. You will appreciate the fact that I've introduced you to the world of Brock Benson once he arrives in town.

My father stared at me and sighed. "You know what your grandpa Aengus would say right now, don't you, Shutter Speed?"

No, but I have a feeling you're going to tell me.

"A married man should never iron a four-leaf clover. He doesn't want to press his luck."

I placed my fork on the table. "Which, interpreted, means . . . ?"

Dad stuck the forkful of potatoes in his mouth and spoke around them. "Means I won't be pressing my luck with you two by insisting on having my own way."

This got a chuckle and a warm smile out of my mama, thank goodness.

Before long our conversation got back to normal. We ate our dinner, then settled down in front of the television. The show got under way with lots of fanfare and zeal from both the television audience and the McDermott clan. Well, all but one McDermott, who grumbled a bit from behind his newspaper. Still, I couldn't help but notice that he lowered the paper every time the judges offered their comments and critiques.

About halfway into the speed skater's awkwardly cho-reographed waltz, the doorbell rang. Mama looked at me. I looked at Dad. He looked at Mama. None of us seemed to know what to do. After all, our doorbell never rang on Monday nights.

"I'll get it." I rose from my spot and made my way to the door. When I opened it, I felt my heart jump. "Drew?"

"Hey, Hannah." There were touches of humor around his mouth and near his eyes as he offered one of those cockeyed grins of his.

"Is everything okay?" I gestured for him to come inside.

"Yes." A pause followed. "Well, mostly. I mean, I guess so. I hope you don't mind that I stopped by. I got your address from Bella."

Ack. He'd been talking to Bella? She must've told him about my fiasco with Sierra's publicist. Otherwise why would he have come here? I braced myself for the inevitable con-versation about to take place. By the end of it, I would most likely hand the gig over to him. But maybe he wouldn't want it once he heard the particulars.

From the living room, the theme song for *Dancing with the Stars* rang out. I heard the announcer introduce Brock Benson, and my heart skipped a beat. I couldn't miss this. No way.

"Would you like to come in? We're watching—"

"*Dancing with the Stars.*" He nodded. "I'm recording it."

"You are?"

"Sure. It's kind of cool to watch someone I've actually met

in person compete on the show. And it's one of my mom's favorite shows. She promised not to watch it till I get home, though." He hesitated, looking a bit nervous, even.

"Right."

Why are you here?

I gestured for him to follow me to the living room. The moment Mama clapped eyes on Drew, I realized we had a problem. They knew each other from the Rossis', but my mother still hadn't told Dad about all of that. Would Drew give away her secret?

Do something, Hannah.

On the television, the music for Brock's tango began. I forced a smile, glanced at my parents, and said, "Mama, Dad, meet Drew."

"Drew." My father rose and extended his hand, but I could read the curiosity in his expression. "Welcome."

"Nice to meet you, sir." Drew offered my father a warm smile, then turned to face my mama. "Mrs. McDermott, good to see you ag—"

"Drew, have a seat," I interrupted. "Brock is about to dance."

"Oh. Sure." He settled onto the loveseat.

Wait. You're sitting in my usual spot.

I paused, then took the spot next to him, feeling a little out of sorts. I forced my attention to the television and watched Brock and Cheryl dance the tango. He did a great job, unless you counted that one part where his shoe came off. Still, the audience seemed to love it, especially his wife, who ended up in a close-up frame at the end of the dance.

"Hey, there's Erin." Drew grinned. "She's just as nice in person as she looks on TV."

"Humph." My father crossed his arms over his chest as he glanced at the television.

The judges gave their critique, and then the show cut to a commercial. Mama got up to make some coffee, and my father wandered off to the bathroom, which left me alone in the room with Drew. Perfect opportunity to find out why he'd really come. Just one little detail to take care of first.

Putting my finger to my lips, I whispered, "I hate to ask you to do this, but please don't mention anything about meeting my mom at the Rossis' house."

"O-okay. Why?"

"It's kind of a long story, but my dad doesn't know she likes to cook."

"Not sure what one thing has to do with another, but I'll keep my mouth shut."

"Thank you." I settled back on the loveseat. "So, what are you doing here, really?"

He wrinkled his nose. "Ah. Well, to be honest, I feel really bad about what I said at your studio today."

"What you said?"

"Yeah. I called you predictable."

I couldn't help but laugh. "Well, I am."

"Maybe, but I don't even know you well enough to make that judgment call."

Squaring my shoulders, I decided to place a challenge. "Well, since you're so intuitive and all, maybe you should just tell me what I'm going to do next."

So there, buddy.

He laughed. "Hmm. I'm guessing you're going to end up apologizing."

The air went out of my lungs. "Gosh, I really am predictable. I was just about to make apologies for questioning your Irish heritage."

"Guess that puts us on a level playing field, then."

I doubt it. And hey, would you like to take a certain bridezilla off my hands?

"Anyway, I'm sorry if I hurt your feelings," I said. "Will you forgive me?"

"Of course. But just for the record, I'm an Irishman through and through."

My father reentered the room on the tail end of that statement and gave Drew a closer look. "You're Irish, son?"

"Yes, sir. I'm a Kincaid."

Oh. Help. I began to fuss with my necklace.

"Kincaid?" My father mumbled something under his breath, then looked my way, creases forming between his eyes. "Hannah? This is the fella you told me about? The photographer?"

"Yes, Dad."

Please, whatever you do, don't tell that awful story about the clash between the McDermotts and the Kincaids.

Thank goodness my mother entered the room with coffee mugs in hand just as the announcer introduced the next dancing couple. She gave Drew a pensive look as she handed him his coffee. "Here you go. What did you say your name is again?"

The edges of his lips curled up as he responded, "Drew Kincaid," and took the mug of coffee.

Dad muttered something under his breath, but thank goodness, he didn't go off on a spiel about the war between the clans.

The television couple—a soap-opera star and a professional dancer—took off around the floor in a beautiful waltz. I was mesmerized by their grace. "Man, they're going to give Brock and Cheryl a run for their money, aren't they?"

"So. Kincaid." My dad cleared his throat, and I turned away from the television to listen in.

"Yes, sir." Drew looked his way, a relaxed smile on his face.

"You say you're a good Irish boy."

"Well, I'm Irish, sir." Drew took a sip of his coffee.

"We're holding a Bing and Bob party the first Saturday night in November," my father said. "You should come."

My breath caught in my throat. Considering the volatile history between the two clans, I could hardly imagine my dad making such a peace offering. *Go, Dad!* Maybe laying down the sword really was the best option.

Drew hesitated a moment, and I could almost read the thoughts in his head. He already knew about the party, of course, and had been invited that day at the Rossis' home. Still, what could he say?

"Thank you for the invitation, Mr. McDermott. I'd love to." *Whew!*

"Well, hold on a minute," my father said. "I'll have to put you through a little test before you can come, son. Not just anyone can come to a Bing and Bob party, even a good Irish boy such as yourself."

Yikes. Just wait till he met the whole Rossi family. They would never pass his test.

Dad crossed his arms over his chest and stared at Drew. "Favorite Bing Crosby movie?"

"*White Christmas*," Drew answered without flinching.

"Hmm." My dad rolled his eyes.

"What?" Drew looked perplexed. "Oh, let me guess—*The Bells of St. Mary's* is your favorite?"

"You clearly don't know my dad." I chuckled.

"But good guess," my mama said.

"I tend to favor a different sort of fare." My father leaned back in his chair and smiled. "Think about it. Why do you suppose we're having a Bing and *Bob* party?"

"Ah. You like the Crosby-Hope movies best, is that it?" Drew grinned. "Well, why didn't you say so?"

"Saying it now. *Road to Morocco. Road to Singapore. Road to Zanzibar.* Love 'em all." A contented look settled over my father. "Nothing tops 'em in my book."

Drew shrugged. "Yeah, they were okay, but I still say nothing comes close to—"

"*White Christmas.*" We spoke the words in unison, and I laughed.

"Love that part where Rosemary Clooney and Vera-Ellen sing that song 'Sisters.'" I sighed. "Maybe because I was raised in a houseful of sisters. I don't know."

"My favorite scene is the one where Bing Crosby and Danny Kaye slip out the window to avoid being arrested." Drew slapped his knee and laughed. "Best scene in the history of movies."

Hmm. Maybe I should go back and watch that scene again. Might come in handy, should the police come looking for me after Sierra's wedding.

"What about the romantic thread?" From her spot on the sofa, my mother quirked a brow, then went back to sipping her coffee. "I just love a great romance. Makes the songs even sweeter."

Oh no you don't, Mama. No point in trying to plant any ideas in Drew's head.

Drew shrugged. "I liked the romantic stuff okay, I guess. Still, the Army angle really did it for me."

"Pretty sure it was Navy," my dad said.

"Nope. Army. Always thought Bing looked great in his uniform."

"Gotta love a man in uniform," I said.

Drew glanced my way, the edges of his lips upturned. "I was in the Marines."

At this revelation, I almost choked. "You . . . what? No way."

"Yes way. I was in the Marines. Did two tours of duty in the Middle East."

Over the next couple of minutes, as he shared his heart about the years he'd spent in the desert, I found myself discombobulated. This man—this competitive, gorgeous, blue-eyed man—was a war hero?

"I don't like to talk about it," he said. "But I've only been home a few years. Started the business right after my dad died."

"You poor, sweet boy." My mother dabbed at her eyes. She looked at Dad and placed her coffee on the end table. "Michael, what do you say? Can this precious soldier, defender of our great nation, come to our Bing and Bob party, or not?"

A crease formed between my father's brows. "I have one more question, and it's the most important." He looked closely at Drew, who squirmed.

"Yes, sir?"

Dad crossed his arms over his chest. "Favorite Bing Crosby song."

"Well, hmm . . ." Drew stared off into space, which made me nervous. "I guess I would have to say 'Irish Lullaby.'"

My father's near-smile tilted downward. "Hmm."

"Next to 'Danny Boy,' of course," Drew said. "Because nothing can top that one, sir. No way, no how."

My father rose and slapped him on the back, maybe a little too hard, gauging from the pained look on Drew's face. "You've just won your official invitation. Congratulations."

"Well, that's a relief, sir."

My dad extended a hearty invitation to the party, and before long the two were thick as thieves, talking about the party's agenda. I watched from my spot on the loveseat, all the while trying to keep an eye on the television, where a Nobel Peace Prize winner took to the floor with a beautiful redheaded professional dancer. They made an awkward team, at best.

Speaking of awkward, this whole thing with Drew Kincaid showing up at the McDermott house was a little awkward too. In an intriguing sort of way. A girl couldn't help but wonder what her handsome competitor was up to.

Tilting my head to one side, I stole a slanted look at Drew. The five-o'clock shadow, the broad shoulders, the twinkle in his blue eyes . . . this guy was the whole package. I tried to imagine what it would be like to photograph him. I'd probably have him dress in a blue shirt so that his eyes would pop. And I'd definitely choose a foresty background. Rugged guys like Drew always looked great in outdoorsy photos. Not a wood-chopping photo or anything like that, but something believable—maybe at a lake or on the pier overlooking the gulf.

"Hannah?"

My father's voice startled me back to attention.

"You still with us?"

"Hmm?" I felt my cheeks turn hot. "Oh. Yeah. Yeah, I'm here."

"In body only." He rolled his eyes. "You gonna help us plan this party, or what?"

"Party? What party?"

Drew gave me a funny look. "You mean you missed the whole conversation? Man, you really do check out, don't you."

My cheeks flamed with heat. "Well, I'm watching the show. Sorry."

"Yeah, I can see why you're interested." Drew nodded toward

the television as the Nobel Peace Prize winner tripped over his partner's feet. "Spellbinding stuff."

Not exactly. But something—er, someone—in this room certainly was spellbinding.

Stop it, Hannah.

The time passed easily, and then *Dancing with the Stars* ended. Drew rose and said his goodbyes. I followed him to the door, still curious about why he'd come in the first place. Just to apologize?

As we stood in the doorway, he reached to take my hand, and my heart fluttered.

"Thanks for inviting me in."

"For a predictable evening?" I said, grinning.

"Not predictable for me," he said. "Very different from my usual Monday night."

"Mine too, actually." I couldn't recall the last time I'd had a guy over on a Monday night. Or any night, for that matter. "Thanks for not saying anything about my mom and the Rossis."

"Don't you think your dad's going to figure it out when thirty strangers show up for his Bing and Bob party?"

"Yeah." I released a breath. "But I guess that's my mom's problem. I'm sure she's got some sort of plan to tell him."

"Hope so." He gave my hand a squeeze. "But at least we know I'm in, being a good Irish boy and all."

"Yes. And I really hope you'll forgive me for what I said earlier about all of that."

He brushed a finger over my lips, and a delicious chill ran through me.

"Don't worry about it." He smiled. "I'm looking forward to spending more time with your family. Your dad reminds me of my own. Makes me miss him." A wistful look came over him. "Dad was always singing the praises of his Irish roots."

Suddenly I missed my grandfather something fierce. "I wish you could've met my grandpa Aengus," I whispered. "He was a second-generation Irish American, and his heritage meant everything to him."

"Well, of course." Drew gave my hand a comforting squeeze.

"My father is proud too," I added, "but not in the same way Grandpa Aengus was. It's almost like this heritage thing gets weaker with each generation."

"Oh, I don't know." Drew now stood so close to me I could smell his yummy cologne. "I think you do a pretty good job of keeping the Irish gene alive. In fact, you're pretty good at just about everything you do." He traced my cheek with his finger, and I tingled from my head to my toes.

"Wait. Pretty good?" I quirked a brow.

He chuckled. "Okay, very good. And I'm sure the photos you're going to take at Sierra's wedding will blow everyone out of the water."

"Sierra Caswell . . ." I paused and released a slow breath, wondering just what to say.

Something in my expression must've alarmed Drew. "Everything okay with her wedding?" he asked.

"Yeah. I mean, no." Ugh. If I told him, he might use it against me. "I'm just struggling with some forms her publicist wants me to sign," I said after a couple of moments of reflection.

"Industry-standard stuff, or something more?"

"Something more." The familiar feelings of panic gripped me as I thought through the details of George's email.

I must've flinched, because Drew looked concerned. "You need—or want—my help?"

Man. With those blue eyes dancing so close to mine . . . with our fingers now intimately intertwined . . . I almost responded in the affirmative. Almost. Still, the McDermott in me wasn't ready to let go just yet.

"I . . . I'm sure it'll all work out."

"Okay. If you say so."

My insides churned nonstop as I pondered what, if anything, to say next. I couldn't stop thinking about Sierra Caswell's wedding and my eventual curfew. I felt a bit like Cinderella, only without the glass slipper and handsome prince.

Okay, so maybe there was a handsome prince in the room.

Drew gently released his hold on my hand. I could see the concern in his expression. He knew something was up. Still, what could I do?

He turned to leave. A couple of steps outside the door, he glanced back over his shoulder. "Hannah, let me ask you a question. That day at the coffee shop, when we met with the magazine reporter . . ."

"What about it?"

Drew's boyish smile caught me off guard. "Tell the truth. You dropped your coffee in my lap on purpose, didn't you?"

At this accusation, I slapped myself in the head. "Is that really what you think? You think I would make both of us look like idiots in front of someone who could potentially affect my career in such a positive—or negative—way? I would never do that."

His smile faded and his jaw tensed. "So, the whole thing was really an accident?"

"Of course it was."

"Ah." He frowned. "Well, frankly, I'm disappointed."

"Disappointed? Why?"

"I don't know." He leaned against the porch railing. "On

some level it made me feel special to think you would go to such efforts to sabotage me. Maybe you saw me as a threat."

His gorgeous blue eyes held me locked in their gaze—a prison of my own choosing. And those broad shoulders held me captive as well.

I see you as a threat, all right, Drew Kincaid.

After clearing my throat, I managed to speak. "Well, if it will make you feel any better, I'll be sure to drop something in your lap at the party."

"Ha. Very funny."

I gave a funny little curtsy, and he gazed at me until my insides felt like mush. Then he gave me a quick goodbye and bounded down the porch steps. I'd just started to close the door when he looked back at me, the evening shadows framing his gorgeous face.

"Oh, Hannah, just one more question."

Naturally.

I held on to the door, trying to still my heart. "What's that?"

He crossed his arms over his chest and stared at me, creases forming between his brows. "Who the heck is Jacquie Goldfarb?"

Unable to put off the inevitable any longer, I released a slow breath, looked into his gorgeous blue eyes, and stated the obvious.

"You are."

15

My Wild Irish Rose

There are only three types of Irishmen who can't understand women: young men, old men, and men of middle age.

Irish saying

The next few weeks were spent in a state of photogenic schizophrenia, one gig on top of another. My business kept me hopping during the day, and my parents kept me sedentary at night. More than once, Drew Kincaid showed up at my house on Monday night to watch *Dancing with the Stars*. I found myself drawn to him, almost forgetting that he was my Jacquie Goldfarb. And despite that whole "the McDermotts and Kincaids are mortal enemies" story, he and my father seemed to be getting along. Strange.

By the end of October, I'd almost talked myself into signing the forms from Sierra's publicist, believing they couldn't possibly be used against me. The following week, Scarlet had convinced me otherwise. And by Saturday, the day of our Bing and Bob party, I had that sick, pit-in-the-stomach feeling that comes when you realize you're up against a wall but have no recourse. I couldn't sign the papers. And I had to tell Bella, once and for all.

After the party.

The first Saturday night in November arrived, but not without its drama. Less than an hour before the onset of the party of the century, my father's emotion-packed words rang out across the house.

"What do you mean, you invited thirty strangers to my Bing and Bob party?"

Even from the comfort of my upstairs bedroom, where I dressed up as Grace Kelly, I could make out every word as the argument between my parents ensued. In fact, I could almost envision the look on my dad's face with each punctuated word.

I stepped out into the hallway to hear my mother's response to his emotional tirade.

"You're going to love the Rossis, Michael," she countered from the living room below, her words carrying up the stairs. "And they're great cooks. Rosa—she's the aunt, the one with the television show—is bringing some of the food. Isn't that sweet? She's really doing us a favor, you see."

"I will not abide Italian food at my Bing and Bob party. Where would we put it—in the middle of the room? It will ruin the whole thing. Besides, what will the guys from my lodge say?"

"Oh, she's not bringing Italian food," Mama said. "She's bringing a rack of lamb for the Bob Hope side. And from what I hear, it's a genuine British recipe, one even you will approve of."

"Still. This is an Irish-English party. You've got to be one or the other to come, and these people, whoever they are, are clearly neither." He began to grumble—in Gaelic, no less—about the generations of Irishmen who'd walked this road before him, but after a while none of it made sense to me. Or to my mother either, apparently.

"Michael McDermott, I swear, sometimes I think you've got splinters in the windmills of your mind."

My father, for once, did not respond.

"I think, just this once, you could consider doing something differently. It won't kill you."

Again, no response from my father.

"Did you hear me?" Mama said. "Or am I wasting my breath?"

After a lengthy pause, my father spoke. "I'll admit, I'm selective with what I hear."

This, of course, got Mama more riled up than ever. I could hear her in the kitchen now, banging pots and pans, followed by a rousing proclamation: "The problem with the McDermott gene pool is that there is no lifeguard!"

This sent my father into a tizzy. He began to rant in Gaelic. I couldn't make out much of it, but I understood his final comment about Irish loyalties.

"Michael McDermott, don't you think it's time to lay all of that down?" Mama's voice held that same stern tone she'd used on me as a youngster. "I mean, it's all in good fun, so you can't take it too seriously."

"Did the McDermotts of old take being Irish seriously?"

"Yes, and it landed them on the front lines of battle, many of them. This isn't a night for battles. Let's just have a party and relax. Eat good food. Visit with friends, old and new." Her voice softened, and I took a couple of steps toward the stairs. "Please, Michael. For me. You know how disappointed I am that our other daughters can't come tonight. I want to make this special for Hannah, and these are people she works with."

I could hear his groan all the way up the stairs. The silence that followed threw me a little. I glanced downstairs to find my parents wrapped in each other's arms. Ew.

Moments later the music kicked in. Bing Crosby's cool voice crooned from the stereo in the living room below. Maybe my parents had mended fences, at least for now. Still, I could hardly imagine what the rest of the night would hold.

The melody of "My Wild Irish Rose" wafted up the stairs, and I began humming along. I headed back into my room and completed my Grace Kelly ensemble by adding an off-the-shoulder cream dress I'd purchased at Salvation Army for a song. I did my makeup as best I could in 1950s style, adding a bit of liquid eyeliner.

A closer look in the mirror reminded me that I still needed to put my hair up. Working with great precision—envisioning the photos that might come out of this evening, of course—I did just that. The finished look almost took my breath away.

I compared myself to the photograph of Grace Kelly on my laptop and grinned. "Not bad, not bad." My heart lurched as I contemplated what Drew would say when he laid eyes on me.

What difference does it make, Hannah? Really?

Still, a girl couldn't help but wonder.

I heard a ding from my computer signaling that an email

had come through. Two, actually. The first set my head to swimming. A reminder email from George, who seemed concerned that he hadn't received the signed addendum yet. Heaven help me. I squeezed my eyes shut, said a rushed prayer for God's grace, then moved on to the next email, a notice from Facebook that I had a private message awaiting me from none other than the infamous Jacquie Goldfarb. We'd exchanged a couple of quick notes over the past weeks, but nothing earthshaking.

I skimmed her most recent message.

Noticed from your profile that you're single. Good for you, girl. I wasted six years of my life on Matt make-me-sick-to-my-stomach Hudson, and he ended up putting a knife in my back. Be glad you never got married.

Ouch. Her "be glad you never got married" carried a sting. Clearly the girl still knew how to get her digs in, hitting the single gal between the eyes with her singleness.

Scarlet, why did I listen to you? I should never have contacted Jacquie Goldfarb in the first place.

I knew I should probably come up with something brilliant to say in response to Jacquie's note, but nothing came to mind, so I closed the computer and headed downstairs to help Mama with the last of the decorations.

At ten minutes till seven, Rosa and Laz arrived. Rosa looked stunning in her Vera-Ellen getup. What a knockout. My father huffed his way through the introductions but made a bit of polite conversation once he realized that Laz, who had come dressed as a very non–English or Irish Dean Martin, held a pot of corned beef and cabbage in his hands.

"You made that yourself?" my dad asked.

"Sure. Love the stuff. Always have. Lived in New Jersey years ago and couldn't get enough of it." Laz lifted the pan as if to emphasize the point. "Want to show me to the kitchen?"

"Never been inside of our kitchen myself," Dad said, his expression a little forced. "But I think I can find it."

This got a funny look from Laz, who finally caught on that my dad was teasing.

"Just kidding, just kidding." My father slapped him on the back and led the way to the kitchen. I followed closely behind to see if my mother needed any help. The amazing aroma of fish and chips wafted up to greet us. Yum.

"Haven't had fish and chips in a month of Sundays," Laz said. He gave my mother an encouraging smile. "You'll have to give me your recipe." He placed the pan of corned beef and cabbage on the counter and stole a nibble of the fish and chips.

"Really?" Mama's face flushed.

"Well, sure. Maybe we'll even add a fish and chips pizza at Parma John's on St. Patrick's Day. Something to think about, anyway."

He began to fill my mother's ears with ideas for his upcoming special at the restaurant. Not that she appeared to mind. Oh no. I'd never seen her so flattered. Then she and Rosa got busy putting out the foods, including the rack of lamb, which smelled delicious.

At this point, "Count Your Blessings Instead of Sheep" rang out from the stereo in the living room. Rosa paused, her eyes filling with tears. "Well, if that isn't just the best reminder in the world. I have so much to be thankful for."

My mother, God bless her, reached over to give Rosa a hug. "So do I. In fact, I'm looking into the face of someone I'm very thankful for right now."

Before long the women were drying one another's tears

and talking about how wonderful the Lord was to bring us all together. I couldn't help but agree. Had we really known each other such a short time?

By seven o'clock, five of my dad's lodge buddies had arrived. I said a quick hello to Bart, Emmet, Kevin, Riley, and Sean. A couple of them headed to the Irish side of the room to leave their themed snacks.

Across the room, "*Nollaig shona duit!*" rang out, followed by its English translation, "Merry Christmas!" Even Rosa caught on and greeted the others with a bit of an Italian-Irish brogue.

"It's not even Thanksgiving yet," Laz said. "Why the 'Merry Christmas' greetings?"

"Just tradition," I explained. "Something we always do at the Bing and Bob party."

In the midst of this happiness, the three Splendora sisters entered. Two of them—Twila and Jolene—brought along their husbands, who apparently hadn't gotten the memo that they were supposed to arrive in costume. For the life of me, I couldn't figure out who had invited these folks. Still, here they were, the ladies dressed as the Andrews Sisters, no less, and harmonizing to one of my father's favorite songs, "Christmas in Killarney." This, of course, won his favor right away.

I introduced the ladies to Mama, and she took to them at once, especially when they called her Sister Marie. Within minutes they were all standing in front of the Christmas tree, talking about how lovely it was. I gave the tree a quick glance, wondering how anyone could see it as lovely. It looked exactly the same, year in and year out. Nothing changed—not the ornaments, the garland, the lights . . . nothing.

I pulled out my camera and caught a shot of Twila reaching

up to touch an ornament I'd made as a youngster. Somehow, seeing it through her eyes—and the lens of my camera—made it feel special.

At exactly three minutes after seven, Scarlet arrived with her scruffy-looking assistant, Kenny, who carried in the most amazing cake I'd ever seen. A true replica of Bing Crosby. On one side, anyway. He turned the cake around to reveal Bob Hope's smiling face.

"Frighteningly realistic," Laz said, giving it a close look. "But I prefer the Bing Crosby side."

"Not me," Rosa countered. "I think the Bob Hope side is priceless." She began to gush over the cake, which, no doubt, was exactly what Scarlet had hoped she would do. I couldn't fault my best friend for trying to win the favor of the Rossis. She knew a good deal when she saw it.

I helped Kenny settle the cake onto a special table in between the Bing and Bob tables, then went to answer the door, astounded by the mad rush of Italians who greeted me. I threw my arms around Bella, welcomed D.J. with a smile, and ushered them inside, along with their children. All the while I offered up a silent prayer that Bella wouldn't want to talk about the addendum. No point in stressing either of us out on a night like tonight.

Bella's parents entered next, followed by her brothers and their wives and children. Only Armando was noticeably absent. Oh well. Didn't need him wreaking havoc.

Soon the house was swimming in a variety of ethnicities. My dad ventured off to a corner to nibble on some fish and chips and gab with his friend Sean, who seemed equally as puzzled by the influx of Italians. Still, I had to give it to the Irishmen. They didn't boot the offenders.

The song on the stereo changed again, this time to "White

Christmas." Everyone in the room grew silent for a moment. Then, as if on cue, the Splendora sisters chimed in, adding three-part harmony to the song. My father stood, clearly mesmerized by their passionate impromptu performance.

When the song ended, my dad's lodge buddies decided to get in on the singing action. It always came down to this at a Bing and Bob party, but such antics usually waited till later in the night, after the games. Sean, Bart, and Kevin began a rousing chorus of one of their favorites, albeit not in harmony. Not even close, in fact.

"Me darlin' was sweet, me darlin' was chaste, faith, an' more's the pity," they sang out, severely off-key. "For though she was sweet an' though she was chaste, she was chased all the way through the city!"

When they finished, my father hollered out his usual, "*Maith thú!* Way to go!" Several of the other men raised their glasses and cheered.

This, of course, got a laugh out of everyone, especially Laz, who asked them to sing it again. I couldn't help but notice that Bonnie Sue, the only Splendora sister without a mate, had set her sights on Sean, who responded to her attentions by calling her Julie Andrews. Obviously the man didn't know the difference between the Andrews sisters and Julie Andrews, but Bonnie Sue didn't appear to mind. Not a bit, in fact.

Drew arrived fashionably late at twenty minutes after the hour. I couldn't help but laugh when I saw his crazy Bing Crosby getup. The plaid suit. The trademark boater hat. The pipe. What struck me the most, however, was the hair. What little I could see of it peeking out from under the edges of the hat did not appear to be his usual blond.

"Did you—did you dye your hair?"

Why this mattered to me, I could not say. Still, from a

photographer's standpoint, I would hate to see the gorgeous sun-kissed locks go.

"Only my hairdresser knows for sure." He wiggled his brows. "But he's not tellin'."

"Tell me it's temporary."

"Spray on." Drew narrowed his gaze. "But since when do you care about the color of my hair?" An arched eyebrow indicated his humorous surprise.

"Oh, I . . . well . . ." My heart did that weird flip-flop thing. I'd noticed the irregular heartbeat before—usually whenever Drew came around.

He gave me an interested look. "By the way, you look . . ." He took me by the hand and turned me around in a full circle. "Amazing. Just like Grace Kelly."

My father happened by. "That's my girl. Hannah Grace."

Drew gripped my hand. "Wait, your middle name is Grace?"

"Yes."

"So you really are Grace."

"Full of grace and truth," Mama said with a wink as she joined us. "That's always been our little family phrase for Hannah."

"And that's the real reason why you decided to come to the party dressed as Grace Kelly?" Drew asked.

"Yeah." I couldn't help the smile that followed.

"Very cool." The expression on his face told me that he really did find it cool.

Behind Drew, in the doorway, a middle-aged woman appeared, holding tight to a Crock-Pot. "Whew. Want to help me with this, Drew?" She pressed the Crock-Pot into his hands, then flashed a shy smile at me.

Drew gripped the Crock-Pot and squared his shoulders. "Hannah, I'd like you to meet my date."

Date?

"My mom, Corinne Kincaid."

The woman with the delightful smile extended her hand. "Hannah, I'm happy to meet you at last. I've heard so much about you."

You have?

"Drew sings your praises all the time. Glad to finally meet you in person so I can put a face with the name."

"Glad you could come, Mrs. Kincaid."

"Kincaid?" My father's voice rang out from behind me, and I cringed, wondering what he would say next. "Well, at least they're Irish," he said after a pause. "Might as well let 'em in. We need the aid of our countrymen to fight off the outsiders."

He went on to mutter something about how the Kincaids weren't exactly our countrymen, what with them being our mortal enemies and all, but I prayed Drew and his mom wouldn't hear it over the noise as the Irishmen got to singing again.

> "There once was an old man of Lyme
> Who married three wives at a time.
> When asked, 'Why a third?'
> He replied, 'One's absurd!
> And bigamy, sir, is a crime.'"

I looked at Drew and sighed. "You can see that you've arrived just in time."

Mama drew near and whispered in my ear, "Do something, Hannah. I have a feeling that's not decaf your father's lodge buddies are drinking."

"If they get too rowdy, I'm sure Dad will usher them out," I responded.

Or not. Minutes later the "Good health to you!" cheer—

"*Sláinte chugat!*"—sounded across the room, and I knew we were in trouble. Whenever an Irishman wished another good health, he was usually swallowing down something other than coffee or tea.

I opted for a distraction by introducing Corinne to my mother. The two women dove into a lengthy conversation about the amazing scent emanating from the Crock-Pot in Drew's hands.

Corinne's gaze traveled to the ground. "I hope you don't mind that I came without a proper invitation, but I've always been a Bing Crosby fan and just couldn't resist once Drew told me about it." She glanced at the Splendora trio and grinned. "Sure looks like you folks are having a lot of fun."

"We are, and you're in the right place if you're a Bing fan," Mama said with a nod. "Say no more. And just so you know, you're always welcome. I'm accustomed to having a houseful, but with all of my girls married now . . ." She looked my way. "Well, all but Hannah here, anyway, it gets really lonely around here."

Before I could help it, a sigh escaped.

"I hope you don't mind that I brought our stew," Mrs. Kincaid said. "It was Drew's idea. He even helped make it. Then again, he's always been a great help in the kitchen. Gotta love a man who cooks."

Yes. You. Do.

"Smells delicious." Mama took her by the hand. "C'mon and help me. I need to bring more of the food out to the table."

I tagged along behind Drew, who followed our mothers to the tables on the Bing Crosby side of the room.

"You helped your mom make the stew?" I asked.

"Don't tell anyone, but I actually made it." He paused. "Well, mostly. She peeled the potatoes, cut up the lamb, chopped the onions, and threw in the Canadian bacon. But I stirred it. And added the spices. And it was my suggestion, of course." A jovial laugh followed his words, along with a tip of his hat.

"Well, your mom is lucky to have you. I'm glad you brought her along."

My mother gestured for Drew to put the Crock-Pot on the table on the west side of the room. She and Mrs. Kincaid then busied themselves going back and forth to the kitchen to fetch the English foods for the Bob Hope table on the east side of the room. Before long we were all drooling over Jammie Dodgers and potatoes as well as fish and chips. The combination of tantalizing aromas nearly took my breath away. I could hardly wait to dive in.

Mama paused from her work long enough to ask for my assistance. "Hannah, would you go into the kitchen to get those scones you made?"

"Sure." I nodded and took a few steps toward the kitchen, surprised to find Drew right behind me.

I gave him a curious glance, and he shrugged. "Just thought you might need some help."

"My scones are as light as a feather."

"Oh, I'm sure they are." Drew leaned over and whispered in my ear, "Okay, so I used the line about helping you just to follow you to the kitchen. Truth is, I'm still trying to figure out that whole Jacquie Goldfarb thing. It's a mystery, but I plan to solve it before the night's over."

"Ah."

Well, in the meantime, could you lean a little closer? That cologne you're wearing is yummy.

Though I hated to admit it even to myself, nearly everything about Drew Kincaid was yummy. Not just his cologne. Not just his Bing Crosby getup. Not just his kindhearted manner. Truth be told, there was little I didn't like about the guy, apart from him being my competition. And the less I found to criticize, the more I found to admire.

And that fact was just about to drive me over the edge. Then again, with such a handsome fella following on my heels, who needed to hang on? Might as well let go and see where the road would take us.

16

Count Your Blessings Instead of Sheep

May the lilt of Irish laughter
Lighten every load.
May the mist of Irish magic
Shorten every road . . .
And may all your friends remember
All the favors you are owed!

Irish saying

The Bing and Bob party forged ahead, noisier than ever. Now, I'd seen my father in his element before, but never in a crowd of this size. He took to sharing stories about Bing Crosby—after his "Irish Lullaby" solo, of course. His best friends, especially Sean, got along famously with the men from Bella's family. Who knew? Laughter rang out across the room as everyone enjoyed the evening.

And the food! I'd never seen so many people consume so much food in one sitting before. Mama, Rosa, and Corinne scurried back and forth from the kitchen to the serving tables to keep the tantalizing stuff coming.

And speaking of tantalizing, I found my thoughts continually drifting back to Drew Kincaid. When I went to the kitchen to fetch more ice, he joined me. My heart rate skipped to double time.

Good gravy. What's wrong with you, Hannah? There you go again, falling for a handsome guy just because he's . . .

Okay, this one was gazing into my eyes with such intensity that I felt the butterflies in my stomach take to flight. And all the more when he leaned in close to whisper something in my ear.

"I can't take it anymore," he said. "What in the world did you mean when you called me Jacquie Goldfarb?"

"Ah." I reached for the ice, then paused to think through my response. "It's sort of a code name that I use when I'm talking about my competition."

"Wait . . . I'm your competition?" Drew looked confused.

"Well, yeah." I headed out to the living room with the ice, hoping he wouldn't carry the conversation further.

"So, why Jacquie Goldfarb? What's the significance of the name?"

I emptied the ice into the appropriate bucket and turned back to face him. "She's a girl I knew in school. Very pretty. Cheerleader type. Pretended to be my friend but turned on me every chance she got. Dated the hottest guy in the school. You know. Jacquie Goldfarb. Every school has one."

"And I'm Jacquie Goldfarb?" His brow wrinkled. "You're sure?"

"Yep."

"I'll admit, I give off the cheerleader vibe." He quirked a brow. "But I can absolutely assure you I've never been one to date the hottest guy in the school."

"Well, thank God for small favors." I managed a weak chuckle.

"Besides . . ." He leaned in to whisper, "I don't plan to turn on you. And I'm no Goldfarb. I'm a Kincaid through and through." Crossing his arms over his chest, he stared at me. "A good Irish boy, to quote your father."

"True."

"So you've settled that issue in your mind, then?" he asked. "You're ready to admit that I'm 100 percent Irish, in spite of being adopted?"

"Of course."

"All right. Well, while we're casting shadows of doubt, I must confess that I'm not 100 percent sure you are."

This statement almost shocked the breath out of me. Was the boy deaf, dumb, and blind? "Are you serious? I'm a Mc-Dermott." After dropping the empty ice tray onto the table, I raised my chin with a cool stare in his direction. "What other proof do you need?"

"I can't argue with that. McDermott is an Irish name. I've been researching it, by the way. You know what McDermott means, don't you?"

"I'm sorry, what?" *You've been researching my name?*

"Your name. McDermott. It means 'free from envy.'" He shared a story about the etymology of the name, but he lost me after a moment. Only one thing stuck with me from his twisted tale.

"W-wait. You're telling me that my name really means 'free from envy'?"

"Yep." He grinned. "Crazy what you learn when you do a little research."

"So, what makes you think I'm not Irish?"

"Totally kidding about that. I figured if you got riled up when I made the accusation, it would be all the proof I needed that you really are. Get it?"

"Very funny."

"My pleasure. And by the way, just in case you didn't know, the McDermotts came to live in America during the potato famine. My mom helped me with this part. She'd done a lot of historical research for our clan over the years, so she knew just where to look."

"And in all that research, did you somehow miss the part about how the McDermotts and the Kincaids were fierce foes back in the day?"

"Huh?" He shrugged. "Never heard her mention it. Weird."

"Well, it's true. My dad says it was like the Hatfields and McCoys all over again, only worse."

"What do you mean?"

Across the room, "Oh Danny Boy" rang out as my father raised his voice in song.

"Do your family research." I turned back to Drew, lowering my voice. "The McDermotts and the Kincaids never got along. They feuded from the get-go. That explains why the two of us—"

"Are a match made in heaven?" The twinkle in his eye threw me.

"W-what?"

"Nothing. You were saying?"

"I was just saying that, according to my father's research—"

"Our people don't get along?" Drew's eyes narrowed into

slits. "Honestly, Hannah, I don't care what our ancestors did. We're living in the twenty-first century, not medieval times."

"True. But my father says that his father—and his grand-father, and his grandfather's father—all swapped war stories about the infamous Kincaids."

"So what started this feud, if you don't mind my asking."

"My dad said it had something to do with land. I'm not sure."

"Kind of odd that I've never heard this story." He shook his head. "My parents told me all of the tall tales from days gone by. Never heard the one about the feud with the Mc-Dermotts. Strange."

"Stranger still that we're here, hundreds of years later, still feuding."

He put his hands up, as if under arrest. "Speak for yourself, little missy. There's not a feuding bone in my body."

"Well, not feuding, exactly. We're just major competitors. Don't you find that ironic?"

"Ironic that we're both in the same line of work, or ironic that you see me as your competitor?" The worry lines on his forehead deepened. "Because, to be honest, I've never really thought about you as the competition."

"O-oh?" This totally caught me off guard. "You haven't?" *What, you don't think I'm as good as you? Is that it? I'm not worthy of being called a competitor?*

Drew's face took on a pained expression. "I guess I just don't think like that. We have the same interests, sure. But I see that as a good thing, not something to divide us."

I sighed. "It's the only way I think, to be honest. I'm just so . . . so . . . competitive."

"Why is that?"

I shrugged. "Because I'm a McDermott, of course. Haven't you heard? The McDermotts don't go down without a fight."

"You fight to the finish, no matter what?"

"Always have. My grandpa Aengus used to tell a story about his great-great-grandfather and some war he fought. He wouldn't give up his sword, even after being captured by the enemy. Held on to it until they took his life."

"Stubborn." Drew quirked a brow.

"That's one way to say it."

"Don't you think—and I'm not trying to be sarcastic here—that some circumstances would call for dropping the sword and saving your life? What's the problem with admitting defeat when it's staring you in the face?"

His words stung far more than he could've known. I thought about that unsigned addendum and felt sick inside. Not that he knew about all of that. Still, I couldn't give up on the idea that I could somehow salvage the situation with Sierra Caswell, despite all opposition. I was a McDermott, after all.

I closed my eyes and could almost see my great-great-great-great-grandfather clinging to that sword, face taut. Strange, he looked a little like me as I clung to my dying business.

A deep sigh followed. I couldn't help it.

I'd just started to open up and share more of my heart with Drew when Bonnie Sue approached, nibbling on a scone. "This is the yummiest thing I've ever eaten in my life. Might have to have a couple more when I'm done with this one."

"Thanks. I made those myself."

"That's what your mama said." Bonnie Sue finished the scone and licked the powdered sugar off her fingers. "And by the way, I just love your mama. She's precious, honey."

"Thank you." I cringed, mostly because she'd called me *honey* in front of Drew. Something about the word made me feel young. Too young.

The other two Splendora sisters started harmonizing "Thanks for the Memories," with my dad's Irish buddies chiming in. Bonnie Sue took off to the other side of the room and added her voice to the fray. I deliberately took a few steps away from Drew, hoping he wouldn't follow me. I needed time—and space—to quiet the voices in my head.

Somehow I landed at the Bob Hope table, where Bella and D.J. stood, filling plates with food. D.J. headed across the room to talk to Mr. Rossi, but Bella lingered behind. She glanced my way and put her plate down. "Hannah," she whispered. "We need to talk."

"Oh?"

Please, God, not here. I do not want this fiasco with Sierra to ruin a perfectly good night.

"Yes. You're not a very good actress, just so you know."

"What?" I felt my hands tremble as I looked her way. "What are you talking about?"

"I'm just saying . . . when Drew walks in the room, you try so hard to act like you don't notice him, but your acting skills stink. Why don't you just let your guard down and enjoy being with him?" She stared at me with such intensity that I felt exposed. "Or is there something I need to know here?"

"Nothing. Nope. Nada. I got nothin'."

"Oh, you've got something all right." She leaned in to have a closer look at my face. "And for the record, you're blushing. I don't think I've ever seen you blush before. If I didn't know any better, I would say you're twitterpated."

"Twitter?" I shook my head. "I'm a Facebook girl all the way. Don't twitter. Or tweet. Or whatever it's called."

"Hannah, I'm not talking about the internet. I'm talking about your heart. I think you're twitterpated. That's what the Splendora sisters call it when you're falling for someone. You're falling for Drew Kincaid."

I felt the breath go out of me as she said the words. While I'd voiced the idea to myself, no one else on the planet—to my way of thinking, anyway—had a clue.

Till now. How in the world had she guessed my dark little secret? I hadn't even convinced myself. Yet. Sure, the guy captivated my thoughts, my imagination, my curiosity. But he was my competition . . . right?

"You can go on pretending you don't see him. You can even act like you're mad at him because he's your competitor. But I think we both know what's really going on here. You see him and your insides turn to mush."

I gave a deep sigh. I swung my camera around and pretended to take photos so that no one would pay attention to our conversation. Through my lens I caught a glimpse of Bonnie Sue eyeing Sean. Off to my right, my dad and his buddies slapped one another on the back as the songs continued to ring out across the room.

"You've got that crazy 'I can't wait to see you, but I'm terrified you don't feel the same way about me that I feel about you' thing going on."

"Good grief, Bella. You should take up relationship counseling."

I pointed the camera in a different direction, this time catching a glimpse of Mama, Rosa, and Corinne, laughing and talking. Oh, great. Mama had taken to showing the ladies the pictures of my sisters and their spouses. And the grandchildren. Lovely. No telling what tidbits she was adding about me. Likely sharing her woes about my current state of singleness. I cringed just thinking about it.

Mama, please don't show them the picture of me with braces.

"And here's a great picture of Hannah the day she got her braces." Mama's voice rang out, followed by several chuckles from her now-captive audience.

Bella's gaze remained fixed on me. "Trust me, I could take up relationship counseling. After all the couples I've met over the years?"

"I'm awful with relationships, trust me. Well, not that I've had a lot of them, but you know what I mean."

"Actually, I don't," she said. "But I'm ready, willing, and able to talk, if you want."

I turned my attention away from my mother and saw Bella's face etched with compassion. "The only real relationship I've had was with a guy I worked with on board the *Clarity*," I said after a couple of moments of awkward silence. "I met him my first day on the ship. He was—well, I guess you could say he was my boss, though technically they employed me as a freelancer."

"And?"

"And it started pretty innocently. I wasn't used to guys flattering me. I mean, c'mon, Bella. I'm no beauty queen." I gestured to my freckled face and frizzy hair. "Most guys in high school and college walked right past me without even noticing me."

Her eyes narrowed to slits, and for a moment there I felt pretty sure I saw steam coming out of her ears. "Hannah McDermott, don't you ever let me hear you say anything like that again."

"What? I'm just telling you the truth. That's why, when I met Jon and he seemed to like me—to really, really like me—I fell headfirst. Lost all control of my senses." Shame washed over me. "I got caught up in it, Bella. The lifestyle on the ship. The way he made me feel. We were a team. He was going to help me propel my career. Only . . ." Heat rushed to my cheeks, and I glanced across the room at my parents to make sure they were out of earshot.

Bella lowered her voice and leaned in closer. "Only, he didn't. Let me guess. He ended up playing you."

"With about four or five other women. Most of them from countries I'd never even heard of. So my happily ever after kind of faded away. But don't you see? That's my problem. When a handsome guy takes an interest in me, I lose control of myself. I'm like an alcoholic falling off the wagon." Somehow I found myself reaching out to grab a scone off her plate. I nibbled on it, deep in thought.

She didn't say anything for a moment, but I could read the concern in her eyes. "So you're afraid that Drew Kincaid— a very handsome guy, by the way—is going to knock you off that wagon once again? You're going to end up feeling compromised?"

The trembling began again, and I lowered my voice. "I hate that part of it, Bella. I didn't mean to let things go so far with Jon, but they did. And I can't ever let that happen again. You know what I mean?" Another glance across the room landed my gaze squarely on Drew. Yikes.

"I do. And you're right to be careful so you don't have to go back down that road. But Hannah, take a look at your middle name: Grace. That's how God feels about what you've been through. He sees it all through his eyes of grace. If you've gone to him to deal with the past—"

"Oh, trust me, I have."

"Okay, then that part is done. Over. You don't have to think about anything you did or anything Jon or anyone else did to you. You just have to look at where you are today. And when it comes to Drew, I can tell you that he's a great guy.

He's not some sleazy guy on a cruise ship hitting on multiple women at once."

"How do I know that?"

"Because he's the real deal, Hannah. He's solid—in his walk with God and in his reputation with the community. I know because he and D.J. are good friends from church. You want to know why I've shown Drew such favor as a photographer? He sings on the worship team. I've watched him in action with the teens from the youth group. I've seen him take photos at small church weddings where the bride and groom had nothing to pay him. I've done what I could to help him because I'm proud of him."

Wow. In that moment I was pretty proud of him myself.

"Nothing to be scared of here, Hannah." She patted my arm. "So when you think about Jon or anything else from the past, just do what my uncle Laz always says."

"What's that?"

"Fuggetaboutit!" She spoke in a thick Italian accent, which made me laugh. In fact, once the laughter got ahold of me, it trickled over into her. Soon we were both in a fit of laughter.

We finally got things under control, thank goodness. I glanced across the room at Drew, who held the three Splendora sisters captive with his Bing Crosby imitation.

"What about the fact that he's my Jacquie Goldfarb?" I asked, my voice lower than before.

Bella chuckled. "Girl, there's only one Jacquie Goldfarb, and I doubt she's anything like Drew Kincaid."

I shifted my focus to the left, and Drew Kincaid's gorgeous face came into view. Instinctively, I swung my camera around and zoomed in. He must've realized I was looking, because he flashed a Bing Crosby–esque smile, which I saw up close and personal through the eye of the camera. I caught the moment on film, naturally. Any photographer with half an ounce of creativity would have.

Still, I had to admit, Bella was right. Drew Kincaid was nothing like the real Jacquie Goldfarb. In fact, he wasn't like anyone I'd ever known before. And though I couldn't say the words aloud, I could no longer deny the fact that he had somehow—heaven help me—landed squarely in the center of the photo . . . and my thoughts.

17

Put It There, Pal

May you always walk in sunshine.
May you never want for more.
May Irish angels rest their wings right beside your door.

Irish blessing

After wrapping up the heartfelt conversation with Bella, I knocked off a couple of scones and a piece of shortbread. I'd just swiped my sticky fingers against my skirt, thanked God for my gym membership, and given serious thought to my rising blood sugar levels when Drew approached.

"I just had the best idea." His eyes twinkled with mischief.

"What's that?" I pressed aside the temptation to lick the

sugar from my fingertips and clasped my hands together instead. Great. Now I'd never get them apart.

He raised his voice to be heard above the men on the other side of the room, who'd taken to playing my father's favorite game, Name That Tune. "Well, you're dressed to the nines. So'm I. We should take photos of each other."

My heart quickened. "I . . . I don't think so."

"Why not?" He reached for his bag, unzipped it, and pulled out the expensive camera. "You already snapped one of me, right?"

"Oh. Well, yeah, I guess I did."

"Now it's my turn. It'll be perfect. I'll get some shots of you for your website, and you can get some of me for mine. We're both dressed for the occasion, after all. When are your clients ever going to see you dressed up as Grace Kelly again?"

"Not anytime soon, likely."

"Right. And besides, you need a new photo for your website. The one you have on there is outdated. Your hair is longer now."

"Wait, how do you know I need a new photo for my website?" The very idea set my nerves on edge.

A boyish grin lit his face. "I always check out the competition." His elevated right eyebrow had me wondering if he was still referring to my website.

"Oh, you do, do you?" Heat filled my face. "I thought you said I wasn't the competition."

Across the room, one of the men yelled out, "'Anything You Can Do, I Can Do Better'!" Ironic.

"Well, you know . . . I mean . . ." Drew gave me a wink. "I look to see what sort of portfolio other photographers have. That sort of thing. But I happened to notice you don't have an updated photo of yourself on your site, and that's a crime."

"The one I have is okay," I argued.

"Humph. It's buried several pages deep. I had to search for days to find it. You're a photographer, for Pete's sake. You need a photo of yourself front and center."

"Well, yes, but . . ." A deep sigh followed on my end. How could I explain that I hated photos of myself?

From the far side of the room, my father hollered, "'Oh, You Beautiful Doll'!" Another song guess.

"See?" Drew's eyes twinkled as he gestured to my dad. "Even your own father thinks you're as pretty as a picture."

Well, if that didn't make a girl feel good, nothing would.

"C'mon, I know the perfect spot." Drew took hold of my hand and pretty much pulled me along until we arrived in front of the family Christmas tree. "Those colors are perfect with your skin tone."

"My skin tone?"

"Sure." He snapped a photo of me before I could argue.

Talk about a candid shot. I'm pretty sure my mouth was wide open in argument.

Before long he had me posing. Go figure. The Splendora trio squealed with delight when they caught on to our little plan. They asked for photos too. Turned out their little singing trio had a name. And a website. And they needed head shots. Tonight, apparently. So much for my one-on-one time with Drew.

The ladies posed themselves in front of the tree, their voices drowning out the sound of my dad's lodge buddies, who continued to play Name That Tune on the other side of the room.

"We've hired a web designer," Twila hollered out above

the chaos. "Very efficient fellow. He's asked us for photos of the three of us performing together, but we don't have any recent ones."

"We're performing at Dickens on the Strand in a few weeks, so catch some candid shots of us singing in front of the Christmas tree to put our fans in the Christmas spirit." Jolene nudged me out of the way and struck a pose in front of the tree.

After washing my hands, I went in search of my camera, which I'd somehow left on the Bob table near the scones. I picked it up and went to work taking pictures of the trio.

They couldn't just pretend to sing, of course, so they put on another impromptu concert right then and there. I managed to catch several great shots of them. And when I heard Drew's camera clicking to my left, I realized he was photographing them too. For whatever reason, the idea didn't bother me at all. The whole thing threw my dad and his buddies a bit, though. They wrapped up their game and joined the chorus in short order.

Good for you, Dad. Learning to adapt in the moment.

Would wonders never cease?

When the ladies wrapped up their performance, Twila took me by the shoulders and physically moved me in front of the tree. "Now it's your turn, Hannah." She turned to Drew. "Doesn't she look like a million bucks in this Grace Kelly getup?"

"Ten million." He started snapping again, and I tried to resist by putting my hands up in the air and easing my way back.

Twila clucked her tongue. "C'mon now, Hannah. None of that. You've got to lean into the camera, girl."

"Beg your pardon?"

"That's a new expression." Twila clasped her hands together, speaking in a singsong voice. "I just coined it. Lean into the camera. Let go of your inhibitions. See yourself the way God sees you."

Clearly easier for some folks than others. Still, I gave it my best shot, even turning a couple of my poses into possible glam-shot opportunities. Hey, I might not enjoy getting my picture taken, but I knew better than to argue with a buxom country gal who liked to hug.

I'd just offered to snap a few photos of Drew when Scarlet and Kenny announced that they were cutting the cake.

My best friend beamed with pride as she sliced Bing's features into smithereens. "Hope you're all hungry. By the way, Bing is an Irish whiskey cake, and Bob is a chocolate truffle."

This, of course, got an energetic response from Rosa and the other ladies, who couldn't wait to sample both. And sample they did! The expressions of wonder and glee filled the room as the lifelike cake structure disappeared right before our eyes. Even my father, usually not much for sugary treats, dove right in, eating not one piece but two.

As I nibbled on a slice of scrumptious chocolate truffle cake, contentment settled over me. I did everything in my power to push my confusion regarding Drew aside and just focus on the delicious dessert.

Scarlet approached with a relaxed smile, cake plate in hand. "What a great night. Thank you so much for inviting me."

"You're welcome. And I think your cake was a hit."

"Really? Well, since you said that, I might as well ask a favor." She paused and glanced across the room at Rosa. "You're on the inside track with the Rossi family now. Can you just put in a good word for me? Sing my praises? Tell them that I'm working hard to gain a reputation as a cake decorator? I would love to schedule some weddings at Club Wed, you know."

"Scarlet . . ." My words drifted off. "I've told you before, Rosa does most of the cakes for their weddings."

"Emphasis on *most*. Surely there are times when they need a backup. Especially if she's busy with her show on the Food Network."

"Wasn't it just a month or so ago that you said I put too much stock in Bella controlling my future?"

"Well, yeah." Scarlet pursed her lips.

"So, what happened? Now you want me to use my connections to help your business too?"

She sighed. "It's not me, Hannah. It's Aunt Wilhelmina. When she heard about Rosa's ties to the Food Network—"

"Wait. You told her?"

"It just sort of slipped out in conversation, and you know how she is."

"Actually, I don't. I've never met her in person. Just heard stories."

"Well, she's very forceful. Very. You don't want to cross her. So she suggested—*suggested* being a loosely used word here—that I somehow meet Rosa and Laz and get some cake samples into their hands. And that's kind of what I've done tonight by making the Bing and Bob cake." She gave me a pleading look. "Just please let Bella know that I've got my portfolio online. And I'm definitely going to open my own shop."

"Right. I'll help you find a place when things slow down, I promise."

"You might not need to." She wiggled her brows playfully. "Aunt Willy and I looked at a place on the Strand, near your studio. She still wants to fund the whole thing. You know she has the most famous cake shop in Houston, right?"

Scarlet began to fill my ears with a lengthy description of all her aunt planned to do for her. "If I'm going to be half the businesswoman my aunt is, I have to get busy. Besides . . ." Her voice took on a strained tone. "I have to find some way to pay her back. She's the one who paid for me to go to culinary school. Do you have any idea how expensive that is?"

"No."

"It's ridiculous. She's very keen on me succeeding. And it's important to me too. I want to keep the family legacy moving forward. I come from a long line of bakers, you know."

And preachers too. Apparently she'd learned a thing or two about giving a persuasive message, because I felt convicted right now. Convicted to help her, anyway.

"Well, I can't promise anything, but I'll do my best to spread the word—not just to Bella but to all of my clients."

"So will I."

I turned as Drew's voice sounded behind me.

"You will, Drew?" Scarlet clasped her hands together at her chest. "How can I ever thank you?"

"By writing down the recipe for that chocolate truffle cake." He grinned. "My mom's already got a pen and paper in her hand."

"Ooh, I'll be happy to. And that's exactly the cake I'll bake for her birthday too." She leaned my way and whispered, "If I play my cards right, I really can have my cake and eat it too. My business will grow, and I can garner some new friends in the process." She headed over to visit with Drew's mother, who seemed delighted to get the recipe.

"I never understood that whole 'have your cake and eat it too' expression," I said after a moment's pause. "I mean, how can you eat your cake and still have some left? The phrase makes no sense."

Drew jabbed the prongs of his fork into his giant piece of cake, which, strangely, looked like Bob Hope's nose. "That's the point, I think. You can't consume something and still have any left to enjoy after the fact. Think of it like a relationship. If you end the relationship, you can't still have it afterward."

He went to work on the cake, eating it in a hurry. I tried not to watch, the whole thing grossing me out a little. My thoughts remained on his phrase about relationships coming to an end. Visions of Jon shot through my brain. I pushed the images away but must've grimaced.

"Did I hit a sore spot?" He narrowed his eyes and continued to eat, Bob's nose rapidly disappearing before my eyes. "You look like you're in pain over there."

"Maybe. If I want to eat cake, I'll eat cake. Period. End of sentence." I took another bite of the chocolate truffle yumminess by way of demonstration.

"Hmm." Drew took a couple more bites. "But what if you want cake tomorrow?" He pointed to his nearly empty plate and gazed into my eyes.

"I . . . well, I'd call Scarlet and she'd bake me another." I set my plate on the table and shrugged.

"What if Scarlet was out of town? What then?" He stepped closer. "What if what you really wanted required turning on the oven and baking a new one yourself? Or what if what you really wanted was right in front of you, but you just couldn't see it because your vision was clouded over from too much sugar?" He put his plate down and gripped my hand.

In that moment I realized we weren't talking about cake anymore.

Oh. Help.

I stared into his eyes and felt myself melting like butter-cream on an overheated cupcake.

No, scratch that. I'd already used that analogy one too many times. I was lost in those baby-blue pixelated eyes of his, swept away by the perfect, upturned lips and great pho-togenic cheekbones.

Good gravy. I was in over my head. And falling fast.

Quick, Hannah. Change the subject.

Thank goodness my father and his buddies took to playing their Name That Tune game once more. Seconds later, Sean hollered out, "'Some Enchanted Evening,'" and everyone roared with laughter. He might've gotten the song wrong, but it was all right to my way of thinking, because it offered me a great opportunity to segue into a new conversation with Drew.

I glanced his way with a smile. "Hey, speaking of enchanted evenings, I, um, well . . . I want you to know that you've made my father's night."

"What do you mean?"

"I mean you've taken an interest in something that means a lot to him. I'm sure he appreciates it." After an awkward silence, my embarrassment lifted. "For that matter, so do I. It means a lot to me that you would come and bring your mother."

"This has been a great night, Hannah. I'm glad we're here."

"Thank you. Oh, and by the way, I forgot to say it earlier, but you're a dead ringer for Crosby."

"Now if only I had his crooning abilities." Drew laughed.

"I'll bet you can sing." The words came laced with a teas-ing tone. "Give it a try, and I'll let you know if you sound like the real deal."

"No way." Drew's face reddened, a clear sign that I'd embarrassed him.

I couldn't resist the urge to carry it a step further. "C'mon. Just a line or two of 'Irish Lullaby.'"

He gestured to the chaos on the other side of the room. "In this madness? No way." Then a smile turned up the edges of his lips. "Okay. Only if it will lay the issue to rest once and for all. But not in here where everyone can hear me." He took me by the hand and led me out to the front porch.

A chill settled over me and I shivered, so Drew took off his jacket and wrapped it over my shoulders. We stood—very close—with the moonlight shining down on us. His eyes sparkled with a mischief that spoke of more than songs and cake.

"Okay, fire away." I took a seat on the bench and waited for him to begin to sing.

Drew began in a tentative voice. The first couple of notes cracked. By the time he got to the second line of the song, however, I had to admit he sounded a bit like Bing Crosby. Oh, maybe not the same velvety tones. But he had a good, strong bass voice, one that carried across the starlit sky and wrapped itself around my heart.

My heart. Hmm.

Listening to "Too-Ra-Loo-Ra-Loo-Ral" in the moonlight would be touching enough, but hearing it pour from Drew's lips made the whole experience seem otherworldly. It also served as the perfect way to wrap up the night.

When the song finished, Drew took my hand and I rose. My twitterpated heart took to racing as he slipped his arms around my waist and drew me close . . . so close that I could feel his heart hammering away underneath my palm, which I'd somehow—heaven help me—placed on his chest. His very solid chest. Yowza! Those beautiful eyes locked into mine, holding me spellbound. When his lips opened to speak, I almost lost my breath.

From inside the house, a muffled version of "Yes Sir, That's My Baby" rang out.

"Hannah, I just want to tell you . . ." Drew reached up to trace my cheek with his fingertip, and I felt myself lost in a dreamy haze. "That first night when I stopped by your house . . ."

"Yes?"

He shook his head. "I really just wanted to see you."

"O-oh?"

"Yes, I—"

At that very moment the front door flew open, and a couple of my dad's buddies staggered out. One of them looked our way and hollered out, "*Slán leat. Go mbeannaí Dia duit.*"

Drew took a step back and responded with an embarrassed, "Goodbye. May God bless you."

My poor, trembling hands nearly gave away my nervousness as a couple more of the fellas walked out.

Sean slapped his knee and turned to Riley. "Pray for me, friend," he said with a smirk.

"Why is that?" Riley asked.

"Me wife. She's developed a terrible habit of stayin' up till two in the mornin'. I can't break her of it."

"Why is that?" Riley asked. "What on earth is she doin' at that time?"

"Waitin' fer me to come home!" Sean doubled over in laughter, slung his arm over Riley's shoulder, and belted out another one of their now-infamous ditties. If they hadn't been walking home—Sean's house being only two down from ours—I might've been worried.

Out of the corner of my eye I caught a glimpse of Drew—handsome, sweet, good-natured Drew—now chatting with my father, who had joined him near the door. A rush of warmth flooded over me. Suddenly every competitive feeling I'd had for him faded away on the salty island breeze.

Still, as our near-miss moment was swept out to sea, I had to face the inevitable. I could not have my cake and eat it too. Not tonight, anyway.

18

Just You, Just Me

May your neighbors respect you,
Trouble neglect you,
The angels protect you,
And heaven accept you.

Irish blessing

Every now and again a girl gets that floating-on-a-cloud sensation. It rarely lasts, but mine lingered through the weekend. Every few minutes I would relive that awesome moment when Drew pulled me into his arms. I could smell his cologne, hear his words whispered in my ear. Ah, bliss! Any questions I might've had about him were no longer an issue. Strange how one evening could change a girl's life. "Some Enchanted Evening" became my theme song.

On Sunday morning, our pastor preached on the love between a husband and wife. Coincidence? I think not. My thoughts remained on Drew, on that near-miss kiss.

Near-miss kiss. Hmm. Next time I'd make sure he didn't miss. In fact, the more I thought about the potential for a kiss from Drew, the giddier I got. The possibilities almost made me forget about the drama with Sierra Caswell's wedding.

Almost.

By the time Monday morning rolled around, I knew I could no longer avoid the obvious. I had to face the inevitable deadline head-on. The reality slapped me in the face when I arrived at my studio at nine o'clock a.m. and checked my email. A note from Sierra's publicist set my heart to pounding. His final demand for the addendum didn't take me by surprise, though. I sensed the anger behind his words, which had taken on a threatening tone. If I didn't fax the signed papers to him by noon, all bets were off.

Still, what could I do? My conscience wouldn't allow me to sign. Even if it meant disappointing Bella. Even if it meant losing Sierra's business and the paycheck of a lifetime. I couldn't. I knew in my knower, as Mama would say.

Using the most professional tone possible, I wrote to George and told him that I could not sign the addendum as it was currently worded. Instead, I suggested several changes, then sent the email on its way, whispering a prayer for God's help. He would give it, I felt sure. Still, facing Bella with my decision was inevitable.

As I sat staring at my computer screen, I put together a plan of action for how to tell her. Later this afternoon. But I might as well get my act together now so that I would look like a pro when the moment came. It didn't take long to gather the necessary paperwork—the original contract, the unsigned addendum, and all correspondence between George and myself. Bella would need to see it all. Then she would understand why I could not do this.

I put the printed pages in an envelope and set it on my desk. Leaning back in my chair, I thought through what I would say to Bella, once I worked up the courage. I would have to tell her, once and for all, that my final decision had been made. Because I would not sign the addendum, I would not be photographing Sierra Caswell's wedding. She would be disappointed, of course, but would have to deal with it.

Feelings of nausea swept over me as I thought about losing the gig. Likely I'd have to give back the front monies they had paid. Thank God I'd socked it away in savings. Well, all but the part I'd used to pay this month's rent on the studio. The idea of losing it made me feel like a complete failure.

Determined to get beyond this, I started to shut down my computer. In doing so, I stumbled across an old email from an existing client, something I'd overlooked in the mayhem of my week. Great. Now I'd need to apologize for not responding sooner. I did my best to clean up that situation, then threw myself into my work, editing photos from a recent shoot. And sweeping the office. And dusting the shelves. And repairing a broken doorknob.

I gave up about halfway into the broken doorknob fiasco. I'd never been one to accomplish multiple things simultaneously. To me, multitasking simply meant messing up several things at once.

Though I attempted to give it my best shot, I couldn't focus. My thoughts, as always, were on the inevitable conversation with Bella. Well, that and the fact that I'd somehow forgotten to put my right earring on this morning.

What's wrong with you, Hannah?

At some point about an hour later, I realized a painful truth. In my attempts to double my efforts to keep this business alive, I'd been cutting things in half: makeup half done, mismatched shoes, cups of coffee and tea poured but never drunk, food half-eaten, earrings half-worn. All of these things I'd done because of distraction. How could a photographer make her way in the world if she went on missing the finer points? The details?

A sigh escaped as I realized how deep this problem went. I'd given my relationships a halfhearted effort, only nodding at them instead of actually enjoying and living them. So many areas of my life had been sacrificed, and all in the name of building my business. And for what? To lose the biggest client of all due to a technicality?

Whatever courage I'd felt earlier in the day waned as I thought about facing Bella with my decision. No doubt this would cause problems with the bride-to-be, which would mean trouble for Bella—exactly what I'd been trying to avoid. Five words shot through my brain, the same five words that always propelled me in instances such as this: *What would Grandpa Aengus do?*

Only one way to know for sure. I had to call my dad and seek out his advice. That meant coming clean. Telling him everything.

And so I did. He seemed surprised to learn that his daughter was being threatened by a major superstar's publicist, but he handled it with grace and ease, even after hearing the nitty-gritty details of my sad story. At the end of my lengthy dissertation about how my life and business were about to come to an end, he cleared his throat.

"You know what your grandpa Aengus would say right now, don't you, Shutter Speed?"

No, that's why I called you.

"It is a long road that has no turning."

"What?"

"This road we travel is filled with twists and turns. But just because you reach a bend in the road doesn't mean you're at the end of the road." His brogue thickened. "Don't look at this as an either-or situation. It's just a turn in the road. There's plenty of travelin' ahead—for you, your business, and your relationship with Bella Neeley."

"But how do you know that, Dad? And how do I keep on going when I'm painted into a corner?" I glanced around the studio, my heart in my throat. Gosh, I'd miss this place when I closed it down. And what lousy timing, losing my business just about the time Scarlet was starting hers.

"Well, honey—"

My gaze shifted to the now-dark computer screen. "I've had it with these people. They've hit me one too many times. Seems like I'm always fighting to prove myself, but I never come in first. I'm a second-placer." A deep sigh followed. "That's what you can put on my tombstone when I die: 'Second to All.' The Jacquie Goldfarbs of this world have won. They've proven their point. I'm not the winner of anyone's race. I guess I should just be happy to be running, right?" My words came faster now, propelled by a rushing current of angst beneath. "Only, I'm not happy unless I prove myself, which is probably prideful, but I can't seem to help it. I want to do well. I want my business to succeed. Is that so bad?"

"Wanting to do well isn't wrong," my father said. "I'd be worried about you if you didn't want your business to succeed. But you can't beat yourself up or compare yourself to others. Remember, the Bible says that the first will be last and the last will be first."

"What does that mean? I mean, really? What does it mean?"

"If you want my honest opinion, I think it has more to do with waiting on God to elevate you in his time, and nothing at all to do with where you fall on the ladder of success compared to your competition. I mean, we can climb the ladder only so far before someone comes along and nudges us down a rung. It happens to everyone. But when God decides the time is right, you'll soar all the way to the top, even if you've been kicked way down to the bottom."

"I've been kicked down, all right."

"Then the timing is perfect. You have no place to go but up." His voice oozed with compassion. "This isn't the end, Hannah. Don't get too defeated just because you've faced a challenge. You're made of tough stuff. After all, you're a—"

"McDermott." I released the word on a sigh. *If I hear that one more time, I'm going to hurl.* "I'm starting to think I was born into the wrong family."

"What do you mean?"

"I can't live up to the name. I'm not the fighter I thought I was. The McDermotts don't go down without a fight—got that. But Sierra Caswell has knocked the fight right out of me. I'm down for the count. Just put a fork in me. I'm done." A pause filled the space between us, and then I whispered, "I know I'm betraying the family name, but I just can't keep this thing going."

My father cleared his throat. "Yes, well, about that . . . There's something I need to tell you, Shutter Speed."

"What's that?" I waited, sensing his next words could change my situation and my life.

My father's serious tone changed, and I could hear the lilt in his voice again as he spoke. "See now, it's really kind of a funny story. I think you'll like it."

"I could use a funny story right about now, so out with it."

A nervous laugh came from his end. "It involves a father with a great imagination, one capable of coming up with a believable story at the drop of a hat."

My stomach began churning. "Go ahead."

"I, well, I haven't been 100 percent honest with you about something."

"Tell me, Dad." Pinching my eyes shut, I whispered, "I can take it."

He released an audible sigh. "Okay. It's like this. The McDermotts . . . um, we're not quite the warriors I've made us out to be."

"What?"

"It's true. All that stuff about the bloody battles and all that, well . . . I borrowed a few tall tales from Grandpa Aengus, but most of them are blown up a bit."

"What do you mean?"

"Truth is, several of the McDermotts did go down without a fight. In fact, if the story your grandmother told was correct, dozens of 'em got intoxicated and ran for the hills when trouble came their way."

"No way."

"Yeah. Happened a long, long time ago. So your grandfather filled our ears with hyped-up blarney to counteract what he knew to be true. And I guess I've done the same thing."

"Are you saying I come from a long line of cowards?"

He sighed. "Well, not a long line, necessarily. But there were a few deserters in the bunch." He mumbled something under his breath, then came back with, "And while we're at it, I'd better go ahead and get something else off my chest too. All that stuff about feuding with the Kincaids . . ."

"Yes, I remember. They fought tooth and nail. Bloody battles raged, all to prove one clan mightier than the other. But we got the land in the end."

"Not exactly."

"Huh?"

"I . . . well, I made the whole thing up."

I felt my lungs deflate. "You . . . what?"

"The two clans have never been enemies. From what I can tell from my research, anyway."

Disbelief coursed through me. "What are you talking about?"

"I'm being honest, Hannah. That whole story about the McDermotts and the Kincaids was something I came up with on the spur of the moment. See, I got really riled up when I found out that some other photographer had one-upped you. Thought it might get you in a fighting mood if I made up the story about the clans. But now I know Drew, and he's a great guy."

"And he's a Kincaid."

"Right." My father cleared his throat, then coughed. "The McDermotts and the Kincaids have always been friendly. But don't think I didn't try to make the story work. I got on the internet and researched, hoping to find some bad blood between the two clans, but I came up empty."

"Dad, you don't understand. I told Drew the whole story. He knows about the feuding between our families. You're telling me now that was all pure nonsense?"

"Yep."

"I made a fool of myself."

"Yep." My father sighed. "You wouldn't be the first person in the family to do that. But if it's any consolation, the Kincaids and the McDermotts are feuding now. At least, their businesses are. That's got to count for something, right? Though, to be honest, you and Drew looked pretty friendly at the party the other night. Not quite the cutthroat competitors I'd expected to see."

"Right."

He's a great guy. A great guy who isn't my clan's mortal enemy.

I couldn't help but feel a bit of relief as I realized the warring between the clans had never taken place. I didn't have to wield my sword or pretend to be strong when I felt like Jell-O on the inside.

Thinking of feeling weak reminded me of the situation with Sierra. Nausea gripped me again as I stared at the envelope on my desk, the one containing the papers.

Before hanging up, my father promised to pray for me, but he offered me the same sage advice I'd already received from Scarlet: "Don't sign that addendum."

"Trust me, I won't. It's too late, anyway." I glanced at the clock and sighed. "The deadline has passed."

"God has a plan." Dad's words were tinged with hopefulness. I latched on to it and tried to smile.

"I'm counting on it."

After ending the call, I decided to call Bella. She didn't answer, so I left a message, letting her know we needed to talk. *Maybe I should just take a chance and drive over to Club Wed. Meet with her in person.* Yes, handling this like a pro was the only thing that made sense.

Courage firmly in place and papers now in hand, I headed to my car. I pulled onto the Strand and turned on a side street, headed toward Broadway. As I drove past Drew's studio, my heart rate picked up. I stared at the sign on his front window, and something occurred to me. I could trust Drew Kincaid with this problem. He wouldn't use it to hurt me. In fact, he might just have the answers I needed.

I tapped the brakes, put on my signal, and turned into his parking lot, my heart in my throat. After checking my appearance in the rearview mirror, I got out of the car and walked to the front door of his studio. I'd just reached for the knob when the door swung open and a stream of customers came flooding out. Perfect timing.

I waited until they passed, then noticed Drew standing at the back of the pack, his hair ruffled by the breeze and drops of moisture clinging to his damp forehead. One lock of hair fell forward onto his face.

He glanced my way, clearly surprised by my unexpected arrival. "Hannah."

"Drew." I waited until he said his goodbyes to his clients, then took a step inside the studio door. "Do you have a few minutes?"

"Sure." He placed his hand on my arm and smiled. "Always happy to see you."

His words gave me the courage I needed.

"Hope you'll forgive the way I look. I've been back in my studio, and it's hot back there. I've been having so much trouble with the heater. Either it doesn't work at all or it heats the place up like an oven."

He led the way through the front office to a tiny room in the back, where he'd set up a small desk and computer. Not quite what I'd pictured, to be honest. Still, I didn't have time to focus on that right now.

"So, what's up?" he asked as we entered the tiny, cluttered office space, loaded on every side with filing cabinets.

"It's more a case of what's down." I leaned against his desk and sighed. "Or, who's down. And that would be me."

"You're down?" He took my hand. "Why?"

"Sierra Caswell."

A hint of a smile graced his face. "Well, at least you didn't say Jacquie Goldfarb this time."

"True. It's Sierra Caswell all the way. There's something I have to tell you. I . . . I can't photograph her wedding."

"What? You're serious?" He didn't look convinced.

"I am. Wish I wasn't. Something has happened and I need your help. But let me just say up front that you're probably going to end up shooting her wedding."

"Me?" He groaned and dropped his head in his hands. "I never wanted that gig."

"You didn't?"

"No. I'm not keen on superstars. They're too much to handle. Give me the ordinary people any day."

"Well, these folks are anything but ordinary, trust me."

"No doubt. Fill me in, Hannah. I want to help."

I was sure he did indeed want to help. Sinking into the chair in front of his desk, I poured out the story. I shared every available detail, adding more emotion than necessary, perhaps, but giving him the whole picture. The whole, ugly picture. I told him about the conversations I'd had with Sierra and the addendum I'd received. I shared with great passion all of my reasons for not signing.

Afterward, I stared into Drew's eyes—eyes filled with compassion—and released a deep sigh. "So, there you have it. I'm finished. Finito."

"So you speak Italian now?"

"Yes. If it means Sierra Caswell will disappear from my life altogether, I will say it in French or Thai or even Swahili."

"Wow." Drew's gaze narrowed. "This is serious. You're changing languages."

"And homes, if she comes looking for me." My nerves almost got the better of me as I thought about the possibilities of that actually happening. "Do you happen to know any place where I could crash for a few days? Someplace where they won't find me? Do you have a spare room, maybe?"

"Be serious. You don't really think she's going to come looking for you."

"No. She'll send George."

"George?"

"Her publicist. Did I forget to mention his name? He's the one who sent the addendum that I refused to sign, so he's the one they'll send. And it won't be pretty when he arrives. There might be attorneys involved. Well, if what he said was true, anyway. The man knows how to threaten a girl, that's for sure."

"That's nuts. You didn't sign the addendum, did you?"

"No."

His expression tightened. "Then you're only liable for what you did sign. They're manipulating you, Hannah. You can't fall for it."

"Too late."

"It's never too late." Drew took a seat behind his desk, suddenly all business. "Do you mind if I . . . I mean, would you feel comfortable having me . . ."

"Look over the contract?" I would never have considered such a thing before, what with Drew being my Jacquie Gold-farb and all, but right now the idea made perfect sense. If anyone would understand my dilemma, a fellow professional would.

I reached for my bag and pulled out the envelope that

contained the papers. Drew opened it and took his time looking over the papers, making comments along the way.

"Okay, see right there?" He pointed to the third paragraph of the original contract, the one I'd signed ages ago. "This contract protects not only Sierra and George, but you too."

"O-oh?"

"Yep. That's why they're so keen on getting you to sign the addendum. It adds a clause where you agree not to hold them liable. See the difference?" He pointed to the addendum. "In fact, it says just the opposite. They're trying to protect themselves, plain and simple, but apparently they don't give a rip about you."

I read it and pursed my lips. "Right. Well, I'm not signing."

"Don't. They've already got a signed contract. You're doing the pictures for the wedding."

"I told you, I don't want to. And I didn't sign the addendum, so I'm out. I missed the deadline."

"Wrong. It doesn't matter. You are still under contract to do the wedding, and they can't say otherwise. You're obligated to, in fact. Read the original contract again. You're the photographer for Sierra Caswell's wedding. Signed in ink, no less."

He grinned, but I didn't feel like joining him in the celebration. In fact, I felt nauseous just thinking about it. I glanced at Drew's desk, noticing a familiar glass-domed cake plate. Inside the dome, dozens of lovely little cake balls just waited for me to grab them.

Really, Scarlet? You've already stopped by with cake samples?

Then again, who could blame the girl for trying? Ready to

pacify myself with a nibble of Italian cream cake, I reached for the dome lid.

Drew's words stopped me cold. "I'll help you, Hannah."

"You . . . you will?" I pulled my hand away from the cake, intrigued by his offer.

"Under one condition. We have to get them to agree to play fair. You won't sign the addendum, but you will agree to perform your duties as originally agreed upon. I'll act as your assistant. They'll have to clear me to do so, but I'm sure they will, especially if Sierra has already mentioned me by name. We'll get some great shots and turn them in, just like they asked."

"But don't you see? They'll still release them to the media. And doing so will ruin my business." I eyed the cake once again, temptation setting in. I could probably eat five or six in one sitting. Then I'd feel better about all of this. Maybe.

"No it won't. If you don't sign the addendum, it doesn't matter. It's just their word against yours. I'm telling you, Hannah, the original contract protects you on every level."

"You're sure?"

"More than sure. But I'll have my attorney look it over if you like. He's really savvy, and I know he wouldn't charge me to glance at it." Drew's lips turned up in a delicious smile as he rose from his chair and stepped in my direction. "He's my cousin. A good Oirish boy named Kincaid."

"A good Oirish boy, eh?" Suddenly my spirits lifted. I rose and found myself standing near—very near—the only Irishman of interest at the moment. Who needed cake to feel better when I had something far more delicious standing in front of me?

"I promise, Hannah. We might be Kincaids. We might be mortal enemies. But we won't let you down."

"Oy. Speaking of which . . ." Time to come clean. My heart began to pound in my ears. "That whole story I told you about the McDermotts and Kincaids?"

"The bloody battles? The fighting and feuding?" He took a warrior's stance and then laughed.

"Yeah, well, about that . . . turns out it was all a lie." I looked at the floor. "A story my dad made up."

"Really?" Drew came close and slipped his arm around my waist. A tingle ran through me as he whispered, "So, you're saying there's no bad blood between us? Nothing to divide us—past, present, or future?"

"N-no."

"Well, that's good to know. Best news I've had all day, in fact." He pulled me close.

I tilted my gaze upward and stared into those gorgeous blue eyes, my pulse racing. With gentle fingertips, he cupped my chin and searched my upturned face, his eyes no longer teasing but filled with hope and longing.

In that instant, every bit of angst I'd ever felt—every twinge of jealousy toward Jacquie Goldfarb or any other—melted away in the joy of this moment. His lips met mine for a kiss that would've made for a perfect photograph, had we cared to capture it.

As the kiss deepened, as the sparks between us began to fly, the words to one of Grandpa Aengus's familiar little ditties went tearing through my brain. I couldn't help my giggles. Drew stopped kissing me and quirked a brow.

"Never knew I had that effect on a woman," he said. "Would've kissed you sooner if I'd known it would bring a smile to your face."

Oh, it brought a smile to my face, all right. My laughter started again, but I didn't bother to stop it. How could I?

Had this ridiculously awful day really ended here—in this glorious place? If so, what had I ever done to deserve it?

Hannah Grace, full of grace and truth.

Where the thought came from, I could not say.

Drew ran his finger along my cheek, sending a tingle through me until I got my emotions under control. Then, with upturned face, I planted a kiss on the boy sure to end any and all feuding . . . forever.

19

The Merry-Go-Run-Around

There was an old fellow at Trinity
Who solved the square root of infinity.
But it gave him such fidgets
To count up the digits
That he dropped math and took up divinity.

Irish limerick

All my life I'd made fun of those stupid romance movies—the ones with the heroine who swooned when the hunky hero pulled her into his arms. Still, as Drew planted half a dozen tiny kisses along my hairline, as he held me close, I reconsidered my position on swooning.

Or, rather, it reconsidered its position on me. For swoon I did.

About halfway into the second swoon my cell phone rang. Until the little "Danny Boy" ditty sounded, I'd almost forgotten about the whole situation with Sierra Caswell. I pulled the phone from my purse, and my heart sailed into my throat.

Bella.

I turned the phone so that Drew could see, and he nodded. "Answer it. You need to tell her."

I'd barely had time for a hello when Bella's anxious voice greeted me. "Hannah?"

"Yes, I—"

"I just had a call from George. You decided not to go ahead with the shoot for sure?"

"Well, actually—"

"I knew you were thinking about it, of course."

"Well, I tried to ca—"

"You should have told me. He said you didn't get the addendum signed in time. He's going to go with another photographer."

Finally gathering my wits about me, I tried to explain. "Bella, I called and left a message. And I was on my way to your place just now but got . . ." I gazed into Drew's dazzling blue eyes and fought the temptation to sigh aloud. "Distracted." Oh, but what a heavenly distraction.

Drew planted a couple of little kisses on my cheek, and I felt my face grow warm.

"You're coming now?" Bella's voice interrupted our little moment.

"Yes." Taking a step back from Drew, I attempted to gather my thoughts once again. We still had a battle to fight, a war to win. I'd wield my bloody sword, I'd . . . "I've got the contract, the addendum, and all of the emails that have gone back and forth between us. You can look over all of them if you like. I have no secrets." Well, other than the one in my arms right now.

"Just so you know, George and Sierra have already asked for Drew by name. So that's the plan, I guess. He'll be the one shooting the wedding."

I put my hand over the phone and whispered, "Sierra has asked for you."

Drew shook his head and extended his hand toward my phone, which I placed in his palm. He spoke with a firm voice. "Bella, you can tell them I won't do it, at least not without Hannah. I won't sign that addendum either. No professional would. It's completely irresponsible. Of course, an attorney could give us more detail, but I wouldn't advise my worst enemy to sign that, let alone someone I care about."

As he said the words "care about," he glanced my way and winked. My heart fluttered into my throat. Oh, how lovely it felt to have someone link arms with me. Someone to fight alongside me.

I couldn't hear the conversation from her end, but I tried to read Drew's expressions as he and Bella went back and forth. His arguments, unlike my own, were spoken with a steady, unemotional voice.

How does he do that?

Eventually he passed the phone back to me. I put it to my ear but kept a watchful gaze on Drew.

"Man. This is a mess." Bella sounded worn down. I didn't blame her. I felt that way too. Or at least I had until Drew kissed my troubles away.

"But the mess isn't on our end, Bella." I tried to sound as confident as Drew had. "And it's not our fault. What they're asking us to do isn't doable. They can try all day—all week, for that matter—but they're not going to find a photographer willing to sign his or her life away. Or career, I mean."

"Still, this fiasco involves Club Wed, so I'm caught up in

it, whether I want to be or not. You know George. He's . . .
well, I hate to admit it, but his conversation almost sounded
like a threat."

"His . . . what?"

"Yes."

I heard the catch in her voice and realized she was really
nervous. Ugh. Just what I'd been afraid of.

"I can't even imagine what's going to happen when Sierra
finds out," Bella continued. "George says that her reaction
could force him to take action against all of us. These are
powerful people. I'm trying not to get frightened, but I have
to admit this one's thrown me for a loop."

At once I slipped off into what I liked to call the white zone,
that hazy place where nothing makes sense. "But why? You
haven't done anything wrong."

"He holds me responsible. I'm the one who recommended
you."

"R-right." For a moment I felt fear snake its way down my
spine. Just as quickly I squared my shoulders and got back
to business. So what if the McDermotts of yesteryear ran
like cowards at the first sign of trouble? I didn't have to take
after them, now did I?

"He's full of hot air," I said. "And besides, he doesn't have
a leg to stand on. The reason no other photographer is free
to shoot the wedding is because I'm still legally bound by
the original contract."

"Are you sure?"

"Yes. Pretty sure, anyway." I glanced at Drew, who nodded.
"Not signing the addendum doesn't make the original null
and void. It just means that they can't hold me liable should
the photos get leaked."

"Okay." She paused. "Well, that's a horse of a different

color. But I'm still conflicted. And a little confused, to be honest."

"I think this is going to end well, Bella," I said. "I really believe that."

"I hope so." She released a breath. "Oh, and before I forget to tell you, Brock called today. He said the *Daily* is going to run a piece on him tomorrow. About the parade, not the wedding. So it's okay to let people know he's coming, just don't tell them he's also going to be in Sierra's wedding, okay?"

"Really?"

My mother would be ecstatic. I could hardly wait to tell her.

I heard Guido squawking in the background, and Bella groaned. "Hannah, I have to go. I'm not sure you would believe what Guido just did. I've got a mess to clean up. But bring me those papers. I'll look over them and we can talk. Okay?"

"I'm on my way. Be there in a few minutes."

I ended the call with Bella, faced Drew, and raised my fist, a mighty warrior. "Okay, here goes nothin'."

"Don't say that." He grabbed my hand and gave it a squeeze. "Where two or more are gathered . . ."

I knew the reference, of course. The Scripture about power in agreement. Well, amen to that.

"Here goes somethin'." I grinned.

Drew gave me a final kiss, then sent me on my way after I promised to call him as soon as I left Bella's. As I drove, a mixture of emotions swept over me—bliss at the very idea of Drew's kisses, and smidgeons of fear as I anticipated seeing Bella face-to-face.

I arrived at Club Wed to find her feeding Guido. Well, feeding Guido, taking care of a toddler's tantrum, and entertaining the three Splendora sisters, who, it turned out, were back on the island to rehearse for their upcoming gig at Dickens on the Strand. Great. How could I talk to her about something so important with so many people around?

The parrot went into his machine-gun spiel and scared the daylights out of me. This got a nervous laugh out of the Splendora sisters, who were apparently more versed in parrot than me. Twila shook her finger at him and recited the opening of a Scripture: "May the words of my mouth . . ."

"Be acceptable," Guido finished, then squawked.

"Wow. He's something else," I managed.

"Don't I know it. Sorry about his erratic behavior. I think he's just picking up on my nerves today." Bella sighed, then scolded the bird, waggling her finger in his face. "Guido, mind your manners."

"Guido, mind your manners," he echoed, then began to trill "Amazing Grace." In perfect pitch, no less.

Bonnie Sue's eyes filled with tears as she reached out to stroke the bird's back. "I don't think it has anything to do with you, Bella. Poor Guido's just missing Sallie so much." She choked out the next words. "*I* miss my Sallie so much."

The women gathered around her for a sympathetic hug and several well wishes.

"Bonnie Sue and Sal were only married a couple of years before he passed," Bella explained. "Took quite a toll . . . on Guido and Bonnie Sue."

No doubt. This put things in a whole new light.

I drew a bit closer. The parrot leaned forward and nuzzled my cheek, then gave me a peck on the cheek.

"Sure seems like we go through a lot in this life." Bonnie Sue dabbed at her eyes. "But I know God's got a plan for me, so I try not to fret."

"Troubles come and troubles go," Jolene threw in, "but we learn to stand strong in spite of them."

Standing strong. Sounded mighty good, especially in light of the strained look on Bella's face. I wondered if she would ask me to come back at a later time, all things considered, but she did not. Instead, she invited all of us into her office, where she asked the ladies to keep our conversation confidential.

Without giving away names or major details, Bella shared what we were facing. Twila took to fanning herself the moment the word *lawyers* came up. For that matter, I did too. The idea of battling Sierra's attorneys made me feel sick inside. Why did I feel like such a coward without Drew's arms around me?

After hearing the twisted tale, Bonnie Sue rose and paced the small office. She didn't say anything for a moment. Turning our way, she finally spoke her mind. "The key is to follow wholeheartedly after God and to listen to his voice. And I believe you have done that, Hannah. You haven't compromised your principles, and God will honor that. Watch and see."

"Thank you." I appreciated her vote of support. I felt a wave of confidence stiffen my backbone.

"I always say we should give God what's right, not what's left," Jolene said. "You've given him what's right. Now if we can just convince those folks of that."

"And with confidence, no less," Bonnie Sue added.

"That's the easy part, actually." Jolene reached over and put her hand on my arm. "Just look those folks in the eye and remember one of my favorite Scriptures: 'Be strong and courageous! Do not be afraid or discouraged. For the Lord your God is with you wherever you go.'"

"Oh, I know that one," Twila chimed in. "It's from one of my favorite Bible stories, the story of Joshua." She reached for her purse and came out with her cell phone. "Hang on a minute. I've got a Bible app on my phone. Perfect for moments like these."

"Are you talking about the story of Jericho?" I asked. "The one I learned in Sunday school as a kid?"

"Well, there is that. But the one I wanted to tell you about was Joshua's battle at a place called Ai." Twila thumbed around on her phone until she found what she was looking for.

"Ai? Never heard of that one."

"Yep." Twila's voice rose in intensity. "See, Joshua and his mighty men had already taken Jericho. But they ran into trouble at the next battle up in Ai. Looked for a while there like they weren't gonna be able to take those suckers down, but they won in the end. Want to know why?"

"Why?"

"Because God told Joshua to see himself as being victorious, even before the battle was won. Reminded him to look back at the battle he'd already won in Jericho so his confidence would be boosted. There's something about remembering your former victories that will stiffen your backbone."

"I see."

"Do you? Problem is, we don't always see ourselves as victors. We give in to defeat before we even give things a chance. We forget the battles we've already won in the past. Fear nabs us and holds us captive."

How many times had I let that happen?

Twila fumbled around on her phone again, finally smiling as she found the right verse. "God said to Joshua, 'You're gonna go on over there and do to Ai what you done did to Jericho.' He said, 'Fear not. Don't get the willies. Stiffen up yer backbone. Why? Because I'm gonna be with you.'" Twila paced the room, now preaching in a full voice. "'And don't you go worryin' about those fellas on the other side of the hill. I know they look like a mighty army, but greater are those who are with us than those who are against us. They won't be takin' us down anytime soon.'"

"Roughly translated, of course," Bonnie Sue said with a twinkle in her eye.

Twila pulled her arm back as if holding a weapon. "Joshua set his sights on the battle and pointed his spear toward that enemy."

"Are you sure he wasn't Irish?" I put my hands up and laughed. "Kidding, kidding."

"Pretty sure he was a Hebrew boy." Twila scratched her head. "But he didn't give up. That's the point. The fight stayed in him till the very end."

"He's soundin' more 'n' more like a good Oirish boy to me," I countered, my brogue intact. "If it's true, he fought till the end."

"Oh, he did, all right." Twila grinned. "Sure, he got scared. We all get scared. But God reminded him of the victories his people had already won in the past. There's something pretty exciting about knowing we've already been victorious once. Beefs us up for the next battle."

Well, amen to that!

"Promise me this, Hannah." She leaned forward and put her hands on my shoulders, gazing intently into my eyes. "Promise you'll not give in to defeat so easily from now on. Doesn't matter what your ancestors did or didn't do. Doesn't even matter what your parents or sisters do. You can make up your mind not to be defeated, even when you feel surrounded on every side. Change starts here." She pointed to her heart.

"And here." Bonnie Sue pointed to her head. At least I think it was her head and not her bouffant hairdo.

"Yes, ma'am," I said.

Suddenly I felt ten feet tall. No longer David facing the mighty Goliath, I saw myself as Joshua standing before the town of Ai. Okay, the town of Galveston. And instead of a spear, I held a digital camera. Still, the analogy held true in most every regard. It also gave me courage like I'd never felt before.

I glanced over at Bella, who had tears in her eyes. "I told you these ladies were something else," she said.

Indeed. No argument there. Any preconceived ideas I'd had about them were now gone, replaced by joy that they cared enough about me to share their hearts.

"Now we're gonna do what the Bible says we should," Twila said. "It's what we always do when we're up against a mighty army. We band together and pray. Where two or more are gathered together, there's power to knock your enemy's head off."

"Roughly translated," Bonnie Sue said with a wink. "But you get the idea."

I certainly did, and all the more as Twila began to pray. In my twenty-six years of living, I had never heard a woman pray the house down the way that woman did. She prayed with the energy and effervescence of an evangelist leading a sinner down the path toward home. Power laced each word—not a hyped-up, made-for-TV power, but true God-breathed energy.

I couldn't speak for Twila, but I was exhausted when her prayer ended. Well, exhausted and electrified. I couldn't remember ever feeling more spiritually charged. Jolene called it a Holy Ghost hangover, and I had to agree.

In that hazy state, I received a hug from Bella, along with her assurance that she would back me up all the way to the lawyer's office if need be. Hopefully it wouldn't come to that, but if it did, we were, as Twila called it, "prayed up and ready."

I thought about the story of Joshua all the way back to

the studio. It stayed with me as I worked and invigorated me for the journey ahead. Who cared if I faced a huge battle? I'd won many in the past, hadn't I? Hadn't the Lord already brought me this far?

Greater are those who are with us than those who are against us. Twila's words raced through my brain, bolstering my newfound confidence.

Change was coming to every area of my life. I could feel it—in the way I walked, the way I talked, the way I held myself. Yes, change was in the air. In my love life. My occupation. My attitude.

My first order of business when I reached the studio? To call Drew and fill him in. My second order of business? To shut down early and head home in time to help Mama cook dinner. Boy, would she be surprised to see me home so early, and loaded with great stories to boot.

I arrived at the house to find I wasn't the only one who'd received the memo to make some changes. I found my mother in the kitchen, cooking—of all things—ravioli. Her hair, usually salt-and-pepper, straight-cut at the shoulders, was now the prettiest shade of auburn I'd ever seen. I couldn't quite get over the difference in her appearance. She looked a good ten years younger.

"Mama?" I drew near and smiled, giddy with delight over what she'd done.

Her hands trembled as she reached up to swipe a loose hair out of her face. "What do you think your father is going to say? You know how much he hates change."

"Surely he will like this."

"Well, do what you can to distract him when he comes in, okay? I'd like to put this off as long as possible."

"Okay." I gave her the *Reader's Digest* version of my day,

then headed into the living room to await my father's arrival. I flipped on the news, got his newspaper ready, and fluffed the pillow on his recliner.

Strangely, six o'clock rolled around and he still hadn't shown up. A few minutes later I could hear the pots and pans in the kitchen, but still no sign of Dad. It just wasn't like him to arrive home late on a weeknight. In fact, I couldn't remember the last time it'd happened.

Dad buzzed through the front door at exactly ten minutes after six, looking winded.

"Dad, you're late."

"I, um, well, I stopped at the flower shop and picked up a little something." From behind his back he pulled out a bouquet of roses, so vibrant and red that they took my breath away. "Think your mama will like 'em?"

"Like them? She's going to flip! What's up? I didn't forget your anniversary, did I?"

"Nope. Just felt like getting the woman flowers. A man can get his wife flowers, can't he?"

Stop the world from spinning. I need to get off. Or at least check my compass to make sure I'm at the right house.

My father—my very predictable father—had done something unpredictable?

He put his finger to his lips and pointed to the kitchen. "I want to take these in to her before dinner and surprise her." He gave me a wink, then headed to the kitchen.

I'd just started to give him a heads-up related to Mama's new hairdo, but then decided to let him find out on his own.

Dad entered the kitchen, singing "Too-Ra-Loo-Ra-Loo-Ral" at the top of his lungs. For a moment, anyway. Just as quickly, he paused and stared at Mama, who turned toward us, a terrified look on her face.

His gaze never left my mother's hair, but he couldn't seem to speak. When he finally did, I hardly recognized his voice.

"M-Marie?" His voice cracked. "Is that you?"

Mama's face flamed, and suddenly, standing there with her auburn hair and pink cheeks, she looked twenty years younger. "It's me, Michael." Her eyelashes took to fluttering, and for the first time I noticed she was wearing mascara. "I, well, I . . ."

"Your hair." Just two words, but they spoke volumes. For that matter, so did the stunned look on his face. I'd never seen my father so perplexed. Or intrigued.

"Yes, well, you see, I've been thinking about this awhile, Michael. You're partial to my hair in its usual state, I know. But every time I looked in the mirror, I felt . . . old. I was ready for a change, honey." She brushed her hands against her apron and shrugged. "You know?"

"Well, you could've knocked me over with a shamrock." He kept staring. "Not quite sure what to do here."

"You could give me those flowers to start with." Mama giggled as she stretched out her hands. "I'm assuming they're for me?"

"They are." He took several slow steps in her direction and passed them off. She blushed all over again, and he leaned down to give her a little kiss on the cheek. "Not completely sure I'm kissing the right woman. Hardly recognize you. Still, I suppose someone will clue me in if I've got the wrong gal. I'm pretty sure the Bible frowns on me kissing someone other than my wife."

"Oh, you've got the right gal, all right." Mama sniffed the beautiful roses, her face just as red as they were. "I'm definitely your wife. Same as always."

"Hardly." He scratched his head as he gave her another look. "Well, you've put me in a real pickle here."

"Oh?"

"Yes. How in the world am I supposed to remember your birthday when you're looking younger by the minute?"

That got a chuckle out of her, and soon my parents were kissing and giggling. I backed out of the room to give them some privacy.

I thought back to that precious moment in Drew's studio when he'd first pulled me into his arms. How strong I'd felt. That same feeling of strength had washed over me afresh when Twila and the other Splendora sisters prayed with me. And now, as I watched my parents embrace, I realized the truth: there really is strength in numbers. No matter what I faced in this life, I could handle it with the people I loved surrounding me.

20

Don't Let the Stars
Get in Your Eyes

May you have the hindsight to know where you've been,
The foresight to know where you're going,
And the insight to know when you're going too far.

Irish proverb

With my parents lip-locked, I headed upstairs, realizing we wouldn't be having dinner anytime soon. I threw myself on the bed, my thoughts fully on the events of the day. Strange how one day could change everything. Not that I minded. Oh no. Change was good. Very good.

The smell of garlic permeated the whole house. Very odd, indeed. I could hardly wait for dinner. Still, as Bing Crosby crooned "Embraceable You" from the stereo downstairs, I knew better than to interrupt my parents, whose laughter and jovial conversation wafted up the stairway from the kitchen below. Heaven only knew what I might walk in on.

Sometime around 6:20 the doorbell rang. I sprinted down the stairs and swung the door open, thrilled to find Drew on the other side.

"Well, hello," I said. I couldn't help the smile that followed. Something about the boy just made me giddy.

"Hello to you too." His grin clued me in to the fact that he was happy to see me too. "I probably should've called first."

"Don't be silly." My mother's voice rang out from behind me. "You're always welcome, Drew." She gestured for him to step inside.

Drew raked his fingers through his hair, a sheepish look on his face. "I hope you don't mind, but Mom asked me to stop by and get her Crock-Pot."

Sure she did. Silly boy.

"Of course, of course." My mother ushered him inside. "Would you like to stay and have dinner with us?" Her eyes twinkled. "I did the unthinkable. I made ravioli."

"Really?" He looked stunned at this news. As he drew in a breath, I could see a "gosh, that smells great" expression on his face. Still, he didn't offer to stay.

"I know, I know." A smile lit her face. "But don't you fret. Michael already knows and he's fine with it, so there won't be a scene. In fact, I think he might even learn to like it. Hope so, anyway."

Drew grinned. "I'm sure it's going to be great, but I really can't stay. Mom's in the car waiting."

"Well, that will never do." Mama scurried out the door, and moments later Corinne entered.

Before long the two women were thick as thieves in the kitchen, serving up a huge bowl of steamy ravioli and pulling hot, buttery garlic twists from the oven. Drew and I could hardly get a word in edgewise as they chatted, Corinne going on and on about Mama's new look. Not that I cared to speak. Something about the smell of garlic on that hot bread nearly rendered me speechless.

We settled in at the table, and my father led the way with a heartfelt prayer. It wasn't quite the same as Twila's prayer, but close. Well, as close as Michael McDermott could come, anyway. After he prayed, Mama passed the ravioli and he gave it a funny look, but he scooped some onto his plate.

"Guess I'd better give this a shot if I want to go on living with the prettiest woman on the island." He gave Mama a wink, and we all held our breath as he took a bite of the ravioli. His eyes widened. "What do you call this stuff again?"

"Ravioli," we all said in unison.

"Remarkable." He took another bite. "You're sure it wasn't invented by an Irishman?"

"Very sure," I said, laughing. "Do you like it?"

"I'm ashamed to admit that I do. Can't believe I've been missing out all these years." He pointed to the serving bowl. "Pass that back over here. Didn't take a big enough serving."

This, of course, made my mother's night. She lit into a fun conversation about the Food Network, and before long we were all talking about Rosa and Laz's show, Mama going on and on about her favorite episodes. She somehow convinced my father to try several other Italian foods over the upcoming weeks, including her favorite, fettuccine Alfredo. Would wonders never cease?

We laughed and talked all the way through dinner. As I

glanced across the table at Drew, as I took in the joy on his mother's face, I flashed back to that day at Bella's house. Seated around her table with so many people gathered around her, I'd felt envious. Now I was living the same life. Okay, a similar life. With ravioli on the plate, no less.

For some reason, this got me tickled. I had to laugh.

"What's up, Shutter Speed?" my dad asked, giving me a funny glance. "You okay?"

"More than okay, actually." I took Drew's hand and gave it a squeeze under the table. He squeezed back, a sure sign that he was enjoying the evening too.

At ten minutes till seven, my father dabbed his mouth, swallowed down the last of his glass of tea, and rose. "Better hurry."

"Hurry?" Mama moved the dirty dishes to the kitchen.

"Well, sure. That stupid dancing show is on in a minute or two."

The whole room grew silent, and we all stared at him.

"Since when do you care about *Dancing with the Stars*?" I asked.

"Who said I cared? Just curious, that's all. Wondering what Brock Benson is going to do tonight. He got the first ten of the season last week, you know."

"Right." I could hardly believe my father had taken note of that.

It didn't take much to convince Corinne and Drew to stay to watch the show, especially with my father on board.

"I've been a fan of Brock Benson's ever since Drew photographed his wedding." Corinne dabbed her lips with her napkin. "Was there ever a more handsome man in the world?"

"Tell me about it." Mama fanned herself, and my father rolled his eyes.

Instead of clearing the table, Mama and Corinne went straight to the living room, pausing only long enough for my mother to show off a new picture of my sister's baby girl.

I rose and began to put the dishes in the kitchen sink. Drew followed me. When we found ourselves alone in the kitchen, he slid his arms around my waist and pulled me close. After giving me a gentle kiss on the forehead, he whispered, "I've been dying to do that all night."

"I've been dying for you to do that all night," I countered, then gave him a kiss on the lips, guaranteed to tide us over until after the show.

By now the sound of our parents' voices rang out from the living room. I popped my head through the door and offered to make coffee. This got a nod from Mama, but her eyes never left the TV.

Minutes later, coffee cups in hand, Drew and I joined them. I took a different place on the loveseat than usual, wanting to give him the better spot. He took it and gave me a wink. Out of the corner of my eye I caught a glimpse of my father as he gave us both a sideways glance. No doubt he would have some questions about my sudden affinity for a Kincaid. I didn't mind, though. Couldn't wait to tell him, in fact.

Settling into my spot, I glanced at the television in time to see Brock coming down the steps with Cheryl on his arm. They were both dressed as pirates. Behind them, the speed skater made his entrance along with his partner, a pretty blonde.

My dad groaned. "For the life of me, I don't understand why that skater is still on there. He's lousy. He fell flat on his face last week and got the lowest scores in the competition."

We all turned to face my dad. He shrugged and said, "What?"

"You've actually been watching, then?" my mama asked.

"Of course not." He reached for his newspaper and opened it. "You all know I wouldn't be caught dead watching a dancing show."

"Mm-hmm." I laughed.

"So what's on the agenda for tonight?" Corinne asked. "Why is Brock in a pirate costume?"

"I'm not sure. I did hear that he and Cheryl are starting with the Viennese waltz," I said. "Must be pirate themed, I guess."

"Ooh, the waltz." My mother sighed. "I just love a good waltz."

"You do?" My father looked amused by this.

"Mm-hmm. And I'm sure Brock will do a great job. He's so—"

"Dreamy," Corinne interjected, then sighed. "I know. I agree."

Drew let out a grunt and focused on the television.

Brock and Cheryl's lead-in package ran, focusing on their antics in the rehearsal room and talking about their characters.

"How cool is that?" I said after hearing the details. "They're reviving Brock's character from his most famous movie, *The Pirate's Lady.*"

Mama released an exaggerated sigh. "That's my favorite movie of all time. He played Jean Luc Dumont, the pirate we all loved to hate."

"I remember that one," Corinne said. "The whole thing was sort of a play on the old *Taming of the Shrew* theme. He looked great in his pirate costume then, and he looks just as great now."

"Wait." My father put the newspaper down. "You're telling me that's the same guy from all of those pirate movies?"

"Well, of course, Dad. I thought you knew that."

My father shook his head. "I guess I do see the resemblance."

"He could capture me and take me aboard the ship, and I wouldn't breathe a word of argument." Corinne released a contented sigh.

Brock and Cheryl took their places center stage, and the camera zoomed in on his face.

I chose that moment to drop my bombshell. "Dad. Mama. There's something I need to tell you."

"What's that, Hannah?" Mama didn't look away from the television.

"Brock Benson." I pointed at the screen as the music for their dance began. "He's coming here."

"What?" Mama paled, and Corinne nearly dropped her cup of coffee.

"Here, to our house?" Mama reached for the remote and paused the television show midstream.

"Looking for a new dance partner?" my father asked.

"No. He's coming to serve as grand marshal at the Dickens parade."

"Oh my goodness." Mama fanned herself. "Well, I read in the paper that we had a special guest star coming to lead the parade, but I never guessed it would be Brock Benson."

"The *Daily* is doing a piece on him tomorrow," I said. "So everyone will know after that. But I wanted to give you a heads-up. Now you can say you heard it first."

"How do you know this?" My father's gaze narrowed.

"Well, I'm not at liberty to say." I grinned. "But you can trust me on this. Brock is coming. And I'm going to do my best to get us a private audience with him."

At this news, I thought my poor mama was going to have

heart palpitations. She began to fan herself, then rose and paced the room, going on and on about how she'd colored her hair just in time.

"Only one thing I can't figure out," Corinne said. "If he makes it through this week of *Dancing with the Stars*, how can he be in two places at once?"

"Yeah, how does that work?" my dad asked.

"I'm sure he'll make it past this week, and if he does it's likely he'll be looking for a place to rehearse while he's here."

"You mean he might bring his dance partner with him?" My father seemed to like this idea.

"Who knows? I'm sure his wife will be with him."

"Erin's great," Drew said. "You're going to love her."

"I've seen her pictures in the tabloids," I said. "And I've followed her character on *Stars Collide*. But what's she like in person?"

He grinned. "She's very . . . bubbly. Fun. One of those overly dramatic types, but in a good way. They seem like a good match."

Funny. As I heard the words "a good match," I realized I'd finally met mine.

"Erin and Brock are both interested in helping people in need. Unlike most Hollywood celebrities, they focus less on politics and they're both people of faith. No doubt about that."

Wow. Made me want to meet Brock even more.

But first we needed to watch him dance the waltz. Mama grabbed the remote and pressed Play. Soon all of the ladies were sighing and the men were rolling their eyes.

The rest of the show passed in record time. When the final dancer took the stage, my cell phone rang. I reached for it, surprised to see Bella's number. My heart sailed to my throat as I anticipated what she might say. Just as quickly, I calmed down. I thought about Joshua at Ai and got a visual of Twila praying the house down earlier today. With a woman like that on my team, I could face any news Bella might have for me.

Drew gave me an "everything okay?" look as I scooted out of the room, and I nodded to reassure him. Once inside the safety of the kitchen, I took the call.

"Hey, Hannah." Bella's voice rang out. "Glad I caught you. Sorry to call during *Dancing with the Stars*. I know it's a mortal sin."

"Actually, I believe it's a cardinal sin, but I don't suppose that matters." I chuckled, relieving the tension between us.

"Just wanted you to know that I called our attorney."

"You . . . you what?"

"I called our attorney. Actually, he's my second cousin twice removed. But having a good attorney comes in handy during situations like this. Just wanted you to know that you were right. Sierra and her publicist don't have a leg to stand on. So don't sign the addendum. Stick with the original and we'll move forward, no matter what they threaten to do. If George kicks back on this, I'll get the attorney involved. But I doubt I'll have to do that."

Relief trickled through me, and I suddenly felt as if I'd lost twenty pounds—ten from each shoulder.

"Are you . . . are you mad at me?" I asked. "I never meant to cause any trouble, I promise you."

"Of course not." She paused. "I'll admit, I kind of panicked when I thought about what George might do. He's pretty intimidating. But I know Sierra better than that. She's a great girl."

"Humph." Might be better not to chime in here.

"No, really. She's a diva for sure. And a little flighty too. But I'm telling you, the reason she's been so picky about the photos is because she listens too much to what George has to say. All it took was a phone call to Sierra to straighten this whole thing out. Once she figured out what George was asking you to do, she changed the plan."

"Really? Is she mad?"

"You worry too much about whether or not people are mad. She's not, by the way. But I want you to know that they still plan to release the photos, only now they won't say they were released against her will. It will all be done in the open, and you'll be given credit for your photos, wherever they appear."

"No one will think I went behind her back?"

"Not at all. And she's fine with that."

"You're sure?"

"Definitely." Bella sighed. "Hannah, the truth is, she's so caught up in the wedding plans that she's overwhelmed. That's all."

"Still . . ."

"She's a bride, Hannah. Brides miss most of the details of everyday life when they're in wedding-planning mode. I'll tell you, a bride-to-be's house could go up in flames and she would only think about one thing—making sure she didn't lose her guest list. Or her gown. Or her shoes." Bella laughed. "There's just so much to keep up with. That's why people hire me, so I can fret over that stuff for them."

"You've worked with a few overwhelmed brides, I see."

"More than a few. And I've handled my share of crises, but none that could've ended up in a courtroom—till now. Well, unless you count that time Brock and I ended up in jail, but that's kind of an anomaly."

"Thank goodness." I grinned. "Because I thought for a while there that I might end up in some serious legal trouble if I signed that addendum."

"You probably would have. Thank God you had the foresight not to sign."

Indeed. I thanked God for that little detail as we ended the call. And as Drew and I said our goodbyes less than an hour later—our parents looking on—I thanked God for him as well. And for parents willing to change. And for ravioli. Basically, for every good thing the day had brought my way.

Minutes after saying good night, I headed up to my room and reached for my laptop, curious to glance at my email to see if George had ever responded. He hadn't, but I saw a note from Jacquie Goldfarb. Weird. Signing onto Facebook, I sent her an instant message.

"I'm here now. What's up?"

Took a minute to get a response, but she finally came back with, "Me. Having trouble sleeping tonight."

I thought about my words before typing, "Aw, sorry."

"You?" she typed in response.

"Just finished dinner with the family." I fought the temptation to add, "And the guy I'm crazy about."

She responded with "*sigh*."

"Why the sigh?" I asked.

"Oh, just the mention of your family, that's all. You might as well know, I was always so jealous of your family."

I stared at the screen, blown away by what she'd written. I finally managed one word in response: "What?"

"You had the perfect life. A great family. Wonderful sisters."

True. But she'd never hinted at being jealous of my life before. Why now?

"I was so jealous I couldn't see straight." She followed this with a smiley face, though I had a feeling she wasn't smiling as she typed.

"Wait." None of this made sense. "You were jealous of me?"

After you got every position I ever wanted and ended up with my date to the prom?

"Well, yeah, you had the one thing I didn't—parents who loved you. And sisters. I had a mom who didn't think anything I did was good enough, a dad who was away on business trips most of the time, and a brother who basically made my life miserable. So from where I was sitting, your life looked pretty ideal."

She ended up signing off after that, but her words stuck with me as I dressed for bed. In all the years I'd known her, it had never occurred to me that Jacquie Goldfarb might be jealous of me. I could hardly comprehend such a thing. It stood in direct opposition to everything I'd believed about the girl.

A mixture of emotions danced through me as I snuggled into bed. When I closed my eyes, I saw the day in little snatches, sort of like a string of photos. There was the shot of George's email and the shiver that ran through me as I read it. There was the snapshot—a close-up—of Drew kissing me. Yum. Then the shot of driving to Bella's. Next came the shot with me holding a spear in hand, pointed in victory as Twila prayed the house down. This was followed by a snapshot of the McDermott and Kincaid clans eating ravioli. An odd photo, indeed.

The last frame—well, that was the one that threw me a little. In that one, I saw a weary Jacquie Goldfarb, tearstained cheeks and sad countenance, seated at her computer, completely alone. Somehow, that last little glimpse put everything else in perspective.

21

Once in a Blue Moon

Blessed are those who can laugh at themselves,
For they will never cease to be amused.

Irish saying

I couldn't remember spending a happier holiday season. Thanksgiving approached and I found more than usual to be thankful for. We celebrated with all of my sisters and their children, but we also invited Drew and his mother, who took to them with both joy and ease. My sisters gave me the thumbs-up once they got to know Drew. Deidre even called him my perfect match. So much for my years of envying my younger sisters for their picture-perfect lives. Looked like my days of "almosts" were truly behind me. Now, to conquer that wedding and move forward with my life and my business, apart from diva country singers.

The week after Thanksgiving, Galveston Island prepared herself for the annual Dickens on the Strand event. You couldn't go anywhere on the island without feeling the Victorian celebration of Christmas. I always loved this time of year. So much so that I decided to do some over-the-top decorating at my studio so it would match the other businesses in the area.

Capping off the holiday for me? I would get to meet Brock Benson in person. My thoughts turned to mush every time I thought about it. Not that I cared to replace my hunky Drew with the handsome dancing/singing/acting star. Oh no. Brock Benson might be superstar material, but he couldn't hold a candle to my guy.

On the day before Brock's arrival, I drove to my studio early in the morning, anxious to tidy up and then deal with the day's work in a hurry. A heavier-than-usual agenda included a morning photo shoot involving twin baby girls. In Christmas attire, of course. They arrived early, and I dove right in, catching some of the best shots imaginable.

Around eleven, just after wrapping up the shoot, I received a phone call that caught me off guard. I didn't recognize the number on the phone right away, but I took the call anyway. The words from the other end of the line threw me a little.

"George is gone."

"What?" I struggled to recognize the voice on the other end of the line. Didn't sound like Bella.

"George. My publicist. He's gone. I fired him."

Sierra Caswell . . . calling me? Personally?

"You . . . you did?" *But George handles everything for you.*

"Yeah." She sighed. "If you want the truth, he was all about promoting me, not about caring for the real me."

Well, that's kind of what a publicist does.

Still, I couldn't argue with the fact that letting him go was the best news I'd heard in a while. Thankful that my clients had already gone, I settled into my chair and leaned back, anxious to hear what she might say.

"So it's just us now, Hannah," Sierra said, her usual practicality waning. "And I might as well tell you that the whole music video at the wedding thing . . ."

I pulled the phone a bit closer to listen.

"Ain't happenin'." She chuckled. "Every time I mentioned it to David, he looked like he wanted to hurl. I mean, the guy can hardly stand being on camera under the best of circumstances. Apparently the idea of landing in the middle of a music video on our wedding day was giving him cold feet and he was too afraid to tell me." She giggled. "Can you imagine someone you love being that afraid to tell you what they really feel?"

"Actually, I can. I tend to run on the overly cautious side too. When it comes to sharing what's on my heart, I mean."

"Really?" She laughed. "I guess I'm the sort to just blab whatever's on my mind. Maybe that's why George was paranoid about protecting me, because he knows me so well. I guess, on some strange level, he was really looking out for me."

"I'm sure he was." *At everyone else's expense.*

"Anyway, I'm glad David finally told me what he was feeling. It helps to know we're just having a wedding and nothing more. The whole thing was starting to feel a little surreal."

Tell me about it.

"So here's what I'm thinking. I know we said you couldn't photograph me from the left side. But honestly, I kind of like my crooked nose. George wasn't into letting people see my imperfections, but I don't mind them. I want my fans to know me and love me for who I really am. If I go on hiding my flaws, they'll fall in love with someone who isn't real. You know?"

"I do." *More than you can imagine.*

"Hey, and speaking of keeping it real, I want you to know that David and I are coming down for this parade thing that Brock's going to be in. I'll be staying at Bella's place. David is going to stay at the Tremont."

"Seriously?"

"Yep. Our rehearsal dinner is that same night, you know, so we'll be there already. Might as well go to the parade. I haven't been to Dickens on the Strand before, so give me some ideas of fun things we can do while we're there."

Sierra Caswell was asking me for advice? Outside the realm of photography? Girlfriend to girlfriend? Crazy.

"There's no better season on Galveston Island than Christmas." I closed my eyes and could almost envision it. "The whole thing is like a picture book. Like stepping back in time. Imagine a Victorian Christmas, one with music and costumes and food and every good thing."

"Sounds amazing," she said. "So, I should show up in a costume?"

"Well, you get in free if you do." Not that Sierra Caswell needed to get in free, but whatever.

"What do we do, though?"

"Shop, mostly. And eat. We have the best funnel cakes in the world. There's a costume showcase. You can win all sorts of prizes for dressing up as the Loveliest Lady or the Best-Dressed Family. That sort of thing."

"Sounds like fun."

"Oh, it is. My grandpa Aengus won the Most Dapper Gent contest once, years ago. The cool part is, if you win, you get to show off your costumes in Pickwick's Lanternlight Parade.

But if you're not really into coming in costume, don't worry about it. There's plenty to do. They've got madrigal music, live musicians, jugglers . . ."

I went off on a rabbit trail about the jugglers, but then worked my way back to the topic at hand. "Oh, and some couples even get married at Dickens on the Strand. There's always a group wedding at noon on Saturday. You can get married there or renew your wedding vows. Whatever you like."

She laughed. "Well, if things get any crazier with my wedding, I might go that route. Sure would be easier than planning my own ceremony."

I couldn't help but laugh. "Well, look on the bright side. You won't ever have to go through this again."

"You're right." She sighed. "I can't wait for you to meet David. He's the best. He's been through so much, being engaged to me. You have no idea how stressful it is, especially with the paparazzi involved. Sometimes I wish I could go back to the way things were before any of this fame stuff ever started." She paused. "Not that I'm complaining, mind you. I feel so . . . lucky."

"No such thing as luck, girl. I'd have to say you're blessed. Or as my grandpa Aengus would say, 'Blessed by the best.'"

She laughed. "Is your grandpa a Texan?"

"He lived in Texas, but his heart was still in Ireland."

Her voice softened. "Has he passed away?"

"Yeah." A catch in my throat made me stop. "I . . . I miss him a lot."

"I miss my grandfather too. He was always so good at giving me advice. I didn't always take it, but his heart was in the right place."

"Mine too."

We both sighed in unison and then laughed.

"Didn't mean to get off on all that," she said. "I just wanted to give you a call and tell you about George. I've already told Bella. She's happy, I think."

Me too. But I wouldn't say that out loud.

At this point the conversation continued to how cute Bella's children were. I filled her in on the details of little Rosie's new tooth. Before long I had Sierra laughing with some of my stories about the antics the Rossi children had pulled.

Just before we ended the call, I thought of something I'd better share. "Hey, do you mind if I ask a favor?"

"Sure."

"You remember Drew Kincaid?" I asked.

"Of course. You're not still worried that I'm going to hire him instead, are you?" she asked. "I feel really bad for telling you all of that."

"No, just the opposite, in fact. I want to ask if it's okay for him to help me out at your wedding."

"No way. I get two for the price of one?"

I chuckled. "Yeah, I guess you could say that. Drew and I are . . . well, we're . . ."

"No way. You're dating?" She let out a squeal and lit into how cool it was to have both of us on the same team. I couldn't agree more.

As we prepared to end the conversation, I thanked Sierra for sticking with me. She countered with, "Girl, it's the right thing. I can feel it. I can't wait to meet you in person, by the way. You seem like my kind of girl."

"You . . . you too."

Who knew? The diva wasn't such a diva after all. Bella had been right all along.

After ending the call, I raced to Drew's studio to tell him all about my day, especially as it pertained to Sierra's wedding plans. I found him under the sink in the bathroom, working on the pipes, his hair a mess and smudges of dirt all over his face.

"What's happening here?" I asked.

He groaned and sat up, nearly smacking his head as he did. "Same thing as before, only worse. The plumbing is shot. When the freeze hit last night, the pipes froze and then split off at the seams. I had a water leak like you wouldn't believe. Water went under the wall and soaked my office. Almost ruined the power adapter leading to my computer."

"Oh no. You caught it in time?"

"Just." He crawled out from under the sink and raked his fingers through his messy hair. "It doesn't make any sense, as much as I pay to rent this place. You would think they'd take better care of things. I've tried talking to my landlord, but he just loads me up on more stories of things he's going to do next week. But next week never comes."

"It's an old building," I observed. "Probably needs a complete overhaul."

"Yeah, plumbing, electrical . . . everything." Under the sink, the steady *drip*, *drip*, *drip* of water sounded, and Drew groaned again. "It's not 'quaint old,' like your place. Far from it, in fact."

I shrugged, unsure of what to say. My heart went out to him.

"Just seems like a lot of money with little to show for it."

"I've got the same problem. Sort of, anyway. I pay a lot for my studio but don't spend much time there. So much of my work is out on location. Weddings, family events, personal photos. I only spend about half of my time indoors, if that."

"Same here."

He appeared to be thinking—I knew it because the tiny

crevices between his eyes deepened. After a moment he snapped his fingers. "Hannah, that's it."

"W-what?"

"We should share an office space. I've got some great backdrops. You've got a great location. I've got a wonderful marketing strategy. You've got the best ambience in town. We both do at least half of our work outside the studio, so we wouldn't be tripping over each other."

My heart raced as I pondered his words. "I—I'm not sure what you're saying. You think we can run two separate businesses out of one location? Won't that confuse people?"

"No." He grabbed my hand and gave it a squeeze. "Not two businesses. One business."

"One business?"

Was he talking about merging . . . everything? At this news, I wanted to sit down. Only, I couldn't find a chair that didn't have some sort of plumbing supply on it.

"Think about it, Hannah. It would be half of the rent but double the proceeds. We'd have each other to lean on. If I didn't have time for a shoot, you could cover it, and vice versa."

"I don't know, Drew." Releasing a slow breath, I began to pace the room.

But the idea did hold some merit. With the rent on my place so high, splitting it down the middle would give me some breathing room. I wouldn't have to depend on large photo shoots to cover my expenses. We could split them. And who better to split them with?

"We've competed against each other for too long." He drew near and took my hand again, which caused a delicious shiver to wriggle its way down my spine. "We need to be working with each other, not against. We can pull from each other's strengths."

I had to admit, the idea held merit. How long had I searched for the chink in his armor so that I could bring him down? If we merged forces, I could let all of that go.

Merge forces. Hmm.

Gazing into Drew's gorgeous baby blues, I had to conclude one thing: letting go of my competitive spirit was getting easier every day. No telling what Grandpa Aengus would say . . . but did it really matter?

"Okay, I like this idea," I said after a moment's reflection. "But I have to ask you something first. And answer me honestly."

"Of course."

"I just have to know . . . do you put your business first?"

He shrugged. "I would guess that most new business owners do, especially those who don't have large families. I mean, I've got no siblings to distract me, ya know?"

I laughed. "I have three married sisters, two parents who know every detail of my life, and a best friend who still thinks that having a slumber party is a good idea. I'm drowning—at home and at work. I want to give 100 percent on all fronts, but there are only so many 100 percents you can give before you realize there's nothing left. And I hate to admit it, but I feel pretty . . . I don't know . . . blah inside. Sometimes, anyway. I mean, I'm energized about the business to the point of thinking about it nonstop. But I don't have as much energy left over to give to some of the things that really matter. Or, rather, things that used to matter."

A wave of guilt washed over me as I remembered how much I used to enjoy taking photos at church, or going on mission trips. "Years ago, I would've been out on the streets at Christmastime, doing outreaches with the homeless. Now I'm so busy taking pictures of people who have everything that

I don't see the people who have nothing. It's like I've cropped that image out of my life. I can try as hard as I want, but in the end, something's gotta give."

"I hear ya." He held up his wrench and sighed. "It's too much, isn't it?"

"Yeah. And the real reason I asked if you put your business first was because I'm tired of doing that." My words came with more passion now. "I want my life to be about God first. And then the people he's put in my path. And then, somewhere down the line, the business."

"I totally agree with that, Hannah. And I think we would hold each other accountable, don't you?"

I nodded as I thought it through. "So, you're serious?" I asked. "Because if we merge forces, there's no turning back. Not if we get mad at each other. Not if one of us has a bad day. Not if one of us outshines the other."

"Hey, I'm counting on you outshining me." He grinned. "Won't hurt my feelings a bit."

"I doubt that." I slipped into his outstretched arms and gave him a gentle kiss on the cheek, overwhelmed by the feelings of peace that enveloped me. So much for the so-called feuding between the McDermotts and the Kincaids. We'd put an end to that tall tale once and for all.

"Want to talk about all of this over a pizza?" He flashed a boyish smile. "I'm starved."

"I thought you'd never ask."

We got into his car and headed to Parma John's, and my phone beeped. I glanced down to see that a message had come through.

"Anything important?" Drew asked.

"Not sure." I opened it, and my heart flew to my throat as I read the note from Jacquie Goldfarb.

"Everything okay over there?" Drew looked concerned.

"Um, yeah." I closed the phone and leaned back against the seat, my thoughts in a whirl.

Oh. Help.

"So . . ."

"Not sure you would believe me."

"Try me." Drew's brow creased, and I could read the concern in his eyes.

"It's Jacquie Goldfarb," I whispered. "She's coming back to Galveston for Dickens on the Strand, and she wants to see me."

22

Learn to Croon

May the road rise to meet you.
May the wind be always at your back.
May the sun shine warm upon your face.
May the rains fall soft upon your fields,
    and until we meet again,
May the Lord hold you in the palm of His hand.

Irish blessing

A girl never forgets two things: the day she started her period for the first time, and the day she met the love of her life. In my case, adding a third life-changing event was unavoidable. The day I met Brock Benson in person.

I'd prepped for this, of course. Had rehearsed what I'd say when introduced. Practiced the angles I'd use to shoot his photos, based on internet pictures I'd found of him. All of this I'd done. But somewhere along the way I'd forgotten to remember that he was just an ordinary guy. Well, maybe not ordinary like my predictable dad, but ordinary in his own Hollywood-esque way. Just a regular guy, according to my awesome and irresistible Drew—who, it turned out, was anything *but* a regular guy.

Bella invited us to her place to meet Brock a couple of hours before the parade began on the first Saturday in December. Drew did the driving, what with me being so nervous and all.

"You okay over there?" He glanced at me from behind the wheel as I touched up my mascara.

"Hmm?" I giggled. "Oh, um, yeah." Unfortunately, I lost control of the mascara wand at about that time and left a big smudge on my right cheek.

Drew rolled his eyes. "I don't know if I should be jealous or just very, very aware."

"Aware?" I reached for a tissue and did my best to remove the mascara, but it didn't want to budge.

"That you're twitterpated."

"Who taught you that word?" I looked away from the mirror and straight at him.

"Who do you think?" He wrinkled his nose and pointed at my face. "Oh, and you've got a little something right there."

"I know, I know." More swiping continued until I left a red patch under my eye. Black and red. Great combo. Now it looked like I'd been punched. "Well, I'm not twitterpated. I guess you could just say I'm starstruck. I've been a fan of Brock's ever since . . ." Visions of his earlier pirate movies flooded over me. And his most recent episode in *Stars Collide*. And that gorgeous, graceful Viennese waltz on *Dancing with the Stars*. "Well, for a while." A lingering sigh escaped.

"He's married, you know."

I slugged Drew in the arm. "I know. Don't be silly. I don't

like him like that. I just . . ." Another deep, lingering sigh. "Admire him."

"From afar."

"Only, not so far today." I giggled and gave my reflection another glance. "Because I'm going to get to meet him in person."

"Looking like you just came out of the ring after facing Muhammad Ali."

"That bad, huh?" I groaned and wiped the mascara smudge with my tissue once more.

"Nah. Just kidding. It's looking better by the minute."

He turned his attention back to the road and began to whistle a little ditty. It took me a minute to recognize the theme song to *Stars Collide*. This reminded me of Sierra Caswell. If everything went as planned, I would meet her today as well. And again tonight at her wedding rehearsal. This would be a day for the record books, for sure.

By the time we arrived at Bella's house, Mama had texted me seven times, Scarlet nine. I had promised both that I would do my best to arrange a private audience with Brock, but I couldn't be sure that would actually happen. Unless Bella intervened, of course. Then again, she was already doing me a favor by inviting me over to meet him.

She and D.J. met us on the veranda of the Rossi home, children in tow. The baby's face lit up the moment she saw me, so Bella placed her into my outstretched arms. Drew knelt down and scooped up Tres, then began to wrestle with him.

Before long they were laughing so hard that Bella put a finger to her lips. "Shh. Don't want my family to know what we're up to out here."

"What do you mean?" Drew rose and gave her a curious look.

"Well, they know something's stirring, but they aren't sure what. I just told Rosa to make an extra-special breakfast because we're having company. She has no idea who or she would've flipped."

"No way. You kept it a secret all this time?"

"I can't believe it, but I did. Nobody around here seems to read the paper or they would've known."

D.J. chuckled. "I nearly blew it for her last night. Said something about Brock's scores on *Dancing with the Stars* and how his travels might affect his ability to perform well this coming Monday night."

"Anyway, I don't think anyone suspects it's Brock coming." Bella slipped her arm through D.J.'s and grinned. "They just know we've got a surprise for them."

I'd just opened my mouth to say, "When is he going to get here?" when a car pulled up in the drive. I watched in rapt awe as Brock Benson—*ooh-la-la!*—emerged from the driver's side, then walked around to the passenger side and opened the door. The prettiest blonde stepped out, petite and loaded with energy. She came bounding our way and threw her arms around Bella's neck.

"Bella!" The young woman let out a squeal, which frightened the baby, who chose that very moment to spit up all over my new teal blouse. Gag me.

Of course, Brock picked that very moment to join us on the veranda. I'd prepped myself for seeing that gorgeous face up close, but nothing could've prepared me for the real deal. The man was *g-g-gorgeous*. And taller than I'd expected too.

I half expected him to turn his nose up at me, what with the mess the baby had made of my blouse, but he did not. Instead, he took little Rosie from my arms and began to tickle her until she cooed with delight. Go figure. Some folks just had the magic touch.

While I used an old tissue from my purse to clean my blouse, Bella made quick introductions. With my heart in my throat, I greeted Brock and his lovely bride, Erin. After a broad-smiled hello, Brock turned to Drew for a handshake. Drew gave me a funny look and pointed at my shirt. Only then did I realize I'd used the mascara-covered tissue to dab away the baby spit-up. Perfect. Now I had a black eye and a gooey blouse with weird smudges on it.

The front door flew open and Rosa came out onto the veranda, broom in hand. She waved it madly and spouted several lines in Italian.

"Don't strike! I didn't do anything!" Brock put his hands up in the air.

Rosa tossed the broom across the railing and into the yard and sprinted—like a much younger woman, I should add—toward him, planting kisses all over his cheeks. She then turned to Erin, giving her nearly as many kisses.

At this point, the entire Rossi clan spilled out from the house to join us. The noise rose to a deafening level, and I decided to reach for my camera and snap a few photos for posterity's sake. Hopefully Brock would be okay with it. He probably got enough of that from the paparazzi. But he didn't seem to mind, so I kept on, catching a great shot of him with Rosie, one sure to melt her mama's heart.

Bella loaned me a clean blouse, and then we all spent the next hour eating more food than should be allowed by law and talking about the upcoming day—both the Dickens event and tonight's wedding rehearsal.

I secretly worried that the paparazzi would show up at the wedding facility this evening, especially if they got wind of the fact that Sierra was already tucked away at Bella and D.J.'s place, but I did my best to press those fears away as I nibbled on my breakfast. Not that I could eat, mind you. What girl could actually eat in the presence of Brock Benson, megastar?

Turned out, as Bella said, he was a pretty regular guy. A guy who really liked Rosa's cooking, from the looks of things. He scarfed down a huge breakfast, then leaned back in his chair and rubbed his stomach.

I wanted to say so many things—to compliment him on his dancing, for one, and to tell him how much I loved his character on *Stars Collide*. Still, Brock didn't appear to be the sort to talk about himself. Most of his conversation was about his after-school facility for children and on how cute Bella's babies were. Go figure.

By the time we wrapped up breakfast, I felt a little foolish for being so starstruck. Drew asked me to help him take photographs of the parade, so we stopped by my studio to grab a few more things. By the time we got to the parade site, my attention had shifted back to where it probably should have been all along—on Drew.

"Bless you for that," I whispered as we worked our way through the crowd to the spot where the parade would kick off.

"For what?" he asked.

I gave him a little kiss on the cheek. "For letting me get away with acting so silly. Brock is a great guy, no doubt about it. But I've already got the greatest one in the world."

Drew stopped in his tracks and turned to face me, a smile lighting his face. "Thank you." In spite of the crowd, he swept me into his arms and gave me a kiss sure to convince me that I needed to look no further for love. Saints preserve us, could that boy make me swoon, or what?

"When this weekend is over, we're going to focus on the two of us," he whispered. "Okay?"

"Of course." That idea sent a little tingle down my spine. Seemed like I spent a lot of time tingling these days.

We found the Rossi family a few minutes later and settled into our places at the street's edge, hoping to get some great shots of Brock leading the parade. Moments later my parents arrived, and my mother's nerves were clearly frayed in anticipation, from her wild-eyed look and the strange job she'd done buttoning her shirt.

"Have I missed Brock?" she asked.

"No." I pointed to her buttons, suddenly realizing that I wasn't the only one in the family who got a little discombobulated when stressed. "He should be coming soon, though."

Mama glanced down and gasped, then started fixing her buttons.

"You like my costume?" My father pointed to his crazy getup, and I laughed.

"I can't believe they let you in here dressed like a leprechaun."

"Hey, leprechauns were around during the Victorian era." He started to tell a story about Grandpa Aengus, but a cheer from the crowd surrounding us drowned him out.

Seconds later my sister arrived with her husband. I gave Deidre a hug and introduced her to the others, then watched as Brock—now dressed à la Dickens, complete with top hat, Victorian suit, and cane—climbed aboard the horse-drawn carriage that would lead the parade. The women, including Mama and my little sister, screamed so loud I thought my eardrums would burst. Brock looked our way and flashed a smile, then gave a little wave. Ordinarily, my heart would've skittered into my throat, but I was too busy looking at Drew to make sure he caught the shot on his camera. He had a better zoom than I did.

The music kicked off just as Corinne arrived, breathless and red-cheeked. She squeezed in next to my mother, who grabbed her hand and released a girlish giggle. Behind her came the three Splendora sisters, Twila leading the pack. The women had apparently taken the "come in costume" part seriously. Surely they would win the prize for their over-the-top regalia.

The horses let out a loud whinny as they pulled Brock's carriage forward. Brock waved to those who'd gathered along the sides of the street, his face all smiles as he noticed Twila, Bonnie Sue, and Jolene. All around me, girls let out squeals in abundance. Well, if you could call the women in our little group *girls*. They yelled loudest of all. I glanced at Erin to see how she was taking this. Not too badly, from the looks of things. She hollered right alongside them.

I didn't whoop or holler—snapping photos was the order of the day. Thank goodness Brock didn't care if I shot them from the front, back, side, or otherwise. So when I happened to catch a really goofy moment of him high-fiving a juggler, I snapped it.

Scarlet arrived wearing her Let Them Eat Cake apron atop a weird hot pink and lime green Victorian dress. Typical colorful Scarlet. She scooted into the spot behind me just as Brock's float passed by.

"Oh, I can't believe I missed it!" She groaned. "I was busy baking samples for you to give Brock Benson. Left them at your studio. Hope you don't mind that I used the key you gave me awhile back."

"Not a bit." Though I rather doubted I'd be going to the studio anytime soon, and I suspected Brock Benson would never taste those cake samples. Still, I would help spread the word about her business, no problem. When things slowed down, anyway. Right now I had bigger fish to fry. Er, bigger cakes to bake.

As the parade moved forward, I got as many photos as I could of the various carriages and floats as they passed by me. The Victorian costumes took my breath away.

Turning, I caught a glimpse of Drew in my lens. I saw the sparkle in his expression, the pure God-breathed joy radiating from his bright eyes, the zeal for life. I began to click shot after shot, knowing that he didn't realize I was catching him in action.

As I paused to glance at one of the photos, the truth poured over me like water rushing over the shore. Brock Benson, awesome as he might be, couldn't hold a candle to the amazing, godly man in the photo I now stared at. Brock might be a superstar—he might even be a hot, hunky superstar—but he wasn't the guy for me. No, to find the man God had dropped down from heaven just for me, I needed to look no further than three feet to my right.

23

High Society

> May your troubles be less
> And your blessings be more
> And nothing but happiness
> Come through your door.
>
> Irish blessing

When the parade ended, I could hardly wait to spend a few hours with Drew. I clutched his hand in mine, photographer no more. For the first hour we walked the Strand, the place where I'd done business for over a year. Seeing our little island all done up in its finest, offering pomp and circumstance worthy of the British Empire, made me proud to be a Galvestonian.

I had always enjoyed the Strand, but never so much as during the Dickens event. Costumed vendors peddled their wares—many of them tantalizing my taste buds with their delicious scents. From rolling carts and street stalls they called out to us, begging us to have a sample of this or that. I had a little of this and a lot of that. Talk about a feast for the eyes and the stomach! Sweets in abundance. Candy-covered apples. Caramel pecan apples on a stick. Yum.

We stopped in the children's area to watch as the little ones frolicked and played. To our right, D.J. helped Tres climb aboard an elephant for a ride. The youngster squealed with pure delight. Or was that terror? Hard to tell with so much going on around me. Several of the Rossis' older children played in the fabricated snow yard, joining an overly made-up Scrooge for a wacky Dickens-themed scavenger hunt. Pure joy radiated from each face. Well, joy mixed with red cheeks from the heat. Who could've predicted temps in the upper seventies this close to Christmas?

At two o'clock we paused to enjoy the Victorian Bed Races down Mechanic Street, cheering on the participants and laughing when the team dressed in the Ghost of Christmas Past attire took the prize. When that ended, we headed to the main stage near the middle of the Strand, where I heard angelic voices ringing out in perfect three-part harmony.

Drew gave my hand a squeeze and smiled. "We're right on time."

He waved at Brock and Erin, who stood near the stage, surrounded by paparazzi, of course. As we approached, Brock managed to convince the reporters to hightail it. He then gestured to the Splendora sisters and smiled.

"This is going to be the highlight of my day," he said. "Three of my favorite ladies, dressed to the nines and singing their hearts out. The last time I saw them, they were doing the same thing, only at a Renaissance-themed wedding."

"No way."

"Yep. My best friend's wedding, to be precise. At Club Wed. They brought the house down then, and it looks like nothing's changed."

Sure enough, the crowd clapped and cheered as the ladies sang. Still, I couldn't get over the fact that Brock knew the three Splendora sisters. And boy howdy, did they ever look fine in their Victorian costumes. Twila in deep-green brocade, Bonnie Sue in vibrant red, and Jolene in the prettiest shade of eggplant I'd ever seen. I caught shot after shot, knowing there would be plenty of good ones for their website. My favorite was the close-up of Twila's feathered hat.

When the show ended, we took to the street again. I kept a watchful eye on the time, knowing we had to be back at Club Wed at six for the rehearsal. Oh, but I didn't want this to end. We now tagged along behind the Rossis and Brock and Erin as they browsed the shops. The paparazzi trailed us all the way.

Bella sidled next to me. "I know everyone dreams of being a superstar, but I couldn't live like this." She shuddered. "Surrounded on every side? I don't know how they do it."

"Me either." *Give me my privacy any day.*

"Hey, speaking of superstars, I wanted you to know that I got a text from Sierra. She and David are here."

"At Dickens?" I glanced around, wondering if I would recognize her.

"Yeah. They're incognito. I think she's wearing sunglasses and a hat and scarf. Over gray sweats and tennis shoes, I mean. She said no one would recognize her. But she's having the time of her life. Said to tell you thanks for the suggestion about the funnel cake, but now she wonders if she'll still fit into her wedding dress."

I laughed. "Cool."

As I thought about the fact that Sierra cared enough about me to share something like that, a wave of contentment rippled over me. Well, that and a hankerin' for a funnel cake, which I purchased at the next booth.

I nibbled on the tasty delight as Her Majesty Queen Victoria paraded by, surrounded by her guard of Beefeaters. Okay, so it wasn't the real Queen Victoria, just someone dressed up to look like her. Still, as she made her way by in a fabulous horse-drawn carriage and greeted us, her royal subjects, I almost felt I was in the presence of royalty. Then again, I pretty much was. Brock and Erin garnered even more attention from the people surrounding us than the queen herself.

We passed the street musicians and paused—well, my father paused, anyway—when we reached the bagpipers. This, of course, led him to a rollicking good story, complete with thick brogue, about Grandpa Aengus. Mama and Corinne were too busy looking at the Victoria-themed crafts and jewelry to pay him much mind, though. I did my best to smile and encourage him as the story poured out. If I wanted to pass on these tall tales to my children, I needed to pay attention.

Children? Hmm. Where that came from, I had no idea.

Ahead of us, Brock and Erin walked hand in hand, pausing at the various shops to take a peek in the window. I couldn't help but notice when they stopped in front of my studio.

Erin turned my way with a smile. "This is it, Hannah? Your place?"

"Yep."

"Very cool. Can we go inside?"

"Of course."

I hadn't planned to show off the place just yet, though. With so many recent shoots, the studio wasn't at its finest.

Complicating the situation further, a crowd of people thronged around us as we made our way inside. Drew managed to stop them before they entered the place by handing out a bevy of Scarlet's cake samples and putting up the CLOSED sign. Before long I was safely inside with Drew, Brock, and Erin, talking about the various photographs on the walls.

"I just love this one." Erin stood in front of a photo of a newborn baby boy. I'd posed him in the sweetest position, curled up and wearing feathery angel wings. Her eyes misted over. "Brock, what do you think?"

"I think . . ." He stared at the photo, then back at her, his eyes now twinkling with mischief. "We'll have to come back in about seven months and let her do the same for us."

"W-what?" I stared at Erin, who broke into a broad smile.

"You won't tell anyone, will you? We've been trying to keep it a secret." She giggled. "Our producer doesn't even know."

"And if the powers that be at *Dancing with the Stars* find out, everyone on the planet will know. You know it will hit the news in a hurry." Brock shrugged. "Still, it's going to come out sooner or later." He quirked a brow. "Literally."

This got a laugh out of all of us. With dreamy eyes, Erin began to share her excitement about the baby. It was all so sweet, so girl-next-door, so non-Hollywood, so . . .

Tick-tock, tick-tock.

Oh no. There it went again.

A quick glance at my watch startled me to attention. Four o'clock. I still had a lot to do before tonight's rehearsal. I should probably head home and get showered and changed.

We moved to the front of the studio, and I reached for the door. At that very moment someone opened it from the outside and an unfamiliar woman stepped inside. For a second I thought she might be a potential client or something. Then, in an instant, I realized who it was.

Jacquie Goldfarb.

I did my best not to gasp aloud as she took several steps toward me. I recognized her face, of course. Same dark eyes and high cheekbones. Same gorgeous dark hair. But something else had changed, and it stunned me. Clearly the girl's profile picture on Facebook needed updating. She was easily fifty pounds heavier in real life than in her photograph.

"Hannah." She opened her arms for a hug, which I gave. "Hope you don't mind that I came inside. I saw the sign but could see you through the glass." She gave me an admiring look, then shook her head, her eyes misty. "You haven't changed a bit. You look just like the girl who tried out for the drill team."

Tried out but didn't make it, you mean.

"Jacquie. You look . . ."

"No, don't." She put her hands up and smiled. "No point in acting like I'm the same girl. I've changed in a thousand ways, not the least of which is this body of mine." She sighed. "It turns out I'm an emotional eater. Marrying Matt put me on a roller-coaster ride—one filled with cream pies, Ding Dongs, and Twinkies. Every time he would break my heart, I'd turn to food." Jacquie chuckled. "But never fear. Now that he's gone for good, I've been dieting. What you're seeing here is the leaner, trimmer version of my former self. I've dropped twenty-three pounds since the fall."

"Congratulations."

She glanced at Drew and smiled, then turned toward Brock. For a moment she didn't say anything. Then her eyes widened, and she finally managed, "Oh! Oh, oh, oh!"

Brock grinned and turned my way. "Hannah? Friend of yours?"

"Yes. I'm sorry, I should've made introductions. Everyone, this is my friend from high school, Jacquie Goldfarb." Somehow I didn't even flinch as I uttered the word "friend." I really meant it.

To my left, I noticed the look on Drew's face as he took in Jacquie's appearance—compassion laced with intrigue. No doubt this wasn't what he was expecting.

"Y-y-you're B-B-Brock Benson!" Jacquie now stood in front of Brock, babbling.

"I am." He extended his hand, and she reached for it.

"Hannah?" Jacquie turned my way. "You know Brock Benson?"

I fought the temptation to brag on myself or my business, opting instead to simply nod. The old, insecure me would have given her an earful, perhaps, but not the new, improved me. Or should I say the Drew-improved me.

Brock, it appeared, was happy to take care of bragging for me. "Oh, sure," he said. "Hannah's business is really taking off, so she's got a lot of well-known clients. You know she's shooting Sierra Caswell's wedding, right?"

"What?" Jacquie looked at me again. "Seriously? Why didn't you tell me?"

"It never came up." I shrugged, hoping no one would make a big deal out of it.

"You're . . . you're doing really well for yourself, Hannah." She gestured to my studio. "I'm so . . . proud of you."

"Nah. Don't be. Just doing what I love. God is blessing me, for sure."

"Still . . ." She paused, her eyes filling with tears.

I slipped my arm through Jacquie's, determined to turn

this conversation around. No longer needing to prove myself, I simply wanted to be her friend. It certainly looked like she needed one.

We spent the next several minutes laughing and swapping stories about the good old days. Strangely, they suddenly felt good. In fact, I could barely remember the pain of the past. Spending time with Jacquie Goldfarb in person put a lot of things in perspective for me. In only a few minutes I realized that all of my former jealousies and insecurities were pointless. Why had I ever compared myself to her in the first place?

I thought about that Scripture, the one about putting away childish things. Maybe that's all God required of me here—to put away my childish, petty feelings and live in the moment. Yes, that's exactly what I would do, for in this moment Jacquie Goldfarb looked and sounded very much like someone I would enjoy getting to know.

But I didn't have a lot of time with her at the studio. By 4:30 I had no choice but to return home to prep for the wedding rehearsal. I changed into something presentable.

Drew picked me up at 5:00. By 5:45 I'd met Sierra in person and found her to be as delightful as she'd been during our latest phone call. And even prettier in person than I'd imagined, in spite of the crooked nose. She gave me a hug that left no doubt in my mind about where she stood regarding our relationship. Then she greeted Drew with a handshake, gave me a wink, and mouthed, "He's a hottie!" when he turned around.

I had to agree. More than that, he was a great guy, and the perfect one for me. Still, this hardly seemed like the time or the place to share all of that information. Instead, I tucked it away in my heart and thanked God for it.

The evening passed from one snapshot to the next. I managed to catch several great shots of Sierra and David during the run-through, and even more at the rehearsal dinner afterward. By the time Drew dropped me off at my house that night, I was so exhausted I barely had the strength to download the photos onto my computer so that I could start up again the next day.

I'd just settled into bed when I realized I'd forgotten to set my alarm. I reached for my cell and had just set it when the phone rang. I almost dropped the crazy thing as it went off in my hand. When I finally stopped shaking, I answered it, tickled to hear Drew's voice.

"Hey, you."

The lilt in his voice made me smile.

"Hey, you too."

"Long day, huh?"

"Yeah, but a great one." I sighed and leaned back against the pillows.

"Still going to church in the morning?"

"Mm-hmm." I stretched. "Early service instead of our usual eleven o'clock one. Pick me up?"

"Sure." He paused. "Hey, I just wanted to tell you something, Hannah. For the record."

"What's that?" I yawned.

Another pause followed on his end. "We joke around a lot about Jacquie Goldfarb, but I wanted to tell you that I'm really proud of the way you acted when she showed up at the studio today."

"Oh?" This certainly got my attention.

"Yeah. After all she put you through, you didn't have to be so nice to her. It tells me a lot about your character that you were. And it's obvious you weren't just putting on a show or anything like that. You really care about her."

"I always did. Maybe too much. It's a flaw I have." I gave a nervous chuckle.

"No. Caring about people, especially people who've hurt you, isn't a flaw. It's a sign that you understand God's grace."

"That's me. Hannah Grace. Full of grace and truth." I stifled another yawn. "I guess I'll never outgrow that phrase."

"Hope not. It's perfect for you."

"Aw, thanks." My eyes grew heavy, and within seconds I started to drift off.

"Hannah? You still with me?"

"Hmm?" I yawned. "Yeah . . . I'm here."

"Okay, sleepyhead. You go on to bed. But dream about me, okay? Not Brock Benson."

"Brock Benson?" I stifled another yawn. "Who's that?"

"Perfect answer. Now get some sleep. We've got a big day ahead of us tomorrow."

Sleep tugged at me like waves calling me out to sea. "Yes . . . we . . . do."

"And just for the record," he said, his voice now softening, "I'm completely and totally twitterpated."

"Twitter? Hmm?" I mumbled, now half asleep. "Oh, me too. But I'm more of a Facebook girl myself." The phone slipped out of my hand, and I drifted off, all of the events of the day rolling together in a delicious, hazy dream.

24

Winter Wonderland

Two shorten the road.

Irish saying

On Sunday morning I woke up shivering. At some point overnight a cold front had settled in over Galveston Island, bringing with it a dense fog and a bit of drizzly rain. Thank goodness Sierra's wedding would be held indoors. And since it didn't start until two o'clock, I had time to pray the fog would lift.

My morning ritual moved along at double the usual speed. I showered and then dressed in my favorite skirt and blouse, then plugged in my curling iron and got to work on my hair, alternating the curling process with the task of putting on my makeup. Everything had to be perfect today. Well, the Hannah McDermott version of perfect, anyway.

Still buzzing with anticipation, I headed downstairs for a bite to eat before Drew arrived to pick me up for church. I found Mama in the kitchen cooking scrambled eggs and bacon. On second glance, she appeared to be adding garlic to the eggs. Oy. What would my father say?

As I opened the refrigerator, she looked my way, worry lines appearing on her forehead. "Um, Hannah?"

"Yes, Mama?" I grabbed an orange from the bowl in the fridge, then reached for a container of yogurt, my thoughts tumbling. Should I eat heavy or light? Load up for the big day ahead, or avoid the calories and carbs so as not to feel overloaded? Decisions, decisions.

"You going to church this morning before the wedding?" Mama wiped her hands on her apron and turned toward me.

"Yep. Early service. Drew's picking me up in ten minutes. I think he's really enjoying our church." I opted for the yogurt, setting the orange back inside the fridge and closing the door. "Why?"

"Honey, have you looked in the mirror?" Mama pursed her lips and leaned against the counter.

"Well, of course. I just finished putting on my makeup." Goofy question to ask a girl who'd spent the morning prepping for the day of her life.

"Ah." The little crinkles around Mama's eyes deepened. "Well, I guess it's a new trend or something. Guess I'm just getting old. Don't know fashion when I see it."

"What do you mean?"

"Your hairdo." Mama turned back to the stove to tend to the eggs now sizzling in the pan. "Never seen anything quite like it."

"My hairdo?" I made a quick dash to the hallway to have a look in the mirror. A gasp escaped as I saw my hair—

completely curled and styled on one side but straight and long on the other. "What in the world?"

Mama, you just saved my life. And my reputation.

My mind shot back to that awful day at the Starbucks on Harborside when I'd shown up in two different shoes. Nothing like a little public humiliation to get a girl's day started.

But not today. Oh no.

I raced back to the bathroom, reached for my curling iron—still turned on, of course, since I hadn't finished using it—and whipped the left side of my head into shape. By the time I arrived back in the kitchen, my parents were seated at the dining room table eating their breakfast, and Drew had arrived. Mama gestured for him to join them, and he took a large helping of bacon and eggs.

Drew greeted me with a whistle and wide eyes. Guess I passed his test. Thank goodness he hadn't shown up any earlier.

"You guys coming to church?" he asked my father.

"Of course. We go to church every Sunday. Never miss." My father took a bite of his eggs, then pulled the fork out and examined it. He looked my mother's way. "Did you do something different with the eggs today?"

"Yes." Mama nodded. "That's for me to know and you to find out. But speaking of doing things differently, I want to talk to you about church."

"Talk to me . . . about church?" he asked.

"Yes. It's almost the new year."

"Right." He scratched his head, then sniffed the plate of eggs, his nose wrinkling.

"Things are going to be different around here this coming year," Mama said. "I'm a new woman, transformed. And this new year is going to reflect that."

My father's face paled a bit. "O-oh? In what way?"

"For one thing, I want to go to the eleven o'clock service at church, starting this morning." She took a large bite of the eggs and leaned back in her chair, a satisfied look on her face.

"The contemporary service? The one Hannah usually goes to?" My father dropped his fork and gripped the table. "Are you serious?"

"Very." My mother dabbed at her mouth with her napkin, then looked him in the eye as if giving him an ultimatum. "I love contemporary worship music and would like to give it a try. I know it's not your cup of tea, but you don't seem terribly fond of the traditional service either, so what's the difference?"

"Who says I don't like the traditional service?"

"You leave every Sunday with a scowl on your face. Maybe this new music will liven you up."

"Give me an ulcer, more likely. Just like these eggs." He folded his newspaper and stared at Mama. "What in the world has gotten into you, Marie? You've . . . changed."

"Thank you for noticing. I'm long overdue."

"Humph."

"I'm a new woman, Michael. Tired of doing the same old, same old. Just because our parents and grandparents looked a certain way or spoke a certain way or ate certain foods doesn't mean I have to. I'm me. Myself. An individual."

He rose and tossed his napkin on the table. "But you're a McDermott, and we McDermotts—"

"That's another thing," she interrupted. "I married into the McDermott clan. If you recall, I was born a Lockhart. We Lockharts are amiable. Fun. Unpredictable. You've shaped me into a McDermott—and I haven't objected—but the Lock-harts have always been more free-spirited. Unique."

"You're unique, all right." He waggled his finger. "It's those Rossis. They've gotten their hooks into you. I hardly recognize you anymore."

"Thank you. I'll take that as a compliment."

My father dropped back into his seat, completely silent.

Drew looked back and forth between my parents and then glanced at me, worry lines creasing his forehead. I shrugged, unsure of what to do or say.

Mama grinned, then rose and gave my dad a peck on the top of his head. I looked on, wondering if my father would blow his top. Instead, he jabbed his fork into the garlic-infused eggs and swallowed a huge bite.

Mama moved back to her chair and took a seat. "We're going out to lunch with our Sunday school class today, by the way. They're eating at a Chinese restaurant."

"Chinese?"

"Yes. And just for the record, I'm ordering chicken chow mein," Mama announced. "You can get whatever you like. Or not. It's up to you, of course."

My father began to mumble something about how a man should be able to eat what he likes.

"I heard that, Michael," Mama countered. "And just so you know, we've got leftover stew in the fridge, so you can help yourself to it when we get home if you decide not to join the rest of us. The microwave is that funny little rectangular box in the kitchen, on the shelf to the right. Push the button on the bottom to warm the stew."

Out of the corner of my eye I caught a glimpse of Drew snorting. He coughed, likely in an attempt to cover it up. Still, he looked like he might burst out laughing at any point.

To his credit, my father said nothing, but his mouth, hanging wide open in surprise, left nothing to the imagination.

"One more thing," Mama said. "As you know, I'm on a quest to diversify our foods."

"Well, I'm willing to go along with that." He glanced down at his plate and sighed. "To a point."

"I might ask you to watch Rosa and Laz's show with me sometimes," she said. "I record it and watch when you're at work, but I'd rather watch it together. And you might as well know . . ." She squared her shoulders. "They've asked me to be on their show this spring." Mama took another nibble of her eggs.

"W-what?" My father's eyes widened. "You're going to be on television?"

"Yes. And I would be thrilled if you would be happy about that fact. In fact, I'm hoping you'll come along and support me when I'm on the air."

"I—I—" He couldn't seem to finish his sentence. Still, I could see the admiration in his eyes and could almost hear "just wait till I tell my lodge buddies" clicking through his brain.

Mama began to hum "Too-Ra-Loo-Ra-Loo-Ral" as she breezed from the dining room into the kitchen. I could hear pots and pans clanging and banging, not in an angry way but in a happy "let's get this show on the road" sort of way.

"She's very happy." I gave my dad a pat on the shoulder.

"Glad someone is." He groaned and took another bite of his eggs.

"Isn't that the idea, though?" I asked. "You want her to be happy. Seems like she's been pretty quiet about her feelings for years now."

A pensive look came over my dad. "I always thought she enjoyed our quiet, simple life. Maybe I was wrong."

"Maybe. Or maybe she's just at a new stage. She is an empty nester, you know." I paused. "Well, almost. If I ever move out."

My father's brow furrowed, and his eyes filled with tears. "Tell me you won't do that anytime soon, Shutter Speed. Don't think my heart could take that, not with all of the other changes happening so quickly. I don't know if I've mentioned it or not, but I don't handle change very well."

I gave him a kiss on the forehead, but I couldn't promise that things wouldn't change in my situation, especially with Drew and me getting sweeter on each other by the minute.

My father took another bite of his eggs, a satisfied look on his face. A little too satisfied, actually. I daresay his expression now spoke of mischief.

"What is it, Dad? You're up to something."

He glanced toward the kitchen, then back at me. "Just pretending to be upset with your mother. That whole eleven o'clock service thing did throw me a little, but I've been working on a top-secret project. You two might as well know because I'll probably need some help from both of you when the time comes."

"Top secret?" Drew asked.

"Yep. Stick around for the big reveal at Christmastime." Dad rubbed his extended belly. "Hey, and by the way, I love chicken chow mein. I've been eating Chinese food for years, just never told your mama because I thought she didn't like it."

"No way."

"Yep. At the lodge. We order takeout every month. And that whole spiel about not liking change was just a bunch of blarney. Truth be told, I'm giving thought to getting hair plugs. What do you think?"

"Th-that's your surprise?" I managed.

"Nah. The surprise is for your mother. The hair plugs are for me. Vanity is setting in, I guess."

"I'm pretty sure she'd be very surprised if you turned up with hair plugs, Dad. And just for the record, I like your current look."

"Now who's opposed to change?" He narrowed his gaze and then laughed.

A quick glance at my watch clued me in to the fact that we were going to be late to church if we didn't hit the road. Drew and I said our goodbyes to my parents and made the trip, laughing and talking about my parents and trying to guess my dad's big secret.

After attending the early service, we drove back to Club Wed for the wedding of a lifetime. Several times along the way, I ushered up a prayer of thanks for the opportunity to shoot this wedding. Strange how my life had changed over the past few months. I'd been given every opportunity a girl could ask for . . . and hadn't spent much time botching them. Grandpa Aengus would've been proud. Suddenly I got a little misty thinking of him.

"Do you think the media has caught on to the fact that the wedding is today?" Drew asked, drawing me back around to the task at hand.

"I didn't have a chance to look at the paper this morning, so I don't know. I think Sierra was pretty smart scheduling it on a Sunday afternoon. Not many people would expect that."

"True. But I did see on the morning news that she was spotted at Dickens yesterday."

"Oh no."

"Yeah. So don't be surprised if reporters figure it out."

Arriving at Club Wed well ahead of schedule, I sent Drew to check the lighting in the chapel while I headed to the reception hall to see the layout. Bella had given me a sketch of what the room would look like, but seeing it in person was critical.

"Wow." I stared at the gorgeous room, amazed at the transformation.

The tables—dozens of them—were fully decked out in a great Texas-meets-Nashville theme. Very country. Perfect for Sierra, and great for me too. The vivid colors were a photographer's dream. I caught several photos of the room in its current state, then went in search of Bella. I found her on the far end of the reception hall, helping Rosa set up the cake. I also found my best friend.

Scarlet turned to me with a smile. "Hey, Hannah."

"Hey, yourself." *What are you doing here?*

"I asked Scarlet to help me." Rosa pointed to the cake, a fabulous multitiered number with yellow roses. "Her decorations are primo, no?" She indicated the amazing hand-designed music notes that covered the various tiers.

"Primo, yes." I stared at the cake and gasped. "You . . . you did that?"

"Well, just the piping and music stuff. Rosa didn't have time, what with Dickens and all. But she made the yellow roses. Aren't they gorgeous?"

"They're the prettiest I've ever seen."

Rosa blushed. Then she and Scarlet went back to work centering the cake on the table and chattering like best friends.

Bella pulled me aside. "It's such a blessing to have Scarlet here. We haven't told anyone, but Rosa's hand isn't as steady as it once was. She's great at baking, but the decorating and construction have been a problem for a while now. So I'm happy to see she's got someone to call on."

"Me too." In fact, I felt like throwing a little party to celebrate. Only, we were already having a party, weren't we?

"Have you seen Sierra yet?" Bella's eyes sparkled.

"No."

"She's gorgeous. Go and see for yourself."

I located her in the dressing room with her bridesmaids fussing over her hair and makeup. Perfect opportunity to snag some close-ups. When the time came for Sierra to put on her exquisitely beaded gown, I slipped into my comfort zone.

No matter what else happened around me, I could always count on a wedding to calm me down. Strange, I know. Most folks in the wedding biz came unnerved during the actual event, working at a frenzied pace to make sure every detail was in place. Not me. I actually came into my own on the wedding day. There, behind the eye of the camera, I was truly at peace. Nothing could touch me. I saw it all—the smiles, the tears, the wrinkles around the bride's eyes.

Mental note: don't forget to iron those out with Photoshop. Not because I had to, of course, but because it was the right thing to do.

Once I wrapped up in the dressing room, I went in search of Drew to make sure he'd caught some shots of the groom and groomsmen. He gave me a thumbs-up and then headed off to take a picture of the ring bearer.

I found the flower girl—Sierra's littlest cousin—in the kitchen, sneaking a chocolate-covered strawberry out of the fridge. Perfect photo op. Minutes later, I saw the bride's grandmother receiving her wrist corsage from the florist. Shortly thereafter, back in the dressing room, I watched as the father of the bride brushed away tears when he saw his daughter—beautiful, serene Sierra—in her wedding dress for the first time. I also happened to notice the rolled eyes from the maid of honor when one of the bridesmaids grumbled about the color of the dresses. I saw the little smudge on Sierra's white cowgirl boots and even took in the uneven hem on the mother of the bride's expensive dress.

There, through the one-eyed lens, I caught a glimpse of an alternate reality, one the bride never saw unless I captured it for her. And just as I'd told Dani, the reporter from *Texas Bride*, I chose my shots very carefully, only snagging the ones that would leave blissful memories for the bride and groom. One misstep and the happy day could be ruined for all.

With that in mind, I looked beyond the maid of honor's eye rolling and straight to the bride, who gazed in wonder at her reflection in the mirror. I saw the joy in her father's eyes and could almost read his thoughts: *Is this my little girl all grown up?*

The photos that I snagged told the whole story. With uncanny precision, I captured the shots that mattered. And I caught them all with the confidence and speed of an expert.

Expert . . .

For whatever reason, the word made me think of Drew. I found him just outside the chapel, a smile on his face as he caught a random shot of the flower girl sticking her tongue out at the ring bearer. I felt sure he'd managed to snag a shot of the groom's mother arguing with the caterer too. Just for fun, of course.

"You're going to love this one wacky shot I got of David

and his groomsmen." Drew chuckled. "And you're never going to believe what they've got planned for the kiss."

"Oh?"

"Can't tell. Promised I wouldn't. Just be ready, okay? You get the shot of the bride and groom kissing. I'll take care of the rest."

"Okay."

Minutes later, the country-western-themed wedding got under way, familiar twangy tunes ringing out as the various members of the wedding party were ushered to the front of the chapel. I slipped into the perfect spot to capture the moment when Sierra's father lifted her veil, and even got a couple of perfectly lit shots of the unity candle. By the time the vows were shared, I had tears in my eyes. Brushing them aside, I focused on the bride and groom. I didn't want to miss the pivotal moment—the kiss.

Thank goodness Drew had warned me. When the "I do's" were spoken, when it came time for that once-in-a-lifetime shot of the bride and groom sealing the deal with a lengthy smooch, the groomsmen all lifted scorecards rating the kiss. Everything from a 9.5 to a 10.0. I didn't have time to focus on the guys, though. My shots were of the bride and groom lip-locked. Drew caught the rest. I heard the clicking of his camera through the laughter and cheers of the crowd. I'd never been happier to have someone working alongside me.

At some point during the wedding reception, my aching feet forced me to sit down. I found a spot at a table near the back of the room. Drew joined me, a smile on his face. He handed me a plate with a large piece of cake on it, and I took a bite, my eyes rolling back in contentment.

"I like a girl who likes her cake."

"Then you've got the right girl, trust me."

"Oh, I've got the right girl, all right." He leaned over and gave me a little kiss on the cheek.

I heard someone nearby clear his throat. Looking up, I noticed Bella's brother Armando standing nearby with a video camera in hand.

"I, um, I'm supposed to be getting marriage advice for the bride and groom. Thought maybe you two might have something to share."

I paused, deep in thought. After a moment I snapped my fingers. "I know." Turning to the camera, I said, "The Bible says you shouldn't go to bed angry." I chuckled. "So, stay up all night and fight it out. That's my advice."

This got a laugh out of Armando, who eventually got control of himself and turned the camera to Drew. I could hardly wait to hear what juicy tidbit he might come up with.

After a moment, he finally spoke. "I guess I would say, don't get distracted by what's in your peripheral vision."

"Peripheral vision?" Armando shifted his position. "What do you mean?"

"As a photographer, when you're focused, you'll occasionally catch those once-in-a-lifetime shots, the ones that take your breath away. The same is true with a good marriage. The two of you as a couple have to stay focused on God. You can't let the stuff on the fringes throw you off course or you'll miss great *kairos* moments. You know, those 'wow, God brought me to this time and this place so that I could learn this lesson' moments."

Armando nodded as he pulled the camera down, then muttered, "Thanks, guys," as he moved on.

I turned to face Drew, suddenly having my own special *kairos* moment. As he swept me into his arms for a kiss sweeter than Rosa's Italian cream cake, I realized the truth. Everything I'd learned over the past few months, everything I'd been given—from my business to this man in my arms—was a gift from God.

Now I simply had to keep my focus on the One who'd given them to me in the first place.

25

You Keep Coming Back
Like a Song

Health and long life to you,
Land without rent to you,
The partner of your heart to you.
And when you die, may your bones rest in Ireland!

Irish blessing

On the Tuesday morning after Sierra's wedding, I received a phone call from Bella, who bubbled over with excitement. "Hannah, that was the best wedding ever. How can I thank you?"

"Me?" I laughed. "Girl, I should be thanking you. I had the time of my life."

"Same here. It was so sad to see Brock and Erin go. Did

you know that they used our reception hall to practice his dance routines for last night's show?"

"No way."

"Yeah. Late Saturday night after the rehearsal dinner. He didn't want anyone to know, but they flew his dance partner down to practice with him."

"You're serious? Cheryl was here?"

"Yep. She stayed at the Tremont. In fact, they all flew together back out to L.A. late Sunday night."

"I can't believe it."

"Believe it. But Brock was plenty nervous about his dances for last night's show, trust me. They haven't had as much time as usual to prepare."

"We watched it. I thought he did a great job."

"Me too. Man, there's something about watching people dance that just lights a fire under me." Bella paused, and I could hear the baby crying in the background. "Hey, speaking of which, that's the real reason for my call. We're planning a feast tonight to celebrate the finale of *Dancing with the Stars*. Rosa and Mama wanted me to call and invite your family. And Drew and his mother too. Oh, and Scarlet. Rosa likes her a lot."

"Really? All of us for dinner?" I could hardly imagine the chaos that might ensue, but it certainly held some appeal.

"Yes." Bella murmured to the baby, who continued to fuss. "And just so you know . . ." She now spoke over the baby's whimpers. "It's going to be a real party. D.J.'s parents are coming. So are the Splendora sisters and their husbands."

"Sounds like a blast." A loud, crazy, chaotic blast.

"I know, right? We'll record the show and watch it after we eat. That way we can take our time. What do you think?"

"I think it sounds like the best idea in the world. Hope my dad will play along."

"Me too. Six o'clock okay?"

The baby's whimpers now turned to full-fledged screams. This seemed to upset Guido. I could hear him in the background, making his machine-gun noise. Bella offered up a rushed goodbye, and the call ended.

Now, to talk my parents into this.

Convincing my mother to go to the Rossis' house for the finale of *Dancing with the Stars* was a piece of cake. My dad, however, put up a real fuss.

"Now look, Hannah," he grumbled. "I've gone along with these crazy new ideas of your mother's. I've eaten strange foods, watched strange television shows, and met some strange—er, interesting—folks. But Tuesday nights I always watch the Biography Channel. You know that."

"Come with us, Dad," I said with a wink. "You'll get to know some characters worthy of their own show on the Biography Channel."

He sighed, but when the time came, he trudged out to the car and joined us for the ride to the Rossi home. As we drove, my mother shared her ideas on an upcoming vacation spot. I thought my father would croak when she mentioned Grand Cayman. The man never left Galveston Island.

At ten minutes till six we arrived at Bella's parents' home. Most of the others were already there. The delicious aroma of lasagna greeted us, along with the yummy scent of Rosa's garlic twists. By 6:40, we'd gathered around the table—actually, tables, since it took three large tables to accommodate everyone—where we enjoyed the meal of a lifetime. To my right, Drew dove into his lasagna. His mama chatted with the other ladies, especially Bella's mother. Turned out the two were friends from the Grand Opera Society. Go figure.

As I enjoyed my meal, I thought about that day when I'd

eaten at Bella's house the first time. My, what a difference a few months could make. That day, Drew Kincaid had been my archnemesis, my Jacquie Goldfarb. Today—I smiled as I glanced at him out of the corner of my eye—he was the man who made me happier than the tiramisu Rosa now served.

We enjoyed fun conversation over dessert, but I was itching to get to the television. After Brock's stellar performance last night, I hoped—dreamed, even—that he would win. Watching him take that mirror ball trophy in hand would be the icing on the cake.

Speaking of cake, I had a second piece just for luck.

No, not luck. I'd already established that luck had nothing to do with it. I ate the cake simply because it was amazing.

By ten minutes after eight, the youngest children were sleeping in a bedroom upstairs and the rest of us had gathered, coffee in hand, in the living room around a huge plasma TV. Rosa stood in front of the television and offered up a prayer for Brock's feet. None of us bothered to tell her that the show was recorded. Her prayers lagged behind the real-time event by over an hour, but she didn't need to know that.

Drew and I squeezed into a chair really meant for one. He didn't seem to mind being so close. I cuddled up against him, happy to have his arm around me for this special night.

Watching my favorite show at Bella's parents' house was a little different from watching it at our home. For one thing, they commented on absolutely everything from the costumes to the guest stars, who provided music and entertainment. As the judges gave their comments, Rosa, Laz, and the others chimed in with their thoughts, often speaking so loudly that I couldn't hear the judges. Still, I had a blast, watching it all take place and listening to the various opinions from those in the room.

Bella and D.J. laughed like hyenas during the funny bits before the dances, which were mostly a repeat of routines we'd already seen this season.

Twila wrung her hands. "I'm just so nervous for Brock."

"Why is that?" Bella's mother asked.

"He told me on Saturday that he was worried about having to repeat this dance because he stumbled the first time they did it. I think we should stop right here and pray for him." Twila hit the Pause button on the remote and dove in, praying the house down in her Southern voice. Once again I bit back the temptation to explain that the show was recorded.

As the emotional "Amen!" sounded from Twila, Rosa hit Play. Seconds later, Brock took the floor, dancing a near-perfect jive.

"Now you see?" Twila clasped her hands together and let out a squeal. "That, my friends, is the power of prayer!"

Bonnie Sue and Jolene chimed in with a rousing "Amen, sister!" and we were back to the show once again.

The evening flew by at warp speed. When the moment finally arrived for the winner to be announced, you could've heard a pin drop in the room. I held my breath, feeling a little woozy. Only when a shout went up from all in attendance did I realize they'd actually called Brock's name.

I looked on, heart in my throat, as the camera zoomed in on his face. In that moment I thought about my once-upon-a-time infatuation with the handsome superstar, the picture-perfect Brock Benson. How goofy it all seemed now. Not that any other woman in the country would blame me. Didn't every girl dream of living her happily ever after with the perfect fella?

Cuddling up against Drew, I felt contentment settle over me. I'd found mine, no doubt about it.

When the roar of the crowd—both the one on television and the one in the Rossis' living room—settled down, my father rose and stretched. "Well, that was great fun," he said with a half smile. "But now I have a little announcement to make. Hope it gets you just as excited as the show did."

My mother's eyes widened. I'm sure this impromptu move of his had her nervous. I certainly wondered what he had in mind.

"It's almost Christmas," my father said, reaching into his back pocket. "And I have a little gift I'd like to present. Early, I know. But appropriate under the circumstances." He took my mother by the hand and asked her to join him.

She rose, looking plenty nervous. "Michael, what are you up to?" she whispered.

"Watch and see." He handed Mama an envelope.

She opened it, and her eyes widened as she pulled out a notecard inside and read it. Tears sprang to her eyes. "Michael, am I reading this right?"

"You are." He bowed and grinned. "I've signed us up for ballroom dancing lessons. A twelve-week course, lasting through much of the spring."

"W-what?" I stared at him, blown away by this news. "Are you serious?"

"Sure am." He turned to face Mama, who brushed away tears. "I planned to wait until Christmas to tell you, but I figured this would be the perfect night, since everyone is in a dancing mood. And who knows . . . maybe next year we'll be so good at the tango that we'll get invited to be on that crazy show." He did a funny little jig across the room, and everyone erupted in laughter.

I didn't bother to tell him that one needed to be a celebrity to be considered for *Dancing with the Stars*. Let the man reach for the stars. He might very well find himself dancing on one. After all, he did have connections now.

My parents took to kissing, which got a couple of whoops and hollers out of the men in the room—as well as Bonnie Sue, who seemed to get a kick out of it. Mama blushed in my father's arms, which got me tickled. And a little embarrassed.

Bella rose and faced the group. "Well, while we're on the subject of good news, I have something to share. I got a call from Brock this morning. He wanted to let me know that he snagged twenty tickets for next season's *Dancing with the Stars* premiere show. He's sending them to me and told me to give them to whoever I wanted."

We began to talk on top of one another, voices overlapping as everyone vied for a chance to land the tickets. This, of course, led to a debate about who loved dancing more. I listened in as the ladies in the room took their turns, sharing their love of the show and of dance in general.

At one point, Bella looked my way. "What about you, Hannah? You want to go to Hollywood to watch the show?"

"I'm a dance fan, no doubt about it." A little sigh escaped as I thought about that. I gave her a smile. "Do you remember that day at Parma John's when I told you that I wanted my lilt back?"

"Sure do, honey," Twila chimed in. "I've been praying about that very thing, but I daresay you've found it." Her brows elevated as she looked back and forth between Drew and me.

"Thank you." I couldn't help the grin that followed. "That's why I like dancing so much. When you're dancing, you don't have time to fret over anything." I looked at Bella and Scarlet. "It's like when we were little girls. Remember dressing up in anything that even remotely looked like a ballet costume and dancing around the living room? I'm sure you two know what I'm talking about."

"I used to love that." Scarlet sighed.

"Little girls just love to dance, that's for sure," Bella added. "At least, I always did. And I'm sure Rosie will too, when she's old enough."

"Bella would entertain us for hours," her mother said. "I still remember when she danced to *La Traviata*."

"I guess that's my point," I said. "Dance comes naturally to us when we're little but fades when we get older. Too many people let the stresses of life get them wound up. I think there's something to be said for cutting loose and having a good time. And hey, people even danced in Bible days."

"Amen, sister." Twila rose and did a funny little two-step. "The Bible says that King David danced before the Lord."

Before long all of the ladies were up on the floor, showing off their dance moves. We laughed until tears ran down our faces.

At some point, I looked at Drew, who rose and stood off to the side of the room. Not dancing. Looking nervous, in fact. A little nauseous, even.

"You okay?" I whispered.

"Yeah."

But he didn't look okay. He looked . . . ill.

When the ladies calmed down, Drew clapped his hands and got our attention. "I . . . could I ask everyone to take a seat, please? I have a little presentation I'd like to make."

We all settled back into our chairs, and I looked on, wondering what the boy was up to. He went into the front hall and returned with a strange scroll-like paper in his hand. Opening it, he uttered a few words in Gaelic.

The boy knows Gaelic? Sounded like a prayer.

I glanced at his mom, who gave him a nod. Very strange.

Opening the scroll, he switched to English, but his words ushered forth with a thick brogue, one that made him even more appealing. "Let it be known this day amongst all who will hear that the feudin' betwixt Clan McDermott and Clan Kincaid shall cease, both now and forevermore."

"I thought you told him that whole feuding thing wasn't true," Scarlet whispered in my ear.

I giggled. "Don't think he cares. He's trying to make a point, I guess."

As he continued to read the proclamation, I started wondering just what sort of point the guy was trying to make. When he got to the "till death do us part" line, I realized this was more than a simple proclamation written in fun.

The room now came alive as the folks around me began to speculate.

Drew took several steps in my direction and reached for my hand. I gave it to him, feeling shaky and flushed, then rose to join him. He went to the front hallway and returned with a sword, which he placed on the floor between us.

"What are you doing?" I whispered.

"It's the age-old tradition of the merging of the clans."

"Merging of the clans?"

His eyes sparkled with merriment. "Go with me here, Hannah. I saw this once in a movie."

"O-okay."

He knelt down in front of the sword, reached into his back pocket, and came out with a tiny box. My heart sailed to my throat. All around me, folks began to cheer—some in Tex-Italian, others in Gaelic. I couldn't make out any of it. My eyes were firmly planted on the handsome clansman in front of me.

Drew's eyes twinkled as he opened the box, revealing a beautiful princess-cut marquise. Wowza!

"Hannah McDermott of Clan McDermott, I'm askin' ye for yer hand in marriage."

My thoughts reeled and I couldn't seem to speak. "I . . . I . . . I . . ."

"Is that a yes?" he asked, his gaze narrowing. "Because if it's not, I'll have to rethink my speech."

"Yes!" I stood in rapt awe as he slipped the gorgeous ring on my finger. "Oh yes!"

Drew wrapped his arms around me as the room came alive with cheers and laughter. "Yer gonna be a Kincaid from now on," he said. "Now, how does that make ye feel?"

My hands trembled nearly as badly as my voice. "Like I'm getting a fresh start. Though I can't help wondering what Grandpa Aengus would've said."

My father rose and gave me a hug. "He would've said, 'Health and a long life to you. Land without rent to you. A child every year to you. And if you can't go to heaven, may you at least die in Ireland."

This got another round of laughter from everyone in the room. Well, everyone but Bella, who told me I might want to reconsider that "child every year" line. I couldn't help but agree with that one. But it looked like I had a lot more to consider than that. Like a wedding, for one thing.

Wedding?

Oh. Help.

I looked back and forth between Scarlet and Bella, my heart in my throat. They approached and wrapped their arms around me, all laughter and smiles.

"Don't fret, Hannah," Bella said, looking far more confident than I felt. "Just leave the details to me."

"And leave the cake to me," Scarlet added. "I've been planning your wedding cake ever since the Bing and Bob party. You liked that chocolate truffle recipe, right?"

"Right." I chuckled. "Well, I'm glad one of us knew this was coming."

"Of course I knew, silly." She offered up a little sigh. "You and Drew are perfect together. You're the cream to his coffee, the garlic in his twists, the icing on his cake."

I didn't know about all of that. Still, as he swept me into his arms for a crazy spin around the living room floor, I did have to admit we made a pretty good dance team, one even my grandpa Aengus would be proud of. And I would go on dancing with Drew Kincaid . . . for the rest of my life.

26

True Love

Here's to the wings of love.
May they never molt a feather,
Till your little shoes and my big boots
Are under the bed together.

Irish wedding blessing

Twenty minutes after Drew Kincaid asked me to marry him, I telephoned my sisters and asked each one to serve as a bridesmaid. Their squealing—and affirmative reactions—nearly deafened me. Afterward I used my cell phone to change my Facebook status to "Engaged." This, of course, got a bevy of comments from my online friends, including Jacquie Goldfarb, who seemed genuinely happy for me. So happy, in fact, that I offered her an official invitation to the wedding.

She accepted right away.

As that decision was made, peace settled over me. No more angst. No more looking back. Only happy days from this point forth.

Scarlet and Bella pulled me into the dining room of the Rossi home, where we shared more tiramisu and lots of girlish chatter about the upcoming wedding. They flowed with ideas, more than I could possibly comprehend.

"I still can't believe you're getting married," Scarlet said as she took a big bite of her tiramisu. "I'll be the last single woman on Galveston Island. Promise you'll toss the bouquet my way."

"Why do you need the bouquet?" I giggled. "You've got Kenny."

"Hmm." She looked at her plate.

"What?" I asked.

Glancing up, she shrugged. "I didn't want to tell you, but we broke up."

"No way." My heart twisted at this news.

"Yeah. I guess we weren't really much of an item, anyway. He's always been sort of a hanger-on-er. I guess you could say I was using him." A sigh erupted. "Kind of like I used you to promote my business."

"I never felt used, Scarlet." I reached over to squeeze her hand, noticing the tears in her eyes.

"And look at how that turned out," Bella said with a smile. "Now you get to work with Aunt Rosa."

"True." Scarlet sighed again and turned my way. "But promise you'll toss me the bouquet?"

"First I have to *order* the bouquet," I said. "And the food. And the wedding dress."

"Hannah, remember what I told you. I'll take care of the

details." Bella gave me a wink. "Now, let's settle on a date, okay? I need to get you on the calendar. What are you thinking? Springtime? Early summer? We're booked most Saturdays, but I've got several Friday nights open."

My head swam with possibilities. Half an hour ago, weddings were the farthest thing from my mind. Now I had to plan one?

My heart danced to my throat as another realization set in. "Oh no. I've got to hire a photographer. What am I going to do about that? We can't very well shoot our own wedding."

"True." Bella chuckled. "Well, you'll love this little tidbit. My brother and sister-in-law are coming back from Italy for a few months. She's having a baby and wants to be near the family."

Two emotions washed over me at once—concern that Bella wouldn't need me anymore once Joey and Norah came back, and relief because we now had a wedding photographer.

Not that I had time to worry. Bella whipped out her phone and pulled up her calendar app. She listed off several possibilities for wedding dates, but I couldn't respond until I'd talked to Drew.

Do all brides move this fast?

I headed into the living room to find Drew and caught him in the middle of a conversation with D.J.'s parents about their motorcycle ministry. Not wanting to interrupt, I headed over to the other side of the room to join Mama and the Splendora sisters, who were deeply engrossed in a conversation of some sort. I got there just in time to hear my mother say that she was happy to finally call herself an empty nester.

What?

"Wait, Mama." I narrowed my gaze. "What are you saying? You're happy that I'm moving out?"

A hint of a smile turned up the edges of her lips. "Well, I don't want you to feel like you're not wanted, Hannah. But I'm going through a lot of changes right now." She lowered her voice to whisper the next part. "And not just menopause. I want to get into shape. So I've been thinking about turning your room into a fitness center."

"A fitness center?"

"Yes. As my cooking skills get better, I'll need to focus more on working out. Wouldn't hurt your father to join me. I think it would be fun to get one of those elliptical machine thingies. And Twila told me that she's got some sort of gaming system that has workout software. She uses it every day. It helps her keep track of calories and everything."

"That's right," Twila said. "Maybe we can all get in shape together."

Mama patted her midsection. "I figured while I'm changing so many other things in my life, I should go ahead and be proactive with my health. If I'm learning to cook Italian food, I'll need a way to keep it from going to my hips."

My father drew near and wiggled his brows. "I wouldn't mind seeing it on your hips, Marie. Wouldn't offend me in the least."

Ew.

Just one more reason I should be happy to move out.

Drew approached and pulled me into his arms, kissing away any concerns. "Long life to you, the future Mrs. Kincaid."

"Long life to you too," I said and giggled. "We're getting married."

"Yep. Merging the clans." He gestured to my father, who followed D.J.'s parents out of the living room. "Speaking of merging forces, you know what they're up to, don't you?"

"Nope. I have no idea."

"Follow me and you'll see for yourself."

Seconds later I stood on the veranda of the Rossi home, watching as my father climbed aboard the back of a motor-cycle and rode off into the sunset with a Kingdom Riders jacket on to ward off the chilly night air.

I shook my head. "This has got to be some sort of a weird dream. I could have sworn I just saw my father ride off on a motorcycle with a man named Dwayne from Splendora."

"You did."

"It wasn't a weird lasagna-induced dream?"

"Nope."

"Not sure which has me more discombobulated—the fact that he's doing something so out of character, or the fact that he just ate a full plate of Italian food and enjoyed the finale of *Dancing with the Stars*. I don't recall ever seeing the man eat lasagna in my life."

"You never know, Hannah. Could be he ends up with a whole new palate."

I laughed. "Grandpa Aengus would turn over in his grave." Or maybe not. The man was adventurous, after all.

"What would he say on a night like this?" Drew pulled me close and placed several sweet kisses on my cheeks.

"Oh, he'd probably share one of his favorite proverbs. Something about how lucky we are to be Irish." I laughed, then shivered as the cool night air wrapped itself around me.

"I'd say I'm pretty blessed, but I don't really think it has anything to do with being Irish." Drew's arms encircled my waist, and a kiss sweeter than Rosa's tiramisu followed.

As I lingered in his arms, I heard the sound of laughter from inside the house. Then the melody to "White Christ-mas" rang out in perfect three-part harmony. Looked like

Twila, Bonnie Sue, and Jolene were giving another one of their impromptu concerts. Not that I minded. Not at all. In fact, I felt like singing myself. And dancing. And . . .

With Drew's gorgeous blue eyes now fixed on mine, I felt like tossing every care to the wind and celebrating this picture-perfect day.

Bonus Feature

Grandpa Aengus's Favorite Irish Sayings

1. You've got to do your own growing, no matter how tall your grandfather was.
2. Never interrupt your opponent while he's making a mistake.
3. May the Lord keep you in his hand and never close his fist too tight.
4. May the saddest day of your future be no worse than the happiest day of your past.
5. May you be half an hour in heaven before the devil knows you're dead.
6. May you live to be a hundred years, with one extra year to repent.
7. Who gossips with you will gossip of you.
8. A handful of skill is worth a bagful of gold.
9. A friend's eye is a good mirror.
10. Count your rainbows, not your thunderstorms.

11. There are good ships and there are wood ships, the ships that sail the sea. But the best ships are friendships, and may they always be.
12. A toast to your coffin. May it be made of hundred-year-old oak. And may we plant the tree together tomorrow.
13. Here's to Eve, the mother of us all, and here's to Adam, who was Johnny-on-the-spot when the leaf began to fall.
14. Give a man a match and he'll be warm for a minute, but set him on fire and he'll be warm for the rest of his life.
15. Leprechauns, castles, good luck, and laughter. Lullabies, dreams, and love ever after. Poems and songs with pipes and drums. A thousand welcomes when anyone comes . . . That's the Irish for you!

Acknowledgments

A special thank-you to my sweet crit partners: Jeanetta Messmer, Virginia Rush, and Barbara Oden. Ladies, you make my job a lot more fun! Thanks for sticking with me during the eleventh-hour rush!

A huge thanks to my agent, Chip MacGregor, from Clan MacGregor. Life and health to you! Thanks for all you do to propel my career. I'm also very grateful for your prayers and undying support.

To my team at Revell:

Jennifer: Where do I begin? I'm blessed with an editor who truly gets me. That's priceless! Thanks for letting me . . . be me!

Jessica: If I could write a limerick just for you, it would go something like this: "There once was a copy editor named Jess, who cleaned up each fictional mess. She scribbled and tweaked and bit back a shriek as one author put her to the test!" (Now you see why I don't write poetry!)

My publicity team: Michele, Donna, Claudia . . . you've become my support team. How can I ever thank you for making sure readers hear about my quirky tales? I'm eternally grateful.

My sales team: I raise my (nonalcoholic, of course) glass to you! Bless you for undergirding my work.

To my readers: Without you, this book would not exist. You insisted that I bring Bella back, and I did! I would never have had the courage to reshape the Rossi family without your input and advice. I'm especially grateful to the readers in my "dream team." You named Bella's children, for Pete's sake! And you gave me wings to fly. Hugs to you all. Enjoy!

And finally, to the One who made all of this possible: Thank you for giving me a funny bone and teaching me how to use it to your glory.

Janice Thompson is a Christian freelance author and a native Texan. She has four grown daughters, four sons-in-law, five beautiful granddaughters, and two grandsons. She resides in the greater Houston area, where the heat and humidity tend to reign. Janice started penning books at a young age and was blessed to have a screenplay produced in the early eighties, after living in the Los Angeles area for a time. From there she went on to write several large-scale musical comedies for a Houston school of the arts. She continues to direct at a Christian theater and enjoys her time in the director's chair.

Currently, Janice has published over eighty novels and nonfiction books for the Christian market, most of them lighthearted. Working with quirky characters and story ideas suits this fun-loving author. She particularly enjoys contemporary, first-person romantic comedies. Janice loves sharing her faith with readers and hopes they will catch a glimpse of the real happily ever after in the pages of her books.

Come Meet

Janice Thompson

at www.JaniceAThompson.com

Read her blog, book information, and fun facts!

Follow Janice on Facebook and Twitter

A Romantic Comedy That Will Have You Laughing All Day

Don't miss book 1 in the Weddings by Bella series!

When Hollywood's most eligible bachelor sweeps into town, will he cause trouble for Bella?

Don't miss book 2 in the Weddings by Bella series!

Get ready for a double dose of wedding frenzy!

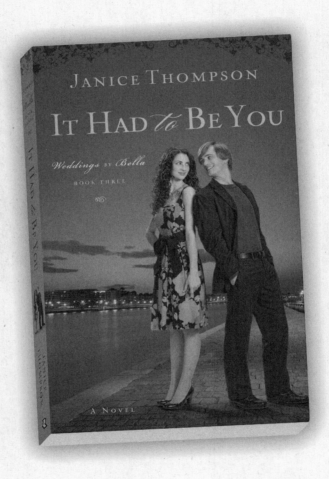

Don't miss book 3 in the Weddings by Bella series!

Catch this hilarious series from
JANICE THOMPSON

★ ★ ★ ★ ★ ★ ★ ★ ★ ★ ★ ★ ★ ★ ★ ★ ★

The *Backstage Pass* series takes you on a wild adventure in Hollywood and on the set of *Stars Collide*.